The Decline of

and other stories

The Decline of the Death Artist
and other stories

David Shaw Mackenzie

[signature: David S. Mackenzie]

•

NAT 1 PUBLISHING
a literary nonprofit corporation
Books that make you question your choices.

This is a work of fiction. Names, characters, places, and incidents are products of the author's imagination or are used fictitiously and are not to be construed as real. Any resemblance to actual events, locales, organizations, or persons—living, dead, or immortal—is entirely coincidental.

THE DECLINE OF THE DEATH ARTIST, AND OTHER STORIES
Copyright © 2025 by David Shaw Mackenzie
Produced by Nat 1 Publishing, a literary nonprofit
www.nat1publishing.com
All rights reserved
v.1: 03.29.2025

ISBN: 9798315943655

Cover Art, Design, and Edits by B.S.Roberts
Title/Heading Font: "Charm" by Cadson Demak
Interior Font: "EB Garamond 12" by Georg Duffner

No part of this book may be reproduced or used in any manner without the written permission of the copyright holder or Nat 1 Publishing, except for the use of quotations in a book review. The scanning, uploading, and distribution of this book without permission from the publisher are illegal and punishable by law. Please purchase only authorized editions—your support of the author's rights is appreciated.

Opinions expressed in this publication are those of the author. They do not purport to reflect the opinions or views of the publishing house or its members. The publisher does not have any control over and does not assume any responsibility for author or third-party websites, social media, or their content.

For my wife, Rachel, with love.

The Tragedies.

i. The Time of Your Life 011
ii. Certain Things about McFarlane 045
iii. Buy or Be Bought 103
iv. Eden Rich 129
v. The Decline of the Death Artist 203

The Time of Your Life.

"SO YOU'RE FORTY-TWO YEARS OLD, is that correct?"

"Yes." A short pause. "To be exact, it's forty-two years, five months, and thirteen days."

"Right. Which means you've got twenty-two years and... let's see..." The assessor consulted the screen on the desk that separated him from Anthony Pilgrew. "Yes, twenty-two years, six months, and seventeen days. That's what you've got left."

"Twenty-two? Actually, I thought it'd be twenty-one."

"Well, no. You're in luck, Mr. Pilgrew. The statutory limit doesn't come down till next month. Everyone can still live for sixty-five years. And whatever you've got before the end of this month can't be reduced."

"Small compensation," Pilgrew said.

"Well, yes. But a whole year... quite valuable." The assessor was a man seventeen years Pilgrew's junior. He glanced at the screen again. "So, in summary, you're forty-two years of age, and you'll be leaving twenty-two years and a few months. I'm repeating myself because I'm legally required to make sure that you know this before we proceed. There mustn't be any doubt or confusion."

"There's none. Not on my part, anyway."

"Good, good. Now... I take it that it's your medical condition that's prompted you to request the final procedure?"

"That's right, yes. I'll be dying very soon."

"I'm very sorry to hear that, Mr. Pilgrew."

The assessor consulted his screen again. "There's a note here—and this is something I have to make sure you've been informed of—it says it's quite possible that you could survive at least two more months without pain."

"I'm aware of that."

"But you still want to proceed?"

"I do, yes."

"And you can confirm that you've made your will, which distributes all items from your estate, including—obviously—your time?"

"All done," Pilgrew said. "One of your colleagues helped me with that."

"Good. So…" He looked at his screen again. "I can tell you that we've created the final procedure narrative as you requested, in all its detail, and so all that remains is for you to make the final payment."

"And how much is it?"

"Well, you did ask for the luxury visual impact model, which is quite expensive…"

"Yes, I know."

"So the full cost is four years and six months."

Pilgrew looked a little surprised at this but took a deep breath and said, "Fine."

"In that case…" The assessor moved his screen to one side and slid a small Timetrader screen across to Pilgrew. "If I could ask you to read out what it says so that there's no doubt you understand the details of the sale."

Pilgrew read, "I, Anthony Pilgrew, agree to a payment of four years and six months to TimeTrad Inc. in return for a luxury visual impact narrative of my final procedure."

"Now, if you could place your hand on the screen, please."

Pilgrew did this.

After about five seconds, the assessor said, "Excellent. All done." He stood. "So, if you're ready…"

He escorted Pilgrew from the small office where the interview had been held. A couple minutes later, Pilgrew was lying on a futon in a small room carpeted and decorated as if it might be a bedroom. The walls were lemon yellow, and the carpet was Persian with rich red and black patterns and tiny areas of orange and green. On the wall were large framed photographs of Swiss mountain scenes, including one of a wooden chalet surrounded by pine trees. The futon was Pilgrew's own, brought to the building earlier in the day. His head rested on one of his favorite cushions, also Persian, whose predominant color was dark blue.

"Are you comfortable?" the assessor asked.

"Fine, yes." Pilgrew shifted his body slightly.

"We've followed your instructions meticulously, and we've designed the narrative exactly as you described. And, obviously, we've used the chalet…" He pointed to the picture on the wall, "as your destination venue and, using the photos you gave us, reconstructed your special friend and recreated your meeting with her. You will enjoy a full twenty-four hours of this wonderful experience."

"That's… that's really good."

"So, if you're ready?"

"I'm ready."

"Right."

The assessor picked up a small package from a table next to the futon and took out a pair of interactive holospectacles. He opened the arms and placed the spectacles over Pilgrew's eyes. He touched a button on the edge of one lens and a pair of side flaps slid down to cover the lens surroundings, ensuring there was no peripheral interference. Both lenses darkened.

"What can you see, Mr. Pilgrew?" the assessor asked.

"I can see… I can see… the forest…" Pilgrew became aware of his heart beating in his chest.

"Is it all very clear?"

"Yes, it is. Perfect."

"Is there a path in front of you?"

"Yes… yes, there's a path." Pilgrew's breathing quickened.

"Good, good. Well, I'm sure you know where that leads. Follow the path, Mr. Pilgrew. Follow the path."

"I will… Yes… I'll… I'll follow it…"

"I'll say goodbye, Mr. Pilgrew."

"Goodbye. Yes. And thank you… thank you." Pilgrew was struggling to remain calm. He looked ahead. The assessor, the bedroom, the TimeTrad building—all had disappeared. Before him, he could see only the forest and the path that cut through it. He was on the edge of another world, one that he'd wanted to return to for many years. The next twenty-four hours were to be the most wonderful he'd ever experience. He could just hear one more instruction: "Step forward, Mr. Pilgrew. Step forward."

"Yes, I…" Pilgrew took one step along the path. "Yes, it's…" He looked ahead and began to feel calm and full of joy as he took the first view of the chalet where he would meet again Anna, the woman he had fallen in love with so many years ago. But the great twenty-four hours only lasted about ten seconds. Within eleven, he was dead.

•••

A nd now we come to the final item."

James Calgary whispered, "About time."

Janice Vandon, sitting on his left, leaned toward him and said, in quiet, cynical tones, "Oh, very funny, Jim. Very funny."

Calgary smiled and said, "You've got to laugh. Got to see the funny side."

"Oh, shut up."

The executor looked up but said nothing for a few seconds. Then he spoke again. "As I said, the final item…"

There were only four people in the large room which was arranged theatrically with a raised dias at one end upon which the executor sat behind a desk, and twenty rows of seats, sixteen seats per row, eight on each side of a central aisle. James Calgary and Janice Vandon, both in their mid-thirties, were sitting in the front row nearest to the dias and the executor. The fourth person, a young woman wearing a red rain jacket, was sitting at the back, as far away from the others as it was possible to be.

"All my remaining time," the executor announced, "I bequeath to Charlotte Daintry."

"What!"

Calgary was on his feet. "Hold on a minute. Tony promised his time to *me*. All of it. What the hell's going on here?"

"The will is quite clear," the executor said. "The recipient is Charlotte Daintry."

"But he told me only two weeks ago. He promised."

"It appears that there were some alterations to the will."

"Oh yeah? And when was that?"

The executor examined the e-documents before him. "On the twenty-ninth of January."

"But… well, that was the day before he died."

"That's correct, yes," the executor said. "But I can assure you that everything was completed in the appropriate manner. All quite legal."

"But he didn't tell me!"

"Well, that is unfortunate, of course…"

"Unfortunate!"

"Yes, but you see, it's not a legal requirement."

"For Christ's sake!"

"Mr. Calgary, please—"

"And who's this Charlotte… Charlotte Dainty, or whatever her name is, eh? Who the hell is *she?*"

The woman at the back of the room stood and began to walk toward the front. "That would be me," she said.

Calgary turned to face her, as did Janice Vandon. Calgary, his expression shifting from anger to mere contempt, said, "So who the hell are you?"

"I'm Tony Pilgrew's daughter," she said.

"Daughter?"

"That's right, yes."

Calgary turned to the executor. "But Tony never had a daughter. No wife, no partner, no offspring."

"I can assure you, Mr. Calgary, that Ms. Daintry is definitely Mr. Pilgrew's daughter."

"What?" Calgary looked at Janice Vandon. "I don't believe this."

"Neither do I," Janice Vandon said.

He looked at Charlotte Daintry again. "Who was your mother?"

"Her name was Anna. They met in Switzerland."

"When?"

"Well, I'm nineteen, and their relationship was quite short-lived, so… not much more than twenty years ago, I suppose. My mother wasn't keen to give me the details. And then… well, Tony only found out about me in the last fortnight."

"Christ." This was stated more quietly than before, with a sense of resignation entering the tone. "But I *need* that time," he said, frustration giving way to despair. "I mean, I've led a shit life, thrown away all my time, sold it off, squandered it. I've got almost nothing left. Tony promised he'd help me out. I mean, how much did he leave?"

"Eighteen years and seventeen days," the executor answered.

"Eighteen? Is that all? But he had a full allocation. Hadn't touched it. He was forty-two, so he should have had twenty-two and a bit left."

"He put aside four and a half years to pay for his final procedure."

"Four and a half years? You're kidding." He paused. "But look, I haven't got any add-ons, nothing at all. I'll be dead next month!"

"Please don't use that word, Mr. Calgary."

"Christ, what do I care? Look…" He glanced briefly at Janice Vandon and then addressed the executor once again. "So he left me nothing at all, did he?"

"I'm afraid that's how it is, yes."

"And nothing to me either?" Janice Vandon asked.

"I'm afraid nothing to anyone else."

"And you!" Janice Vandon turned angrily to Calgary. "You promised me time. *Ten years*, you said. Ten years! Remember that?"

"Well, sure, but—"

"So now I'm in the same shit as you. Christ!" She stepped out into the aisle. "Well, you can all go to hell!" she called out as she started to stride down toward the exit doors.

"Oh, Janice," Calgary began. "Come on, please—"

She turned and yelled back at him, "I never want to see you ever again!"

●●●

Half an hour after leaving the offices of Almack and Blore, where Anthony Pilgrew's will had been read, Charlotte Daintry entered one of the many office suites owned by TimeTrad Inc. This particular suite was on floor 37 of the Trellis in the City of London. Making her way past four security points, she finally knocked on the door of Matthew Krent, one of TimeTrad's senior managers.

"Come in."

She opened the door.

"Well, Andrea," Krent said. "Good to see you. Successful morning?"

Before she could respond, he said, "Wait a minute. Today you were…" He tapped his way through several displays on his desk screen. "Yes, here we are… *Charlotte!*" He looked up and smiled.

"That's right," she replied, "but let's move back to Andrea."

"Sure. Anyway, everything went okay today?"

"One hundred percent."

"Excellent. So—"

Matthew Krent was a man of thirty-two. He was dressed in the company uniform: a pale grey suit, white shirt, and company tie. The tie was darker grey with the company logo—TT— on it in white.

"Shall we?" He placed a Timetrader on the desk in front of him. "Oh, come on, sit down, won't you."

Andrea sat on a chair placed in front of Krent's desk.

"Quite an achievement, you know," he said as he tapped some figures into the Timetrader.

"Thanks."

"How did you manage to convince him?"

"Well, we did a trackback search and found someone he met on holiday about twenty years ago. A little holiday romance. I mean, he never saw the woman again, but I got enough data together to prove I was his daughter."

"Including false DNA results."

"Of course."

"And he fell for it?"

"Yes. But then he wanted it, really. I mean, the idea that he had a daughter... It made him feel great. I didn't even have to ask him for his time. When he was convinced I was who I said I was, he insisted on giving me everything."

"Great."

"And that event—I mean, the holiday romance—well, he asked for that to be the basis for his final procedure narrative."

"Which we supplied."

"Yes."

"Good. Great! Everybody's happy." Krent smiled. "Well, as I said, excellent work. So, shall we?" He pointed to the Timetrader.

"May I ask a couple of things first?" Andrea said.

"Of course."

"Well..." she hesitated. "I mean, I know I've got a long way to go—"

"How old are you?"

"Twenty-three."

"Forty-two years."

"Well, forty-one if they bring it down to sixty-four as they say they will."

He smiled again. "Even if it's forty-one, you've still got quite a long way to go."

"Sure, but... well, one thing that's become very clear to me since I've been doing this job is that there's quite a lot of people who've got no time left. Nothing. Even people my age. They've... you know, they've sold it, been cheated out of it... I don't know, but they're down to almost nothing. I mean, there was a guy this morning—I'd say he was thirty-two, maybe thirty-four, and he thought he was going to inherit all of Pilgrew's time, all of it. It seems they were good friends and Pilgrew had promised it to him. And then, of course, I came along and, well, he was relying completely on that inheritance but now he's got nothing. And if he doesn't get any time soon, he'll be dealt with in a couple of weeks."

Krent responded to this with a shrug. "Are you suggesting we're responsible for that?"

"Well, in a way we are because we took all that time from him. In a sense, he'll be... he'll be dealt with by me."

Krent pushed his screen to one side and clasped his hands on the desktop. "Andrea," he said, in a quiet, comforting tone. "The guy you're talking about is James Calgary, is that right?"

"Yes. How do you know that?"

He waved the question aside. "I try to keep up with all current projects, particularly yours, because you're so good at them. Anyway, was he drunk?"

"Calgary?"

"Yes."

"Not that I noticed, no."

"Unusual. You see, I checked out his background. He may only be thirty-three, but he's been an alcoholic since his early twenties. And he's been bankrupt a couple of times and divorced twice—" Krent raised his hands in resigned disappointment. "What can you expect? He's a disaster area. Hopeless, absolutely hopeless. Been in rehab twice, and he's only thirty-three! I mean, no wonder he's got nothing. And it's all *his* fault, Andrea. Totally his fault. Nothing to do with you. Please don't blame yourself. I mean, I'd be willing to bet that even if he had got all of Pilgrew's time, he'd still be down to nothing in a couple months from now. Please, please, don't feel guilty about it. All right?"

Andrea took a deep breath. "Okay," she said with a nod. "Okay."

"Is there anything else?"

"Yes," she said. "I wanted to check up on my allocation."

"Sure. Let's see—" He pulled his screen back in front of him and tapped a finger on it several times. "So far, you've earned three years, five months, and six days." He looked at her. "Which takes you to sixty-eight."

"Or sixty-seven if the new law goes through."

He sat back in his chair. "Well, it will, of course. But look, you're only twenty-three. You've got *decades* in front of you. Plenty of time to rack up even more time. Can't you see that?"

She shrugged. "Well, you're right, I suppose. And what do I get for this one?"

"Six months."

"Is that all? Come on, you got twenty-two years out of this!"

"Eighteen."

"No, twenty-two. Remember that Pilgrew paid four and a half for his final procedure narrative. He paid TimeTrad."

"Okay, yes. Good point. Well, look, I shouldn't really do this but since you've been so successful—and not just in this project but all the others too—I'll put it up to nine months. Okay? How does that sound?"

Andrea almost managed a smile. "Okay."

"So you got eighteen years and seventeen days. Right?"

"Yes."

"So I'll just take off seventeen years and three months. Agreed?"

"That's fine, yes."

"Right." He adjusted the Timetrader accordingly. "If you'll just read it out, please."

She read, "I, Andrea Norland, wish to transfer seventeen years and three months to TimeTrad Incorporated." Then, without prompting, she placed her right hand, palm down, on the screen. After five seconds, she removed it.

"Well, there you go," Krent said. He moved the Timetrader back to the side of his desk. "I'll say it again, Andrea: Well done. You're brilliant at what you do, and if you stick at it for a few more projects, you'll be thoroughly rich in time. Oh, and money, too. I mean it. Anyway…" He turned to his screen. "I've got another project for you. A guy called Maxwell Elsted. He's fifty-six, and he's got terminal cancer. No add-ons, so we can only get nine years…"

"Eight."

"Eight. Right, maybe only eight. But it's worth it. I'll send you the details, okay? Just get started on it as soon as you can."

●●●

I'd like to introduce you to a new device," Ellerby said. "I think it's going to be very useful. Very simple, very efficient. And here it is." He held up a small object which resembled a toy pistol with a shortened barrel. It looked as if it was made from yellow plastic.

Someone said, "Looks a bit like a gun."

"Oh, it's not a gun," Ellerby said, smiling. "It's far more dangerous than that."

This prompted some laughter.

Max Ellerby was sitting at the head of a table which was in the shape of a narrow oval. A dozen of his senior executives were seated round it. All of them were men. Ellerby was the CEO of TimeTrad Inc.

He was fifty years old—fifty years, eight months, and seven days. He was dressed as all employees of the company were: pale grey suit with a company tie. The only difference being his suit looked as if it cost several times more than anyone else in the room. His thick grey hair was neatly cut and held by expensive oils in a carefully arranged style, which appeared to reduce his age by about ten years. The functional elegance of his appearance suggested that here was someone whose attention to detail might tend toward a level of ruthlessness in his association with his peers.

He picked up the device. "It's an age calculator," he explained. "You point it at someone—it's got to be aimed at skin, apparently—and it'll tell you their age. Then it links to the database, and you can see how much time they've got left. Very handy." He looked to his left. "Would you mind, Henry?"

The man sitting three down on that side of the table said, "Not at all," and smiled. Then he added, "I already know I'm the youngest here."

More laughter followed this comment.

"Well, you are," Ellerby said. "But I know that from our records. Anyway—"

He pointed the device at Henry's head. This created a moment of unease, not only for the man called Henry but for those on either side of him. However, the moment soon passed. Ellerby read from a small screen positioned on the end of the device facing the holder. "Your age is forty-two years, one month, and seven days."

"Sounds about right."

"And you've already racked up two hundred and sixty years plus."

This prompted some amusement among the other executives. Someone said, "Planning to live to three hundred, Henry?"

"I have children," Henry said. "I want to look after them."

"Christ, how many have you got?"

"Five, so far."

"Really? Well done."

"Not sure how to take that," Henry responded.

More laughter.

"Gentlemen," Ellerby said, and attention turned back to him. "It's hardly a critical decision, but I'm trying to decide on a name for this thing." He placed it carefully on the table. "*Age Assessment Device* is a bit long, don't you think? So, I was just thinking of calling it a *timer*. What do you reckon?"

Someone said, "Excellent idea."

"Yes?" Ellerby looked round at the others. Most of them nodded.

"Good. Thank you. It's a *timer,* then."

There were murmurs of approval round the room.

"I suggest we immediately order a million of them. Phase One. Every police officer in the country gets one. This'll be crucial in fulfilling our population management aims. Agreed?"

Everyone in the room voiced their agreement. Everybody except one. "A question, if I may?"

"Yes, Peter?"

The man three down on Ellerby's right straightened up in his chair. His name was Peter Radcot. At fifty-six (fifty-six years, five months, and four days) he was one of the oldest present. "What limits are to be placed on the use of these devices?"

"None."

"None?"

"Peter, these... these *timers*... are very accurate. They can tell you straight away if someone is out of time. And we know, from bitter experience, that people with no time left just hide away and scrounge and, well, they're a burden on the rest of us. What this will do—" He pointed again at the timer. "Is help the police to identify the timeless, round them up, and deal with them."

"Deal with them? Is that the main purpose of those timers?"

"Look, Peter, don't forget that the people of this country voted for this when we offered to sort out the problem which was spiraling out of control. And TimeTrad helped to put through the necessary legislation."

"I just think we're rushing into this, that's all. It's getting out of hand."

"In what way?"

"Well, how many of us expected all these developments?"

"Such as?"

"For one thing, all the implications of time-trading."

"We live in a commercial world, Peter."

"So everything becomes a commodity, is that it? Even time?"

"Peter, for Christ's sake, you work for TimeTrad, don't you? And time is our sale product. Why the hell do you work for the company if you don't like it?"

Radcot said, "I don't like our excesses."

"Ah," someone said. "You're on a mission!"

"Call it that if you like, but look—" He sat forward in his chair and placed his elbows on the table. "Are any of you aware, for example, that there are several other time-trading companies out there—some masquerading as TimeTrad, by the way—who have staff who go out at night searching for down-and-outs, rough sleepers, and so on and offer them accommodation. They take them back to some kind of hostel, clean them up, give them new clothes, something to eat, etc. and then, when they're nice and comfy, are asked for a little time in return. Maybe just a month, that's all."

"That's a good deal!" someone called out.

"Well, I agree," Radcot said. "I mean, if you're in your thirties or even forties, what's losing a month from your life allocation? You can always do a bit of extra work later and earn some time back, can't you?"

"Of course you can. So what's the problem?"

"Well," Radcot went on. "The latest figures show that most people—seventy-three percent, in fact—would need to work for more than a month—in some cases a whole *year*—to earn enough to buy one month. Ludicrous."

"But hold on, Peter," Ellerby said. "These hostels are doing a great job. The homeless are being offered shelter, and the public loves it because these wretches are being cleared off the street."

"Win win," someone added.

"And if all they lose is a month…"

"Yes, but that's just the beginning of the story," Radcot went on. "Remember that a lot of these people are addicts—alcohol, drugs, whatever. And now, once they're comfortable inside the hostel, they're offered the drugs of their choice. But they have to pay."

"No, Peter, no…" Ellerby was shaking his head.

"And after that," Radcot continued. "Well, it's pretty simple to figure out what happens. They take more and more drugs, and the price goes up and up. It gets to the point when they don't care how much they spend, and they've probably lost track anyway, so they wind up losing all their statutory time allocation. And that's great for the trading company because they're obliged by law to report anyone in the hostel who's timeless. So the police turn up, arrest the guy, and he gets dealt with. It frees up a place for someone else to move in, and the whole thing repeats itself. Great system, eh?"

Radcot looked around the room during the short silence that followed. Then Ellerby said, "Well, Peter, I think you've been listening to the wrong people. Nothing like that happens in any of these hostels. I'm quite sure of that."

"Well, I've got proof."

"Really?"

"Yes. I know of a heroin addict who was enticed into one of these hostels where they looked after him very well, apparently…"

"Well, of course, they did."

"For about a week or so, but then they offered him very high-quality heroin, which he couldn't resist. After a couple of weeks, it got to the point where they were charging him two years for a hit."

Someone said, "Two years a hit? You're kidding."

"I wish I was."

"Complete nonsense," Ellerby said.

"I'm afraid it isn't," Radcot went on. "Within three weeks, he'd lost his entire statutory time allocation." He paused. "So he was duly dealt with."

After a short silence, someone said, "Well, he was a heroin addict. I mean, good riddance."

"Come on, Peter, who told you this ridiculous story?" Ellerby asked.

"The man himself."

Someone said, "Before or after he was dealt with?"

Several of the executives laughed at this.

"Not funny," Radcot said. "He told me all about it the day before… well, the day before he was dealt with. I tried everything I could to save him, but I failed."

"Why save him, for Christ's sake? He was a heroin addict!"

"His name was Alistair Radcot," Radcot said. "He was my son."

● ● ●

"How old are you, Mr. Calgary?"

"Thirty-four."

"Thirty-four and?"

"Oh, a couple of months."

"And you say you've got no time allocation left?"

"Fraid not."

"I see. Well, obviously before we can effect a sale, I have to check out all your details. Are you happy for me to do that?"

"No problem."

"Right."

Calgary was sitting in a TimeTrad outlet talking to a salesman named Frederick Barnett, a man who was the same age as Calgary but still had his full allocation of thirty-one years left, plus add-ons he'd gained in bonuses from the company.

"We've got a new device to help us with this. Very quick, very efficient." Barnett opened a drawer in his desk and took out a small yellow timer. "It's an age assessment device. Checks your age just by looking at your skin and links into your database to check your allocation. Are you comfortable with this?"

"Fine. Go ahead."

"Okay. So, if you'll just put your hand on the desk, please."

Calgary did this. Barnett pointed the timer at the back of Calgary's hand, held it there for a few seconds, and then checked the rear screen.

"Well, as you can see here..." Barnett turned the timer around so that Calgary could also read the data. "It says your age is thirty-four years, two months, three weeks, and five days. And a few hours. And your remaining allocation is thirteen days and five hours."

"Christ, is that all?"

"I'm afraid so."

Calgary's sigh was one of resignation with a hint of anger. "I thought I'd got a bit more than that," he said. "I thought I had about six weeks..."

"I'm sorry, Mr. Calgary. But then, we can help you out. That's what we're here for. How much do you want to buy?"

"Well, I've got four thousand six hundred pounds. How much can I get for that?"

"Four thousand six hundred." Barnett looked surprised.

"Yes."

"No other assets?"

"No, but I reckon if I can get six months or something like that, then I'll have enough time to sort things out."

"Six months?"

"Or thereabouts."

Barnett sat back in his chair. He said, slowly, "Mr. Calgary, the current rate is twelve thousand pounds a month."

It took Calgary a few moments to understand this. Then he said, "Twelve thousand? A month? You're not serious."

"I'm afraid that's the rate right now, and I need to make you aware that this is likely to rise at the end of this month to fifteen thousand."

"Fifteen thousand? Christ!"

"I'm afraid the market has changed a lot since you last checked."

"Bloody hell," Calgary said and then, more quietly, "Bloody hell."

"Have you no friends who could lend you some interim time?"

Calgary shook his head. "No. I thought I had, but the guy changed his mind."

"Could he be persuaded to change his mind back again?"

"No, 'fraid not. He's... he's dealt."

"Ah."

"Christ, is it worth doing this?" He took out his cell, tapped in some numbers on the calculator screen, and said, "An hour or two under twelve days, is that it?"

"Let me check," Barnett said. He did his own calculation on a screen at his side. "Four thousand six hundred buys you ten days, seventeen hours, and thirty-six minutes."

Calgary looked up from his phone. "Really? I get it to be about twelve days."

"Well, remember that we always base our calculations on the current month, and we're now in February. But then, in March, with thirty-one days—"

Calgary laughed. "Wow," he said. "So if I waited till the first of March, I'd get twelve days, not ten and a half. Well, isn't that great."

"Except, as I say, the rate is due to rise on March first, so it's likely you'll get less than ten and a half days. Just let me calculate it for you." Barnett reached for his screen.

"No, don't bother," Calgary said as Barnett started to tap in numbers. "Don't bother. You've forgotten something, haven't you?"

"Oh, what's that?"

"Well, I've only got thirteen days left, remember? And today's the sixth of February. I'm not going to make it to March, am I?"

"Ah, I see what you mean. In that case, I take it you want to make the purchase now. Am I right?"

"No, you're not right." Calgary stood up. "You're not right at all. Nothing to do with any of this is right."

Without waiting for a response, he turned away from the TimeTrad salesman and left the office.

Calgary decided to walk home. His travel pass had expired, and he saw little point in renewing it. All he had now was his cell, the clothes he was wearing, plus a few spare shirts, and a bed. The small flat he rented was empty. Not even carpets remained. Next month's rent was due on the seventeenth, two days before the end of his time allocation. Could he persuade his landlord, who was generosity itself, to let him stay in the flat free of charge for the extra two days? No chance.

He continued walking along the quiet streets. When he was about five minutes away from the TimeTrad office, a young man walked quickly past him, stopped, turned, and said, "You need time, don't you?"

Calgary came to a halt and looked very carefully at the man before him. "If I say yes," he asked, "what's it to you?"

"I saw you coming out of TimeTrad," the young man said.

"Really."

The man seemed nervous. He was standing with his hands in the pockets of his rather shabby pale blue quilted jacket—some of the binding threads had broken away, and the cuffs and hem were edged with dirt. He was shifting his weight from foot to foot as if suffering from the cold. He had untidy black hair which was long but not too long in terms of the current fashion. His shoes, Calgary noted, were scuffed and worn.

"Come on, then," Calgary said. "If you've got something to say, say it."

"I can sell you some time."

"Can you."

"Yeah. Real cheap, too."

"That a fact."

"Yeah, and I can do it right now, no problem. I've got the kit." He drew out a shiny red transfer box from his right-hand jacket pocket, held it up for Calgary to see, and then stuffed it back into his pocket.

Calgary noticed that the young man's hand was trembling. The expression on his face was one of resolution, struggling against fear, his eyes wide open, pupils tiny. "I don't need any time," Calgary said and walked on.

The young man fell into stride beside him. "Yes, you do," he said. "I know you do. I'm bloody sure. How about… how about a year for a thousand quid?"

Calgary stopped again, and the young man stood beside him, half-turned toward him, right hand outstretched, not touching him but pleading nevertheless. "I just… I just need some money. I mean, I'm not absolutely desperate or anything…"

"Of course not."

"But I just… I'm…"

"You need a fix," Calgary said.

"My last one, I swear it. Really. I'm nearly off it now. I've got a job starting next week and I just need to get there, you know? Just need to get through a couple of days—"

"How old are you?"

"Twenty-three."

"And how much time have you got left?"

"Oh, lots. Years!"

"When did you last check?"

"Oh, look, does it matter? I know I've got years left. Years…"

"But you don't know the exact figure?"

"No."

"So why don't you check it out?"

"What does it matter to you? Just give me… look, how about *two* years. I'll give you two years for a grand. How about that?"

"I'd be surprised if you've got two years left."

The young man stepped back. "What? Oh, come on. I'm twenty-three, for Christ's sake. You think I've thrown it all away? What is it… forty-two years? Are you crazy or something?"

"Oh, I'm definitely crazy. No doubt about that," Calgary said. "But look, maybe we can do a deal."

"Well, like I said…"

"No, no. Just listen, will you? I'll give you some money on one condition."

"Yeah? Shit, here we go. Maybe I should just tell you to fuck off right now."

"Well, maybe you should, but I don't think you will. Anyway, what's it to be?"

The young man stood there for a few seconds, his nervousness even more apparent than before. His right leg was twitching. "Okay," he said. "Give it to me. What's the condition?"

"Simple," Calgary said. "Just show me how much time you've got left. You've been blocking it, haven't you?"

"Blocking it? No, no. Shit, I've got years left. Years!"

"Fine. Then prove it."

After a few moments' hesitation, the young man took the red transfer box out of his pocket and switched it on. He placed his right palm on the acceptance screen and then looked at the display. "No, no, that can't be right." He wasn't angry, just disbelieving. "Must be something wrong. Must be."

"I bet there isn't," Calgary said.

The young man looked at him. "You don't even know what it says."

"You've got less than a year left."

"Well, that's what it says, but it's crap."

"I'm sorry, but these things don't make mistakes."

"Now look…" This time, he was beginning to get angry.

"What's the actual figure?"

"Look, it's wrong. It's fucking ridiculous."

"Just tell me what it says."

"Well, it says… it says six weeks. Six weeks and three days. But that's ridiculous. It can't be. It's just fucking wrong!" This last sentence was an angry shout.

"No," Calgary said, "it's right. You've just got to face up to the fact that you've been selling off time without keeping track of it. Or throwing it away or having it nicked."

The young man shook his head. "Christ," he said quietly. "Six weeks. How the fuck…"

"Well, I can't buy any time off you, can I?" Calgary said.

The young man said nothing.

"Can I just check what I've got left?"

The young man shrugged. He held the transfer box out to Calgary, who placed his right hand on top. After a few moments, the young man said, "Christ, you're in a worse state than me."

"What does it say?"

"Thirteen days, five hours, twenty-six minutes and... and..."

"That's okay," Calgary said. "That's enough. Forget the seconds."

"Did you know it was that bad?"

"I did, actually. You see, I fucked up my life even more than you did. Anyway, I'll give you thirteen days."

"What?"

"I've no hope of getting any time from anywhere, so I might as well get dealt with now. Get it over with. Five hours is enough to get me back home, lie down, wait for the bastards to arrive..." He paused. "I suppose I could make it a condition that if you accept, then you won't do any more drugs, but... well, it's up to you, isn't it, eh? You want to fuck up more, just go ahead. Anyway, flick it on to incoming." He pointed to the transfer box the young man was still holding in his right hand. He did so. "Now tap in thirteen days." The young man complied. "Now, hold it out."

Calgary checked the figures and then placed his hand on the box. After a few seconds, he took his hand away. "There you go."

"I'll do it," the young man said. "I'll stay clean."

"Good idea."

Calgary turned and resumed his walk back to his flat. The young man called after him, "Thanks a lot, mate. No, really. Thanks. Thanks a million."

Fifteen minutes later, Calgary reached his flat, whose walls were bare and the floor reduced to floorboards. In his tiny bedroom, only the bed remained, with a couple of books on the floor beside it. Calgary knew the drill. All time transactions were logged centrally so the system would already know that he had only five hours and a few minutes left. At exactly two hours to go, his case would be flagged up, his whereabouts noted, and a team would be sent out to pick him up and bring him to the nearest Age Resolution Unit where he would be dealt with.

He thought about going out and buying a huge amount of painkillers so that he could deal with himself. But he knew he couldn't buy enough in one purchase because there were limits, so he'd have to visit several pharmacies in order to accumulate enough pills to do the job. And then he might just vomit them up before they got down to the business of dealing with him. No, he was just too tired even to contemplate all of that.

So he lay down on his bed and started thinking about what he should be thinking about under those circumstances. There was, of course, the mess he'd made of his life, the awful things he'd done. There were the people he'd let down, those he'd hurt, and those who had actually died due to his failures. No, not good to think of all that. Given that he couldn't change any of it, why carry on beating himself up about it right now when his life was about to end? Best thing to do was to think about the positive things in his life. Yes, the positive things.

He thought hard. He thought harder. It was a good ploy because after a minute or so, he fell asleep.

As Calgary had predicted, the team arrived two and a half hours later. He woke up five minutes before they pulled up outside the building. He never needed an alarm to wake him up; some kind of internal clock always ensured that he was awake when he needed to be. When the bell rang, he went to the door and was confronted by four armed men in dark blue uniforms.

"Mr. Calgary, yes?" the team leader asked.

"That's right."

"Just let me check, will you?"

"Sure." Calgary placed his hand on what appeared to be a transfer box or something similar.

"James Algwin Calgary," the team leader said.

"That's right."

"You know your time's up."

"I'm aware of that, yes."

"Right, well. Just one question, though."

"Go ahead."

The team leader consulted the device in his hand. "It says here that you had about thirteen days to go until you gave them all away about... let's see... three hours ago."

"That's right."

"I'm just required to check that the time wasn't stolen from you."

"It wasn't."

"So it was a legitimate sale?"

"It wasn't a sale. I just gave it away."

"You gave it away?"

"Yes. A gift."

"Who to?"

"I don't know. Someone I met in the street."

"I don't understand," the team leader said. "I mean, when you gave these thirteen days away did you know that it would bring your Age Termination forward to... to about an hour from now?"

"Yes, I did. You see, I've got no hope. No friends, no... nobody. No chance of getting any more time, so I'd rather be dealt with now than spend a miserable couple of weeks waiting for you to arrive."

"I see." The team leader made direct eye contact with Calgary for the first time. He hesitated for a few moments, which suggested that the bare, honest, and unemotional responses he was receiving might be new to him. In a relatively quiet and more considerate tone, he said, "We need to go now."

"Busy day, is it?" Calgary asked.

"I'm afraid so, yes."

"Lots of dealings today?"

"Yes."

"A couple of hundred? A thousand? Ten thousand?"

"I'm not allowed to tell you the actual number," the team leader said.

"Well, I realize it's confidential information, but there's not much chance of me passing it on, is there?"

"I need to hand-cuff you," the team leader said, adding, as if in apology, "Statutory rules."

"No problem." Calgary held his hands out.

"Behind your back, please."

Calgary turned around, and one of the other members of the team clipped the cuffs onto his wrists.

"Okay, let's go."

At the front entrance to the apartment block, the group of five men encountered fifty-year-old Jason Framfield, Calgary's landlord.

"What the hell's going on here?" he asked in a tone approaching anger.

"Pretty obvious, I'd say," Calgary said as the group crossed the forecourt toward the white team vehicle.

Framfield walked alongside them. "This is precisely what I didn't want!" he shouted. "You promised this wouldn't happen here."

"Things change," Calgary said.

"Oh yeah, sure. You don't give a shit, do you?"

"Considering what's going to happen to me in about an hour from now, well, I'd say you're absolutely correct."

"Excuse me," the team leader began, "who are you, exactly?"

"The name's Framfield. I own this building, and I don't want word to get around that it's full of wasters like this piece of shit here."

"We're being as discreet as possible, Mr. Framfield."

"Oh, sure. Four guys in uniform armed to the teeth. *Subtle*." He looked at Calgary again. "You said you had at least two weeks left."

"Did I? Well, life's going by real quick these days. Anyway, you're in luck, aren't you? I mean, you can rent the flat out straight away. Double rent for two weeks. Can't be bad, eh?"

They reached the vehicle—a long white van with no side windows. It had a sliding door, which one of the team members pulled open.

"In you go, Mr. Calgary."

"Well, goodbye, Mr. Framfield."

"Good fucking riddance," Framfield shouted as Calgary, helped by one of the team, stepped up into the vehicle.

Someone else shouted, "Wait!"

"What?"

A young woman was running along the pavement toward them. "Wait!" she shouted again. "Hold on! Hold on!" She made it up to the group and, breathing heavily after her sprint, said, "Don't take him away. Don't. I've got some time for him. Really, he's okay."

"Too late," the team leader said. "He's got less than two hours left. Too late for add-ons now."

"No, it isn't." A bit hot following her run, she unzipped her red rain jacket. Then she pulled out an ID card. "Put this on your transfer box." She handed it to the team leader, who glanced at it before placing it on his transfer device. Then, he looked carefully at the data on display.

"There's been a mistake," the young woman said. "I've been charged with sorting out the mess."

"Well," the team leader said, "I hope you understand that even if mistakes have been made, rules about time transfer apply."

"I know."

"We can only abandon the procedure if he's given a minimum of a year, and there's a system charge of two months."

"Yes, I know that, and I agree."

"Okay, but hold on a minute, will you?" The team leader looked through the open side door and said to Calgary, who had heard what was happening but hadn't yet seen the young woman. "Do you know this woman?" the team leader asked him.

Calgary, already seated, leaned forward and looked around at the new arrival. "Are you…" He began and then said, "I recognize you, but I can't remember where you came from."

"Yesterday, the reading of Tony Pilgrew's will."

"Ah, right." Calgary smiled a rueful little smile. "Yes, I remember now. You're his daughter. Charlotte, yeah?"

The young woman paused momentarily and said, "Yes, that's right. And I got all Tony's time."

"You did, didn't you."

"But shortly afterward, the executor found an error. Tony did actually leave you one year. So I've been sent to make the transfer."

"Well, I'm not going to say no."

"Give me your hand," the team leader said to the young woman.

She placed her hand on the transfer box.

"Well, you've got add-ons of four years, two months, and six days."

"Correct."

"Really?" Calgary asked. "But Tony… Tony left…"

She interrupted. "It's perfectly correct," she said firmly.

Calgary shrugged.

"Okay, so…" the team leader looked more closely at the screen, then looked up. "Can you confirm your name, please?"

"Andrea Norland."

"Right. So what's going on here?" Pointing to Calgary, he said, "He thinks your name is Charlotte, and you confirmed it."

"Norland's my professional name," she said. "Please check my ID again and look at my status within the company."

Framfield, who had been merely a spectator up to this point, now decided to speak. "Why do you want to help out this piece of shit?"

She looked at him and said, "Not your business."

"You're throwing it away, you know. A whole year. He's a complete waster."

"I repeat, not your business."

"Actually, I agree," the team leader said. "Just keep out of this, Mr. Framfield."

Framfield shook his head but said nothing.

"If you've still got a problem," the young woman said to the team leader, "You have my authority to check my transaction history."

"Really?"

"It'll confirm my ID and tell you more about what I do."

"In that case..." He tapped in some instructions and then presented her with the transfer box. She placed her hand on it again.

The team leader studied the screen. "Okay," he said. "I see what you mean."

He ordered Calgary to be released from his handcuffs, and the transfer of one year was made. "You're a lucky man, Mr. Calgary," he said. "A very lucky man."

Calgary watched as the team got into their van and drove away. Framfield was already walking back into the apartment block. Calgary stood on the pavement and rubbed his wrists free of residual pain from the cuffs. "Well," he said to the young woman who was zipping up her rain jacket. "Andrea, Charlotte, whatever your name is, thank you very much indeed. A whole year. Wow. Now look, I've got about four thousand pounds in cash. That should stretch to a cup of tea. What do you reckon?"

●●●

There's been a significant development," Ellerby said. "Which is why I've asked you all here this morning. Big changes to the way we work."

"And our income?" someone asked.

"Well, of course." He smiled. "No point in changing anything if we don't increase profit. There's major benefits, no doubt about that."

He was seated as before, at the head of the oval table with his senior executives in front of him. On the table, a few inches away from his hands, lay what looked like a timer but in blue, not yellow.

"This device," he began, "looks pretty much the same as the one I showed you a couple weeks ago, only it's blue, not yellow. But the main difference is that it has an extra application. I postponed ordering the yellow timers because our research team came up with a very simple idea. You see, given that you can now have all the information, completely accurate, about a person's time allocation, or lack of it, why not deal with the timeless on the spot?"

This from Peter Radcot: "Deal with them on the spot?"

"Yes. Reevaluation..." Ellerby shook his head. "That's a lengthy and expensive process, as you know, but now it's completely redundant. A waste of time. New research shows that less than one percent of these re-evaluations are proved to be in error."

"One percent? Is that all?" This was not from Peter Radcot.

"May I point out…" This was from Peter Radcot. "That one percent of a million is ten thousand. So you're happy to deal with ten thousand people just like that?"

"Somehow, I thought you might come up with a statement like that, Peter. Look, of those ten thousand, it's only one percent again whose assessment is out by a significant amount. For the other ninety-nine percent, it's just a few minutes, perhaps an hour or two."

"What a waste of time and money," one of the executives said.

"So deal with them on the spot, is that it?" Radcot asked. "Even those hundred who've got plenty of time left?"

"Peter, what is your problem here? If we don't do it now, someone else will come up with the idea in a few months' time. What I'm saying is that it's quite clear there's no need for Reevaluation Centers anymore. This device can do the assessment and effect Human Despatch directly. Swift, efficient, much less expensive."

"So," Radcot said, and he took a deep breath. "We just kill them straight away."

"Peter!" Several voices called out his name in shock or disgust or both.

"You will apologize for that statement immediately," Ellerby said, repeating, with anger, "*immediately*."

"Okay, okay," Radcot said. "Yes, I apologize for using the word *kill*. Inaccurate. A better word would be *murder*."

"Peter!"

Several of the men round the table now stood up and waved a hand in anger. There were shouts of "No! No! No!" and "Get out!"

"Please! Everyone, please!" Ellerby called out, but the rage continued for half a minute more. Someone leaned over Radcot and said, "What a bastard you are!"

"Please, sit down, everyone," Ellerby said, and the anger began to subside. "Let's just sort this out, shall we? Now, Peter, you've just broken one of the most important rules of society."

Radcot stood. "Fuck society," he said. "And don't worry, I'm gone." He made for the door.

Someone shouted out, "Apology! Apology now!"

Radcot turned. "Fine," he said. "I agree." Then he went silent.

"Come on then."

"Oh, you mean you want *me* to apologize? No, no. I'd like everyone here to apologize to me for supporting a system that murdered—yes, *murdered*—my son. But I don't think that's going to happen, is it?"

He walked out of the room.

Less than five minutes later, Radcot left the building, walked down to Leadenhall Street, and hailed a cab. The cab approached but then swerved away as a black Daimler arrived. Radcot was dragged into the back seat by a couple of men in black uniforms. They sat on either side of him, and the car moved off. They headed down Gracechurch Street to Monument and crossed the Thames on London Bridge.

"I kind of expected something like this," Radcot said. "Though maybe not quite so quickly."

No one replied. In fact, no one said anything the whole time Radcot was in the car.

They headed down to the Elephant and Castle and then turned toward Camberwell. At this point, the man on his left grabbed Radcot's right hand and pressed it down onto a transfer box.

"Removing everything, are you?" Radcot asked. "The whole lot?" He even managed a tiny, short-lived smile. Again, there was no reply.

The man slipped the transfer box back into his pocket. At the next traffic light, Radcot was pushed out of the car, which moved quickly down Camberwell Road, turned left toward Peckham, and disappeared.

"Well now," he said quietly to no one in particular. "What to do next?"

He began to walk slowly toward Camberwell Green. He knew that was where he was heading because a street sign told him so. He'd never been in this part of London before. Twenty years ago it had been busy, full of people and street markets. Most of those who lived here were older and not well off. Now, the place was much quieter. It wasn't yet run down or abandoned. Not quite. But its popularity had clearly peaked. Radcot could see a few empty shops, some *For Sale* signs. And where were all the people? Well, of course, they were elsewhere. Many of them, retirees of a certain age with few assets, had been dealt with.

Radcot realized he didn't have his briefcase. He couldn't remember if he'd left it in the conference room or in the car that had brought him to this place. But then, did it matter where his briefcase was? Not really. Nothing inside it could be of any use to him now. Not even his cell. Who did he want to speak to? No one.

Since the death of his son, he was alone, relative-free. Who was there left for him to care for or to care for him? Well, he had one or two friends, distant ones, who might struggle to remember his name in a year or two.

But he still had his debcard to buy himself coffee. He found a café and went inside.

The café was almost empty. "A bit quiet," he said to the young man behind the counter as he ordered his coffee.

"Closing down tomorrow," was the reply.

"Really? That's a shame."

"Well, you can see why, can't you? Not enough customers."

"Emigration," Radcot suggested.

"Well, if that's what you want to call it."

Radcot took his coffee and sat at a table by the window. He could see one person in the street. A few moments later, the young man who had served him approached and handed him a plate with a very generous slice of chocolate cake on it. "Got a hell of a lot of it left," he said. "It'll just go to waste, so enjoy."

"I certainly will," Radcot said. "Thank you very much."

As he ate the cake, he thought about what had happened over the previous ten years and tried to figure out how the world had arrived at this present state of things.

There had been no big changes, just lots of little ones. *That's how these things go*, he decided. It had all started out if not exactly innocently, then at least reasonably. A world with a huge number of people, not just too many but too many *unproductive* ones; sixty percent of the population supported by forty percent. Unsustainable in the long run. So, a solution was proposed: everyone had an age limit. Compulsory euthanasia at one hundred. And yes, people were happy with that, they actually voted for it! Christ almighty, he'd voted for it himself! Maybe those who were already centenarians didn't vote for it, nor those in their late nineties, but nearly everyone else did. And the care bill for centenarians? Reduced to zero. And then? Well, the next step was obvious—bring the age limit down to ninety-eight, then ninety-six, then ninety-four.

At this point, protests began, and a new amendment to the law was introduced to keep everyone happy. This stated that ninety-four was no longer the maximum age; it was to be the average age. So, if someone died at eighty-four, his or her unused allocation of ten years could be passed on to their partner, who had the chance to live to a hundred and four. Simple, and everyone was happy. Except, it was at this point that general time-trading began.

At first, only unused allocations from those who died younger than ninety-four could be traded, but then everyone got the right to trade their allocation. This meant that, for example, at twenty-four, you could sell all of seventy years if you wanted. In fact, twenty-four was a significant number as, only two weeks after this new law came into force, a man of twenty-four found himself with no time left. He'd sold his entire allocation but had squandered all the proceeds within a few days. He had no money to buy any time back and no friends who could lend him any interims. So, he was dealt with. Soon, hundreds of thousands of people, then millions, were in the same situation, timeless before ninety-four. So, they were dealt with.

Corruption of the system took many forms. Find someone with a big personal allocation, get them at gunpoint to transfer their time, report them as timeless, and then, well, deal with them. Some gangs recruited women to have children who, after registration, were robbed of their allocation of ninety-four years and then *disappeared*. There were whole districts in which incubation lodges had been set up—prisons for pregnant young women who were promised freedom if they handed over their new-born child. Lawyers in the pay of these gangs speeded up the process by ensuring premature babies or even aborted fetuses were registered as citizens and had a full allocation. There was a famous court case in which it was argued that a child born ten weeks premature should have an allocation of ninety-four years and ten weeks. After a long debate, it was decided that this would be a step too far.

The price of time went up and up.

The rich bought time from the less well-off, and soon the difference in life expectancy became very wide: fifty percent were allotted with a hundred and thirteen; the rest seventy-five.

The statutory allocation also fell dramatically. From ninety-four years it slipped to ninety, then eighty-five, then eighty. All very popular with the people in power. They still managed to raise their personal allocation. Now, the statutory allocation stood at sixty-five, due to come down to sixty-four next month. *What the hell will happen next?* For Radcot himself, everything was quite clear.

He had just finished the cake, which was delicious, and was halfway through his coffee when the team arrived. Just two men in black uniforms this time. By now, Radcot was easy to spot because he was the only customer in the café. They came and sat down at his table. One of them shouted to the young man behind the counter, telling him to disappear, which he did.

"Peter Radcot?" the other one asked.

"Well, denying it would be a waste of time, wouldn't it?"
"Just answer the question, will you?"
"Yes, my name is Peter Radcot."
"Right, well, we've got to make an assessment."
Radcot nodded. "Please carry on."
The man took out a blue timer and pointed it at Radcot.
"Ah, you've got one of those new timers," Radcot said.
"No."
"No?"
"Not called a timer anymore. It's called a dealer."
"Ah…" Radcot actually managed a weak smile. "Of course. Of course, it's a dealer, yes."
After checking the screen on the dealer the man said, "Red. Do you know what that means?"
"Let me guess. I've got no time left."
"Even worse. In deficit. You've over-run by thirteen minutes."
"So you're going to deal with me on the spot, is that right?"
"Yes, that's exactly what we're going to do."
"Can I finish my coffee first?"
"No."

● ● ●

"You gave me a whole year?"
"That's right."
"A whole year. Wow." Calgary paused and then went on, "You know I can't pay for that. Not right now, anyway. As I said, I've only got about four grand, and that won't cover it."
"I don't want any payment," Andrea Norland said.
"What?" He looked at her in confusion. "But the rate for a year is about fifteen grand, isn't it? You can't just throw away fifteen grand."
"You think I'm throwing it away? How low is your opinion of yourself?"
Calgary shook his head and smiled. "Pretty low."
They were walking along a quiet street in Chelsea. The area was run down, partly derelict. There was grass growing between the paving stones, pot holes in the road. Nearby, there was a seventeen-story building that had been reduced to thirteen, lots of rubble on the ground around it. There were few vehicles on the

road and not many people. Nearly all of the people that Calgary and Norland could see were beggars sitting on the pavement, some asking for money, most begging for time.

"You live here?" Calgary asked.

"Not far. A couple of streets away where it's not like this. A lot better."

"And you work for TimeTrad?"

"Not anymore. I quit. Let's see…" she took out her cell to check the time. "About forty-three minutes ago."

"What did they say when you quit?"

"Nothing. They don't know about it yet. I mean, I'm supposed to be there, and I'm not, so they'll figure it out soon enough."

"And then?"

"Well, they don't like it when people leave the company."

"I bet they don't."

"They've got special ways of dealing with them."

"Christ."

At the next corner, a man of indeterminate age—somewhere between forty and sixty—was sitting on the pavement, leaning back against the adjacent building. He was bearded, scruffy, wearing a worn-out brown coat with holes at the elbows. He was shivering, but not from the cold. As they approached, he started to call out to them, "Got any spare time, eh? Please, any spare time, even a day or two—" As they passed him, his voice reached desperation level. "I'm done for! I've nothing left! Maybe an hour at most!" He tried to get to his feet but couldn't and fell back against the wall. "Please! For Christ's sake, help me!"

But they didn't stop. They walked on. They could still hear him calling after them at the next junction while waiting for the lights to change. "I've got no one! No one! Please help me!"

To Andrea Norland, Calgary said quietly, "Too late, isn't it."

"Yes," she said. "And there's too many of them."

A white van crossed the junction and passed them, going in the opposite direction.

"Looks like a team to me," Calgary said. He glanced back briefly to see the van slowing down to avoid the potholes.

They crossed the junction, stopped, and turned around to watch. The van had pulled up beside the man, and four black-uniformed men emerged.

The begger shouted, "No, no!" Then his voice rose to a scream. "Please! No! No! Don't do it! Please!"

Then one final scream of "Please" was truncated as he was dealt with mid-word. It was all over very quickly. He slumped to one side, but even before his body had time to stretch out on the pavement he was grabbed, lifted, and shoved into the vehicle via the sliding side-door.

The van moved away, did a U-turn, and then crossed once again the junction where Calgary and Norland stood. The driver ignored the red light as there was hardly any traffic on the street.

Andrea Norland said, "No one's safe anymore."

"No," Calgary agreed. "You're right there. Anything we can do about it? Anything at all?"

"Leave the country, I guess."

"Leave the planet, more like."

They walked on.

A minute or so later, Calgary said, "I think that's the van."

"What?"

"The team." He pointed up ahead. "They're coming back."

"That would be for me," Andrea Norland said.

"What?"

"I told you, TimeTrad doesn't like people leaving."

"No, no, surely..." Then he said, "Okay, if that's what you reckon." He grabbed her by the arm and pulled her across the pavement and down a narrow alley.

"What are you doing?" she called out.

"Taking you where the van can't follow. But the team can, so we need to get a move on."

A few meters down the alley, she dragged him to a halt. "It's a waste of time," she said. "You know it, and I know it. I can't get away. It'll just be a case of a couple of minutes."

"No, no. Come on!" He grabbed her by the arm again. "Come on, we've got to give it a go. We can't just give up."

"I'm going back."

"No!"

She managed to pull away from him. "There's no point," she said. "None at all."

Calgary stood beside her, his face exhibiting the distress he felt. He shook his head. "In that case, I'm coming with you."

"Please, you don't have to."

"Correct. I don't have to." He pushed past her and headed back up the alley toward the street again.

When they both emerged from the alley, they could see the van approaching. It slowed down as it got closer to them. Then, it speeded up again and passed them. It reached the next junction, turned left, and disappeared.

Andrea Norland leaned forward and breathed deeply. "Christ," she said quietly. "Christ almighty." She began to weep.

Calgary put his arm round her shoulders. "How about that cup of tea I promised you?"

A few minutes later, they sat in a quiet café on a narrow street between Chelsea and South Kensington. There were at least a dozen other customers. Andrea Norland confessed everything, including the fact that she wasn't related to Tony Pilgrew.

"Well, I'd figured that out," Calgary said. "But how did you convince him you were his daughter?"

"We checked his history and discovered he'd had an affair with a woman called Anna twenty-odd years ago. It was a holiday romance, and he'd lost touch with her straight away. It wasn't too difficult to manufacture a daughter."

"But he'd have needed proof, wouldn't he?"

"Oh, that was the easy bit. We just faked the DNA test results."

"Wow," Calgary said quietly. He picked up his cup—he was drinking coffee—and drank half of the contents.

Andrea sipped her tea. "It's all a complete fraud," she admitted. "And there's lots of different methods. Quite often, it starts with hospital lists. They look for the ones who are dying young or who've got lots of add-ons and not many relatives. They work out the best way to get the time off them. In Tony's case it was relatively easy, particularly as we promised he'd meet up with Anna again."

"Really? You found her?"

Andrea smiled. "No, no. Of course we didn't. It wasn't going to be the real Anna. We promised him a Super-real Visi on his deathbed. We'd recreate the scene in Switzerland where he met Anna. I mean, he'd be with her again, experience all the emotions—"

"So that's what he got, is it? A reconstructed love-scene?"

"No. It's promised to everyone who goes early because of some terminal disease. We'll make sure you have the greatest experience of your life just before you die. That sort of thing."

"But it never happens?"

"No. Too expensive." She shrugged. "And who's going to complain about it? There's only one person who could possibly say whether it happened or not, and he's dead."

"How do you know about this?" Calgary asked.

"Pillow talk," she said. "I had an affair with one of the IT guys in charge of that project. He wasn't happy about it. A little bit of conscience creeping in."

"Did he do anything about it?"

"Well, he said he was going to, and then he disappeared." She picked up her cup of tea but then replaced it in the saucer without drinking any. "No one knew about our affair, so I kept my mouth shut. I never saw him again."

"Dealt with?" Calgary suggested.

"Almost certainly."

"Well, I'm sorry to hear that."

Neither spoke for half a minute. Calgary finished his coffee.

"It was after that," Andrew Norland said, "that I realized that there's lots of scams. Fake relatives is maybe the most common one. Just a question of data manipulation, persuasion, and playing on the victims' desires."

"Did you think of telling the authorities about this?" Calgary asked.

She laughed. "The *authorities*. Wow, that's an old-fashioned word."

"You know what I mean."

"Yes, but haven't you forgotten something?"

"What's that?"

"TimeTrad are the authorities."

"Ah, well..." He looked at her with an expression of ignorance and resignation. Then said, "Did TimeTrad pay you in time?"

"Yes."

"How much did TimeTrad pay you for getting Tony's time?"

"Nine months."

"Is that all? And you've just given me a year?"

"Yes."

"Well, that was very generous of you."

"It was your case that made me decide to get out. I mean, what I did yesterday was going to kill you, wasn't it?"

"Keep your voice down, eh?" he said, smiling.

"Okay, you were nearly dealt with as a result of what I did."

"Well, it was close."

"Are you an alcoholic?" she asked.

"An alcoholic? No."

"They told me you were. And you've been married twice, or is it three times?"

He laughed. "Haven't been married even once."

"No?"

"I think I would have remembered. Look," he said. "I've certainly messed up my life, no question. I mean, how else could I be left with all of my statutory allocation gone? But it wasn't drink, and it wasn't multiple marriages." His smile was tentative, awkward. "Let's just say it was something much worse than too much drink or too much sex."

Andrea Norland didn't respond to this. Instead, she stood and said, "Look, we'd better go."

At that point, the door to the café opened, and three armed men came in.

One of the men said, "Everyone out, please." Then added, "Except you two." He pointed at Calgary and Andrea Norland.

The café emptied in seconds.

The team leader, a tall man with the posture of an athlete, said, in a loud, pompous voice, "The time you received, Mr. Calgary, was supplied to you fraudulently. So you're out of time."

"I've got about an hour," Calgary said.

"No, I'm afraid not. The punishment for fraud is the forfeiture of any time you have, whether it's seconds, hours, or years. All gone. So…"

Andrea Norland realized that the team leader was going to kill Calgary, and shouted at him to stop. Calgary might have yelled, too, but it was too late. The team leader's blue dealer was activated, and Calgary was dealt with. On the spot. With a grunt which suggested displeasure rather than pain he dropped to his knees and then fell forward to stretch out, face down on the floor.

Andrea Norland knelt beside him and began to weep quietly. She pressed her cheek against his. The team leader stepped across the floor, pointed the device at her head, and dealt with her, too.

Certain Things About McFarlane.

The Decline of the Death Artist, and other stories

> "Fiction reveals truth that reality obscures."
> —*Ralph Waldo Emerson.*

1.

As McFarlane strode across the busy foyer toward the elevator, he thought he might never see Emily again. The elevator doors opened as he approached so he stepped in without breaking stride. He turned and looked back across the foyer.

Never see her again? What a strange thought. Ridiculous in fact. There she was, standing next to one of the Greek-style columns that punctuated the large, red-carpeted area of the foyer. She waved to him. The red carpet, he reflected, was entirely appropriate, given the prestigious event in which he was the most important participant. He waved back and quickly held both hands before him, palms toward her, fingers spread. "Ten," he mouthed. "Ten minutes."

He couldn't be sure if this had registered with her because a group of three delegates chose that moment to cross the foyer, obscuring his view of her. But, as the doors started to close, he saw her wave again. He smiled and pressed for the fifth floor.

The elevator was empty, so he began to speak, albeit in a relatively quiet voice. "Ladies and gentlemen, it is indeed an honor to be invited to give the opening address of the Belvart Conference. Indeed, as the youngest speaker—" No, he'd said *indeed* twice. Scratch the first one. "Ladies and gentlemen, it is an honor to be invited to give the opening address of the Belvart Conference as the youngest speaker ever to be afforded such a privilege…"

Yes, that was it. *Privilege.* Honor and privilege. Of course, saying he was the youngest ever keynote speaker… well, that could be taken the wrong way, but it was merely a statement of fact, not arrogance. Bratley wouldn't mention it in his introduction. Not Bratley. He was a bit of a sad case, really. Only an Associate Professor at forty-two, and he'd never opened the Belvart Conference. And never would. Limited talent, that was his problem. Not like himself, R. R. McFarlane, MBE. Pity about the MBE. Oh, it was *something*, but it was the lowest of the honors. Knighthood next. In a couple years. Maybe before.

The elevator rose very slowly.

He had arranged for his suitcase to be sent ahead and taken to his room. He looked at his watch. 6:30. Just enough time to freshen up, change his shirt—no time for a shower, unfortunately—and get back down again in ten minutes to rejoin Emily at about 6:40. There was time for them to have a drink in the bar—a small one, certainly, for him—before Bratley kicked things off at seven in the main conference hall. Then the big speech—*his* big speech—at about 7:25.

When the elevator doors opened on the fifth floor, he checked the time again and was surprised to see that it was 6:33. Three minutes to travel five floors with no intermediate stops? Unusual. Also, as he stepped out into the main corridor, he could see no room indicator, so he didn't know which way to go. He couldn't see anyone to ask, either. He decided to go to the right.

Soon, he found rooms in ascending order, starting at ten. He continued, on the basis that he would reach room thirty-one eventually. But when he got to 30, the numbers finished. Next to room number thirty was a small lounge. The door was open, and he could see inside. Dark brown leather sofas and glass-topped coffee tables. But there was nobody there.

He walked on past five or six doors marked *private*. He continued, conscious that time was pressing. He glanced at his watch and was shocked to find it was nearly twenty to seven. Had all of ten minutes elapsed since he waved goodbye to Emily? At this rate, it would probably be better if he just gave up and returned to the foyer. In fact, he'd more or less decided to do this when he reached room thirty-two.

So frustrating! In his rush, he'd clearly missed thirty-one, so he went back. He started to run but then slowed down again. It was his haste that had got him into this fix in the first place. He walked quickly but made sure to check every door. And he arrived at number thirty.

His frustration began to slide toward anger. *This is ridiculous*. Room thirty-one on the fifth floor and he couldn't find it. And no time left now. He checked his watch again. 6:45!

Surely he hadn't been going up and down the corridors for fifteen minutes. Nothing to do now but get back to the elevator and go down to the foyer again. He began to run.

McFarlane counted the rooms as he passed them: 29, 28, 27… He reached number ten and then… and then he found himself standing in front of room one.

He gave a little cry of despair as he realized he'd come too far. He turned back, looking for the elevator which, he was sure, should be on his right. But he couldn't find it. He arrived at room ten again.

For a few moments, he stood, hands on his hips in front of this door, breathing heavily from his exertions. There had to be a simple explanation. How could he have… he'd just…

He looked around. There must be stairs. Just take the stairs, sprint down and get to the foyer. Emily may have given up on him, but he could still make it for the start of the conference. Plenty of time for that. He looked at his watch and found it was three minutes to seven. Impossible! No, no, no! Half an hour wandering these corridors? He checked his watch again. No doubt about it: 6:57. And, as he looked, it flipped over to 6:58.

He would miss the start; that was certain. But if only he didn't panic, he'd get himself down in plenty of time to compose himself for his speech at 7:25. But something strange was happening to him. There was no doubt about that. And he realized, with a shock, that since he'd arrived on the fifth floor, he hadn't seen anyone. Not one person. But he consoled himself with the thought that whatever was happening was not of his making. He released himself from responsibility. And he had twenty minutes to get downstairs. He might turn a corner, and there would be the elevator, and he'd be in the conference hall in less than two minutes. "Stay calm," he told himself. "Stay calm."

McFarlane walked along the corridor steadily rather than briskly. Soon, he reached the small lounge he'd passed earlier. This time, however, there was someone there. A boy of maybe fifteen or sixteen wearing a maroon uniform with black piping. He had a pillbox hat, also in maroon, and shiny black patent leather shoes. He was sitting on one of the leather sofas reading a sports newspaper. He stood when McFarlane entered the room.

"You work here, do you?" McFarlane asked.

"Yes, sir," the boy replied. "Hall porter. Can I help you?"

"I sincerely hope so. Just take me to the elevator. I can't seem to find it."

"Certainly, sir."

But instead of coming straight out into the corridor as McFarlane expected, the boy put his newspaper down on the nearest coffee table and opened it out to the middle page as if he were about to realign the pages and tidy it up.

"Look, forget the newspaper," McFarlane said. "I'm in a hell of a hurry, so just get out here and take me to the elevator."

"Of course, sir." He abandoned the newspaper. "Just follow me." He walked swiftly past McFarlane and into the corridor.

The two of them strode out. McFarlane saw the doors marked private, and then those numbered thirty down to ten. They turned left down a corridor McFarlane couldn't remember and then right into another.

"Is it much farther?" McFarlane asked. He had to break into a run occasionally to keep up with the boy whose walking pace was quite quick.

"Nearly there, sir," the boy said without turning round. But he set off immediately down yet another corridor, and McFarlane—following a few yards behind—started to get anxious again. When they reached the end of this corridor, he called out, "Hold on. Wait a minute."

The boy stopped and turned.

"Look, this is ridiculous," McFarlane said. "We've been walking miles. I mean, how far can it possibly be?"

"It's right here, sir," the boy said calmly. He was standing at a T-junction of corridors. He pointed to his right, and as McFarlane stepped forward, he saw the elevator doors around the corner.

"Well, thank God for that." McFarlane pressed the call button, which immediately lit up. The floor indicator showed the elevator to be on the twelfth floor.

"Are you telling me this is the nearest elevator to... to the lounge where I found you?"

"Yes, sir."

"Well, I find that hard to believe. Now, look, this will take me to the foyer, won't it?"

The boy looked surprised. "Of course, sir."

"Well, I bloody hope so." He jabbed at the call button again. "Oh, come on, for crying out loud!" The elevator appeared to have stopped at floor ten.

The boy was now standing behind McFarlane whose attention was devoted to the slow progress of the elevator as indicated by the column of numbers being illuminated in descending order very slowly.

"Oh, come on!"

"May I…" the boy began.

"Yes?"

"May I ask which room you're in, sir?"

"Thirty-one on the fifth. This is the fifth, isn't it?"

"Yes, it is."

"Well, where the hell is room thirty-one? I mean, there aren't any signs anywhere. It's bloody impossible. I can't even find my own room!"

The elevator was on the move again. Floor nine… floor eight…

"There's no room thirty-one on this floor, sir," the boy said quietly.

"What?"

"There's no room thirty-one. Not on this floor."

McFarlane turned. "You're kidding! You mean, I've spent all this time… up and down corridors… all for nothing?"

"May I take a look at your key, sir?"

"What? Oh, for Christ's sake!" He handed his key to the boy and turned to the elevator again. His irritation was now increasing toward crisis point. He pushed the call button several times. "Oh, come on!" he yelled at the elevator doors.

The boy said, "You're on level R, sir. Can you see?" He stepped forward and held the key up for McFarlane to examine. "See? It's R five three one."

"Level R?"

"Yes, sir."

"And where the hell is that?"

"Well, sir, if you…"

"No, no. Hold on," McFarlane interrupted. He looked up at the floor indicator at the side of the elevator. "Level R, you said. But just look up there. It's not even listed."

"There's a level R button inside the elevator, sir." He handed the key back to McFarlane.

"Inside the elevator?"

"Yes, sir."

"But not indicated outside the elevator?"

"No, sir."

"And why is that?"

"Well, sir, that's a good question—"

"I know it is."

"I'm afraid I don't know the answer."

51

"I'll bet you don't. I mean, what kind of place is this, eh? It's completely bloody ridiculous! The whole… the whole thing…" He saw that the elevator was one floor away, on the sixth. But still he shouted, "Oh, come on!" and pressed the call button several more times.

Then he looked at his watch and saw it was half past seven.

"What!" He looked at the boy again. "What time do you make it?"

"Seven thirty exactly, sir."

"But that's impossible! Impossible! I mean…"

"The elevator is here, sir."

"What? Oh."

McFarlane turned as the elevator doors drew apart, and he was enfolded by the sound of several noisy conversations. The elevator seemed very much larger than the one in which he'd reached the fifth floor. There were at least twenty people in it, all talking and laughing in a light-hearted party mood. Many of them were wearing colored paper hats. Some had wine glasses in their hands.

McFarlane hesitated, disconcerted by the sudden arrival of so many people and so much sound. Then someone called to him, "Are you getting in?"

"Oh, of course, yes." He stepped forward into the elevator. Then he turned and just caught a little wave from the boy, the hall porter, and heard the words, "Have a nice evening, sir," before the doors closed.

The crush of people meant that McFarlane could hardly move. "Could you press for the ground floor, please," he called out.

"No problem!" someone replied.

Someone else said, "We're already going there. In fact, we're going everywhere!"

This information was greeted with a cheer. McFarlane didn't join in. He turned his head toward the man who had invited him into the elevator a few moments before. He appeared to be about thirty and wore a smart mid-grey suit and maroon tie—and was one of the few people in the elevator who wasn't wearing a party hat. "Are you going to the conference?" McFarlane asked.

"Conference?"

"The Belvart."

The man shook his head. "Not a name I'm familiar with, I'm afraid."

"No? But it's, well, its world famous. In fact, this year, I'm actually…" He hesitated.

"I'm sorry," the man said, "but I didn't know there was a conference."

"Really? But… are you staying in the hotel?"

"Oh, yes."

"Well, we come here every year," McFarlane said. "I was told the whole place was booked out to the delegates."

The man shook his head again. "News to me."

"Well, that's what they told me, anyway."

The young man turned and addressed the others in the elevator. "Anyone going to a conference tonight?"

This question was met with laughter and some booing. Mostly laughter. Right next to McFarlane, a woman in a pale blue dress said, "Oh, Steve, don't be so boring. A conference! How dull can you get?"

The young man looked at McFarlane and shrugged. "Not a popular choice, I'd guess," he said.

"No, doesn't seem like it."

The elevator stopped and the doors opened. Four more people got in. Although the elevator was large, it was becoming very crowded, and McFarlane didn't like crowds much. Usually, he would have gotten out of the elevator and waited for another one, but this was out of the question right now. He had to get to the conference hall as quickly as possible. He might even make it to the podium within a couple of minutes. They'd certainly wait for him. How could they not? He was the most important speaker in the entire proceedings. They *had* to wait for him. If they didn't, well, he'd have something to say. Especially to Bratley.

"You're actually going to a conference?"

McFarlane turned—as much as he was able—toward the voice. He was pressed, shoulder to shoulder, with the young woman in the pale blue dress. "I'm sorry?" he said.

"You're going to a conference?" she asked again. Her words were very slightly slurred. She wasn't holding a wine glass, but McFarlane thought she was drunk. He was close enough to smell her breath but detected nothing. Her shoulder-length hair was a pale peroxide blonde, and she wore pink lipstick.

"Yes," he said, "It's the Belvart Conference."

"Sounds pretty important."

He heard the irony in her voice and went on resentfully, "Well, it is important, actually. And I'm the principal speaker, as a matter of fact."

"Really? Well, I'm impressed. No, really, I am. So you must be a professor or something. Am I right?"

"Actually, yes, you're right," McFarlane said. "I am a professor."

"Wow!" The young woman smiled. Then she called out, "Hey, everyone! We've got a real live professor here!"

This prompted further whooping and cheering.

Then, more quietly, to McFarlane she said, "I've never met a real live professor before."

McFarlane found this hard to believe. After all, most of the people he knew were professors or at least senior academics. Those he worked with, socialized with, had dinner with and corresponded with, most of them were professors. The idea that there were people in the world who'd never even met a professor was a very strange one. Was it possible this woman, who sounded reasonably well-spoken—apart from being drunk, that is—had never been to university?

"What are you a professor of?" she asked.

"Polypragmatics."

"Polly... *what?*"

"Polypragmatics."

"And what on earth is that?"

"Well, it's a bit difficult to explain in just a sentence or two, actually..."

"Is it pretty?"

"Pretty? What do you mean?"

"Pretty Polly Pragmatics." And she laughed.

McFarlane did not find this funny. "Actually..." he began but he was interrupted by the elevator itself as it halted at the third floor. Two people got off, but another five got on.

"Popular conference," the woman in the blue dress said. She leaned toward McFarlane and winked.

The elevator stopped at the second floor as well and McFarlane found his frustration and anger rising again, particularly when he checked his watch and saw that it was a quarter to eight. "No!" he shouted out. "I don't believe it!"

"What's the problem?" the woman in the blue dress asked.

"What time do you make it?" he said.

"No idea," she replied. "I never wear a watch. Such ugly things. Anyway, I find there's always someone around who can tell me the time. Hey, Steve, what time do you make it?"

"Seven forty-eight."

"There you are," she said to McFarlane. "Seven forty-eight. That any good to you?"

"No," he said. "I'm late. I'm very, very late. I just can't believe it. It's hopeless."

"Oh, come on, Professor, why don't you lighten up? Things can't be that bad. Anyway, we're nearly there."

The elevator came to a halt again. The indicator above the doors confirmed that they'd reached the ground floor. However, any relief McFarlane might have felt was overwhelmed by the bitter knowledge that he was more than twenty minutes late. Hundreds of people were waiting for him to deliver the most important speech of the entire conference and he was twenty minutes late. He tried to calm himself as he waited for the doors to open. But half a minute later, the doors were still shut, and he certainly wasn't calm. "Why aren't the doors opening?" he asked loudly but got no reply.

Then, inexplicably, the elevator began to move again. But McFarlane's anger gave way immediately to confusion because he had the strange feeling the elevator had begun to move sideways. *Sideways?*

"Here we go!" someone called out.

"What the hell's happening?" McFarlane said in a tone some way between frustration and despair.

The woman in blue said, "Isn't this fun?"

"Fun?"

"Yes, fun!" she said as the elevator began to pick up speed, or so McFarlane believed.

There was a slight swaying sensation as if the elevator were running on rails. Everyone seemed to be enjoying it. Except McFarlane. Of course, the girl was drunk—he was sure of that now—and most of the rest of them were drunk, too. But what on earth was happening to *him?* There didn't seem to be anything he could be sure of anymore. In his frustration and anguish, he turned to the girl in blue and asked, "Why are we going sideways?" He was aware, even as he said it, how ridiculous a question it sounded.

"Sideways? What do you mean?"

"We're... we seem to be going sideways."

"Have you been drinking?"

"No, I haven't! Certainly not."

"Hey, Professor, please don't get upset."

"Upset! I've every right to be upset! This is the most important moment of my life, and I'm late! Because of this bloody elevator!"

The woman in blue ignored this tantrum and said, "Let me tell you something, Professor. In confidence."

McFarlane took a deep breath, mastered his anger, and said, "Go on."

She leaned toward him and spoke into his ear. "Lifts can't go sideways, Professor. They can only go up and down." Then she laughed out loud again.

McFarlane didn't have time to respond because the elevator drew to a halt, the doors sprang apart, and everyone tumbled out, including McFarlane, who was close to the front and therefore had little choice. He was aware of people pressing from behind. He was some yards away from the elevator when he realized he wasn't in the foyer. He was standing on a wide carpeted area behind the top row of seats in a banked auditorium that led down to a curtained stage. For a moment or two, he thought he might be in the conference auditorium itself, but no one had taken their places yet, so that was unlikely. Besides, he could see private boxes to the right and left of the stage. This was quite definitely a theater, not a lecture hall. He turned and looked back toward the elevator. The doors had closed and it had already departed for other floors.

The man in the grey suit, who had spoken to him in the elevator, was standing close by. McFarlane said to him, "This isn't the foyer, is it?"

"No, I'd say not."

Then, rather weakly, he asked, "Do you know how I can get there?"

"I'm afraid not, no."

"Somehow, I thought that's what you would say."

The man turned to him. "Look," he said. "Do you really need to get to the foyer? Is it really that important?"

"Important?" McFarlane asked. "Oh yes, important." But all anger had left him now. He wasn't resigned to what was happening to him, but he felt defeated. For the moment, at least. He thought he might scream or perhaps just start weeping. He looked at his watch and, with little surprise now, saw it was ten past eight. He'd missed Emily, he'd missed Bratley's introduction, and he'd missed his own spot by, well, by three-quarters of an hour. Nothing could redeem the situation. They couldn't possibly have waited for him—he was foolish to think they would. If he turned up in the conference hall now, he'd be a laughing stock.

He said, "I don't know what's happening to me. Something very, very strange is happening, but I don't know what it is." His voice was bleak, tinged with sorrow and confusion.

Maybe the man in the grey suit sensed this. He put a hand on McFarlane's shoulder. "Why not enjoy the show," he said gently. "Just take a seat with us and enjoy the show."

At that point, the young woman in blue joined them. "Hey, Professor!" she said. "You staying with us after all?"

McFarlane said, "I'm not sure."

"Oh, you don't want to go to that stuffy old conference, do you?"

"Well, I'm a bit late…"

But she cut him short. She stepped up to him, grabbed his face in her hands, and kissed him quickly on the lips. "There," she said. "You know, I've never kissed a professor before."

McFarlane looked shocked.

The young woman said, "Oh, come on, Professor, it wasn't *that* bad, was it?"

"Well, no, I'm sorry if I gave that… that impression…"

"Oh, I get it. You only kiss professors, right? I bet your wife's a professor, too, isn't she?"

"Well, as a matter of fact, she is, yes."

"You see! I knew it. I knew it. Anyway, look, why don't you just come with us." She held out a hand toward him. "Come on, Professor. We'll take care of you, won't we, Steve?"

The man in the grey suit nodded.

"Just come with us and enjoy the show."

McFarlane reached out and took her hand, and the three of them—the woman in blue, McFarlane, and Steve, the man in grey—made their way slowly down the right-hand aisle toward the front row of seats.

2.

The theater filled up rapidly. McFarlane and the young man in the grey suit were sitting in the front row of the stalls, very close to the orchestra pit and the stage, separated by a railing only a few feet from their knees. They had to stand up frequently to allow people to pass to other seats in their row. The seats themselves were the old-fashioned flip-up style. McFarlane noticed the dark red plush upholstery was wearing thin.

He was disappointed the young woman in the pale blue dress was not with them—she had chosen to sit with other friends farther back. But disappointment was not the main emotion he felt. His anger and frustration about missing his speech at the conference had given way to a kind of despondency that edged toward despair. He could not say he was ruined—that would be going too far—but all that he'd striven for was in jeopardy, of *that* he was sure. However, there was nothing to be done this evening; he resigned himself to the fact that tomorrow morning was when issues would be resolved or not.

"So, what's the show tonight?" McFarlane asked with feigned interest.

"You know, I'm not exactly sure," the man in the grey suit said. "It's something called *Burning You*."

"Never heard of it."

"It'll be a surprise, then."

"Tonight's been full of surprises," McFarlane said. "I'm not sure I can take any more."

"Oh, just relax and enjoy it. You can always leave at the interval if it's really bad."

"Can I?"

"Well, of course you can."

"I doubt it," McFarlane said.

"Well, it's a free country, isn't it? Oh, by the way—"

"Yes?"

The young man turned toward him. "The name's Steve," he said, extending a hand.

"Steve, well, my name's McFarlane." He felt that *Professor McFarlane* was a little bit too formal, given the circumstances, but he disliked handing out his first name to total strangers.

"McFarlane? Really? You know, I used to have a friend whose name was McFarlane, and everyone called him Mac. Okay if I call you Mac?"

It wasn't okay. He despised the convention of shortening names or using nicknames. He loathed the diminutive *Mac*. And yet he found that he was saying, "Sure. Mac's fine. Pleased to meet you, Steve."

They shook hands.

"So, what brings you here?" McFarlane asked, but before Steve could reply, the house lights went out and the curtains parted to reveal a brightly lit bare stage—white floor, white walls—on which two men stood, facing one another. They were young men, perhaps in their early twenties, wearing blue jeans and white tee-shirts. The man on the right had his arm stretched out taut, pointing a gun at the other's chest.

In quiet, even tones, unnerving precisely because they were so gentle, the man with the gun said, "Tell me why I shouldn't kill you. Come on, give me a reason."

The audience had no way of knowing how far into this conversation the playwright had chosen to begin his play, but the other man—the one the gun was pointing at—was shaking. His questioning hands were trembling as if he had been under threat for some time. "Because it wasn't me," he said.

"I don't believe you," the man with the gun said.

"But you have to believe me. I mean, it couldn't possibly have been me. I wasn't even there."

"No? So where were you?"

"I was at home. I keep telling you I was at home!"

"Can you prove it?"

"Prove it? Well, I was… I was alone, I was by myself, so—"

"So you can't prove it."

"I was at home! You've got to believe me!"

A sharp metallic click indicated the gun was cocked and ready for use.

"Please… please…" the other man pleaded. His fear had reached the point of terror and panic. He dropped to his knees and raised his hands in supplication.

"Too late," the man with the gun said, and he fired into the other man's chest.

There were yells and screams from the audience because the report from the pistol was very loud indeed. In the front row, McFarlane found his ears stinging from the shock. He quickly covered them in case there was to be more firing, and he closed his eyes.

A few seconds later, when he dared look, he saw that the man with the gun was prodding his victim with the tip of his foot. McFarlane's heart was beating quickly and he very much wanted to leave. But he couldn't.

The gunman began to roll his victim toward the edge of the stage. Both men, one vertical, one horizontal, were right in front of McFarlane, who could see blood oozing from the victim's chest. One final push and the man tumbled with a crash into the orchestra pit.

"My god," McFarlane said, gripping the armrests of his seat tightly.

"What do you think?" Steve whispered. He was smiling.

"My god," McFarlane repeated.

"It's very realistic, isn't it?"

"Realistic? I don't—"

"All that blood. It's amazing what they can do."

The man with the gun resumed his initial stance just to the right of center stage, looking toward the wings on the left. "Bring in the next one," he shouted.

Two heavily-built men dressed in black and wearing black balaclavas entered the stage. They dragged between them another man in jeans and a white tee-shirt. They threw this second victim to the floor at the gunman's feet and then withdrew.

The gunman leaned over to speak to this new victim. "So what have you got to say for yourself?"

The man, who was breathing hard, pushed himself up on one elbow. "It wasn't me," he said.

"You know, I rather thought you'd say that."

"It could't have been me. Really." His voice trembled.

"That a fact?"

"I wasn't even there!"

"You were at home, right?"

"Yes!"

The dialogue continued, but McFarlane's attention was diverted to the orchestra pit.

Sounds of someone clattering about in pain reached him, and then he watched in horror as, right in front of him, a blood-stained hand reached toward the lower horizontal bar of the railing that separated the front row of seats from the pit. Slowly, the first man shot dragged himself out of the pit. He managed to pull himself up so that he was leaning over the railing. At one point, his head came down and landed on McFarlane's right knee. McFarlane recoiled in horror and disgust.

The man raised his head again, and McFarlane could see the glazed eyes, the blood trickling from his mouth, his white tee-shirt almost entirely red. There was a large hole in his chest from which blood pulsed out. "Help me, please help me." He tried to clamber over the railing, but further movement was beyond him. But then the railing itself collapsed and the man pitched forward to land on top of McFarlane, who screamed.

Steve said, "Wow!"

Trapped by the weight of the dying man and the railing that was pinned down between them, McFarlane shouted, "Get him off me! Get him off me!" He could feel blood being pumped across his chest and his waist and his knees. The man's head rested on his shoulder, his hands curved upward to grab McFarlane by the throat.

"Get him off me!" McFarlane screamed again.

A quieter voice responded, "That won't be a problem, sir, but there's something I need to do first."

This was the gunman who had walked over to the edge of the stage and was standing about ten feet away from McFarlane, looking at him and the first victim from across the orchestra pit. "I thought I killed that bastard," the gunman called out, "but apparently not." He raised his gun again and fired two shots into the back of the man who was lying on top of McFarlane.

"No!" McFarlane screamed. He had felt the body of the man shudder with the impact of the bullets. "No! No! No!"

"Don't worry," the gunman said. "He won't be bothering you anymore."

As if in response to this comment, the shot man slid off McFarlane and lay lifeless at his feet.

Steve said, "Never been to a show like this before."

McFarlane couldn't speak. He looked at the blood on his jacket and shirt.

Someone shouted, "That's him!"

This was victim number two, who was still alive and still on the floor of the stage, though he'd pulled himself up into a half-sitting position. "That's him!"

"I know," the gunman said. "That's why I finished him off."

"No, no, not him. *Him!*" The man pointed again.

He was pointing at McFarlane.

"Well, this should be interesting," Steve said.

"What? No, no, no… this is not… it's not funny…" McFarlane said, in a voice breaking with fear.

"Oh, come on, Mac, it's only a play."

"A play? A play? Look, I felt the bullets! I felt his body jerk when they hit him!"

"Yeah, it's great, isn't it, how they do it."

"For Christ's sake, I'm covered in blood!"

"And there might be a bit more of that," the gunman said.

"What?"

"Get him."

The two masked men who, only a minute or so before, had dragged the second victim onto the stage, appeared in the aisle adjacent to where McFarlane was sitting. First they picked up the dead man and dumped him into the orchestra pit. Then they pulled the railing upright but, finding one section had separated itself from the rest, wrenched it out of the floor and flung it into the orchestra pit on top of the dead man. Then they grabbed McFarlane.

The audience didn't know what to make of this. Most appeared to believe that McFarlane was a member of the cast, and his protestations an indication of the quality of his acting skills. Others, particularly those sitting within a few seats of McFarlane, shared McFarlane's horror and seemed unsure of what was happening. But Steve was enjoying the show immensely.

McFarlane was dragged up onto the stage, all the while shouting, "Let me go! Let me go! This is outrageous! Let me go!"

But they didn't let him go until they'd pulled him to center stage and pushed him to the floor to kneel in front of the gunman. In the battle between anger and fear, it was fear that won. "What are you doing?" he said to the gunman. "I can't believe— I can't believe this is happening."

"Oh, it's happening all right," the gunman said. He pointed his weapon at McFarlane's head. "So tell me why I shouldn't kill you."

"But... this is preposterous," McFarlane said. Quite suddenly, anger overruled fear. "I'm getting out of here. Now." And he stood up. But the two men who'd dragged him onto the stage grabbed him from behind and threw him roughly to the floor again.

Someone shouted, "Shoot him! Shoot him!" This was the man, the not quite second victim, who was still on stage, sitting cross-legged on the floor.

The gunman leaned over McFarlane. "You know, I think I'll have to do something special with you."

"Just let me go, you bastard," McFarlane said, and he lunged forward only to be dragged back by the two masked men standing over him.

"Yes," the gunman said. "Something special. You see, it would be very easy to just kill you like I did that other bastard." He nodded toward the orchestra pit. "Yes, I could kill you easily enough. End of story. End of *all* your stories. But that would be a bit of a waste in your case, I reckon. So what do you think, eh? What could be worse than me shooting you? From your point of view, obviously. What can I do that would really make you suffer? What do you think?"

"I'm fed up of your games," McFarlane said. "Just let me go."

"Oh, these aren't games," the gunman said. "This is for real. No, no, I mean it. Let me show you. You see that man over there?" He indicated the man sitting on the floor a few feet away, the one who had denounced McFarlane a couple of minutes before. "See him?"

McFarlane gave a barely perceptible nod. "Yes," he said quietly.

"Well, watch." The gunman turned quickly and fired. The man was struck in the face. His head jerked back, flinging blood and bone and brains across the rear of the stage. His body spasemed, feet kicking out at imaginary targets before he subsided and lay still. Some of the audience were screaming. Others rose to leave the auditorium. The gunman came to the front of the stage. "Nobody leaves," he said. His voice was loud, but he wasn't shouting. With or without the gun it was a voice of authority. "If anybody leaves, I'll kill everyone in the front row, starting with this piece of shit here." He pointed to McFarlane. "So, get back to your seats. Now."

The people who had risen to leave did as they were told.

McFarlane was shaking again.

"You see. I can do it," the gunman said to McFarlane. "I can do it, but the question is, can you? Tricky one, eh? What do you think? Here, try it." He took hold of the barrel of the pistol and held the handle out to McFarlane. "Why don't you shoot me? I think you've got reason enough to do it, don't you?"

McFarlane felt his heart beating; could hear it pounding in his ears.

"Take the gun," the gunman said. "Take it and shoot me."

McFarlane was still kneeling on the floor. He was shaking as if he had a fever. His little burst of anger and resistance was now gone. He didn't know what to do. Blood from the head of the second victim was spreading across the stage.

"Take the gun."

McFarlane felt he was about to weep. He reached out a shaky hand and took hold of the pistol. Then, hand and pistol dropped into his lap. He looked down at the weapon, which was already blood-stained.

"Now shoot me," the gunman said and smiled. "You can't do it, can you?"

McFarlane raised the gun and fired point blank into the gunman's chest.

The roar of the weapon was even greater than the earlier shots, and McFarlane felt the sudden sharp recoil in his elbow. He dropped the gun on the floor. Everything was now in darkness; the lights had gone out when the shot was fired. McFarlane was aware of screaming close by and shouts of anger and fear. He couldn't see anything but sensed that the audience was in panic. He didn't know what to do. He couldn't believe he'd actually shot someone. He was afraid and exhausted and bewildered. Then he felt a hand on his arm.

"Come on, Mac. Time to go." It was Steve who helped him to his feet.

"I can't see anything," McFarlane said.

"Don't worry. Just hold onto my arm. We'll be out of here in no time."

In an awkward tandem procession, the two stumbled to the back of the stage, McFarlane hanging on to the elbow of Steve's jacket. They pushed on through a couple of anterooms, brushing past stage props and rails of brightly colored costumes. They emerged into a white corridor with neon lighting. McFarlane was momentarily blinded by the sudden brightness, and let go of Steve's arm.

"Not far now," Steve said, rushing ahead. McFarlane followed. About a minute later, Steve opened an unmarked door and said, "This is it. For the moment, anyway."

The room was a well-appointed bathroom with a shower stall, toilet, bidet, and bath. There was a wardrobe and a towel rail. The walls were tiled in pale green with a motif of swaying palm trees. There was a mirror above the bath, and when he looked at himself, McFarlane struggled to believe what he saw. "Christ, is that me?"

Here was a disheveled, bloodied figure, hair and face streaked with dust, shirt and jacket torn and covered in blood.

"You know, you were terrific, Mac," Steve said.

"What?"

"You were great. I wouldn't have believed it."

"Wouldn't have believed what?"

"That you were actually in the play. My god, powerful stuff!"

"But I wasn't in the play. What are you talking about? There wasn't a play. Christ, that was the most terrifying experience of my life!"

"You see, there you go, staying in character. I admire that, I really do."

"No, no, look…" McFarlane began stabbing the air with the index finger of his right hand. "I was *not* part of the play! There was *no* play! They actually got murdered! Those people got killed! And I killed someone myself. God—"

Steve smiled. "Good one, Mac. You know, you nearly had me fooled there."

"No! No! No! Listen, I felt the shock, okay? When… when that guy who fell on top of me, when he was shot in the back, I felt the shock to his body when the bullets hit him! I felt it!"

"I know, yeah. Well, I could see that myself. But it's all special effects. I mean, it's amazing what they can do these days."

"Christ, I…" But McFarlane's tirade had lost momentum. He could see he was getting nowhere. More quietly, he said, "Okay, so what's this, then?" He took off his jacket and threw it on the floor. He took hold of the front of his bloody shirt. "What's this then? Strawberry jam?"

"Oh, something like that, I'm sure," Steve said. "It's a bit of a mess, certainly. Why don't you take it off? I'll get you another one. Pair of trousers, too." He went over to the wardrobe and drew out a small pile of shirts and underwear, a few pairs of trousers. "Must be some stuff here that'll fit you."

McFarlane unbuttoned his shirt. "All this blood," he said. "All this blood. And I shot someone. I actually killed someone. Christ…" He sat down on the floor and leaned back against the bath. "God almighty, what have I done?"

"Okay, Mac, you can give it a rest now," Steve said. "You're not on stage anymore. Give me your shirt."

McFarlane handed him the shirt. Steve dumped it in the wash-hand basin.

"Now, look," Steve said. "If this was real blood, you'd never get it out, right? I mean, white cotton shirts and blood? They don't go well together. But look at this."

He turned on the cold tap and let it run over the blood-stained shirt. He moved the shirt round in the basin so that all parts came into contact with the flow. In less than a minute he was holding up the dripping shirt, completely white. "See?" he said.

McFarlane got to his feet. He saw. He realized that the little understanding that he'd had of what was happening to him had now gone.

"Tell you what," Steve said. "I'll wait outside. Why don't you just freshen up and put on some new stuff. Take whatever you want. Dump your old clothes in the bath. Okay?" He left the room.

Five minutes later, the two men walked along the bright, white corridor. McFarlane was wearing a dark grey suit, which might have been tailored for him. He'd remembered to transfer everything from his old jacket to the new one. Most importantly, he had the key to the room he hadn't yet reached: R531. Feeling more comfortable in his fresh clothes but still troubled in mind, he said, "So where are we going now?"

"Back to the theater."

"Now hold on." McFarlane grabbed Steve's arm and pulled him to a halt. "I'm definitely *not* going back there."

"Oh, come on, Mac. Relax. It's not what you think."

"It's never what I think," McFarlane said. "I don't even know what to think. It's all gone. Everything."

"Trust me," Steve said. "Trust me, it'll be fine."

"Trust you? Why should I trust you? I only met you five minutes ago."

"Well, that's not a very nice thing to say. But look—" He put a hand on McFarlane's shoulder. "I don't like to be blunt…"

"But you're going to be."

"Well, yes. I mean, it's like this. You don't really know where you are, and you don't know where to go. So you've got no option, right?"

"And you do know where we are?"

"Oh, sure. And anyway, they're all waiting for you."

"Who's waiting for me?"

"Everybody. Back there. They want to see you."

"Don't be ridiculous."

"Just follow me," Steve said, and he started down the corridor. After a few seconds, McFarlane set off in pursuit.

Three minutes later, they walked through the property and costume rooms again and reached the door that gave way to the rear of the stage. Steve held the door open for McFarlane. "After you," he said.

"I don't like this, you know. I don't like it one bit."

"Look, it's okay, Mac," Steve said quietly. "Really it is. Just walk out onto the stage."

"You actually want me to go back there?"

"Yes. Look, you can do it. Just walk onto the stage. Nothing is going to happen. It'll be fine, absolutely fine. Just walk to the front of the stage."

"And if I don't do it?"

Steve shook his head. "Your loss, Mac, your loss. Just walk to the front of the stage and take a bow."

"Take a bow?"

"Yes. Just do it." He pushed the door open.

McFarlane was now close to tears. He felt he had no will left. Not only that, but this issue of will was irrelevant anyway. Whatever he did, whether he walked onto the stage or not, he was bound to encounter more pain. In that sense, then, everything was equal, and nothing mattered. He stepped through the door.

At first it was dark, but after he'd taken a few paces forward, the stage lights went up. The curtains were closed, so he couldn't yet see the audience. But he could hear them. In fact, a great deal of noise came from the auditorium, lots of cheering and shouting, scarcely muffled by the heavy velvet curtains. McFarlane took a few more steps to the front center of the stage, and as he did so, the curtains parted before him. He could see the audience now. They were applauding wildly. They were shouting and whistling. And, by the time the curtains were fully drawn back, they were on their feet. He could hear the thump thump thump of the tip-up seats as they jerked upright, and then the noise rose to another level. "Bravo!" the audience began to shout. "Bravo! Bravo! Bravo!"

McFarlane looked round. He was the only one on stage. They seemed to be applauding... *him!* For a few moments, he stood there, bewildered. He looked around again and saw Steve applauding from the wings. Steve gestured to him. "Bow!" he shouted. "Take a bow!"

McFarlane turned to the audience, but he couldn't bow. Why should he bow? *What have I done to deserve such acclaim?* Then, he became aware of people approaching from the wings. With a shock, he saw the gunman. Then he saw the first victim, not a trace of blood on his chest. The second victim was there, too, his head completely unmarked. And there were the two men in black, their balaclavas removed. All were smiling at him and applauding him. Their applause continued for a full minute. Then they all joined hands, with McFarlane in the middle. They took a step forward to the very edge of the stage. And they all bowed.

3.

McFarlane was applauded again ten minutes later when he entered a room where a party was taking place. Most of the guests had been to the play, or so McFarlane deduced, as his arrival was noted, and he was the focus of much cheering and clapping.

As the applause subsided, the general noise level rose again, and party poppers were set off, and champagne corks flew. There was much laughter, shouting, and clinking of glasses. McFarlane was not fond of parties, but he was glad that, for the moment at least, he was no longer the center of attention.

"What'll you have, Mac?" Steve asked as they approached a table on which were laid out bottles of wine and spirits and glasses of different shapes and sizes.

"Water," McFarlane said.

"Oh, come on, Mac, you can't just have water."

"Why not?"

"Well, for a start…" Steve examined the rows of bottles. "There isn't any! Now there's a good reason."

"In that case, I won't have anything."

"Aw, Mac, lighten up. Enjoy yourself. Things are going so well here."

"Are they? Are they?" McFarlane was becoming exasperated again. "You just don't understand, do you, eh? I've been through hell!"

"It certainly looked that way." This was said by the young woman in blue who had just joined them. She was carrying two flutes of champagne. She handed one to McFarlane who accepted it before he could find words to decline the offer.

"I mean, it went beyond method," the woman continued.

"Method?"

The Decline of the Death Artist, and other stories

"You know, *method acting*. Stanislavski and all that." She stepped forward and, having disposed of one glass of champagne, put her right arm round McFarlane's neck and kissed him on the cheek. "I'm a little drunk," she explained.

McFarlane took a sip of champagne. He was still being held in a kind of sideways embrace by the woman in blue whose right hand held onto his neck. She rested her head with its pale blonde hair on his left shoulder.

"My name's Sophie," she said. "What's yours? I mean, other than Professor?"

"He answers to Mac," Steve said before McFarlane could reply.

"Mac," Sophie repeated. Then she broke away from him. "I'm sorry. I'm embarrassing you, I know."

"Not at all," McFarlane said.

"No, you're being kind. You've got a wife. It's not fair. And I'm a bit drunk. Not very drunk, you understand. Just a bit. What's your wife's name?"

"Sandra."

"Sandra. Well, that's a very English name, don't you think?"

"Is it?"

"Very sort of Home Counties. Sandra. Ha! I bet she wears jodhpurs and rides horses, doesn't she…"

"Actually…" McFarlane began, but Sophie cut him off.

"I'm so rude!" she said as if this had come as a sudden revelation. "I'm sorry, I'm so sorry. No really… It's—" She looked at her glass of champagne. "It's this stuff!" she said. Then she drank what remained in her glass and held it out to Steve. "Get me another one, won't you, Steve?"

"Not sure you should have another one, Sophie."

"Neither am I, but just one more. Please."

Steve shrugged and then took her empty glass over to the drinks table.

Sophie put her arms round McFarlane's neck and held onto him tightly. With her head pressed hard against his, she said, "Why don't you come with me, Professor, eh? Would that be nice?" She released him, grabbed his free hand, and dragged him toward the door.

When they were out in the corridor, she let go of his hand, turned to face him, and said, "You do want to come with me, don't you?"

She seemed to be entirely sober. No slurring of words, her eyes intensely upon his face. "Come with me?" she said again.

"Yes," he said. "Yes, I will."

"Good."

She grabbed his hand again and led him down the corridor. As earlier with Steve and even before that, with the young hall porter, McFarlane was hurried along corridor after corridor. "How much farther?" he asked after a couple of minutes.

"Oh, not long now," Sophie said. "Look, the elevator's over there." She pointed.

McFarlane found the sight of the elevator doors comforting. He'd spent so much time earlier in the evening looking for one. "Great," he said.

"I'm just popping in here for a moment," Sophie said. They were close to a door marked *Ladies*.

"Sure."

"Won't be a moment." She pushed the door open and went inside.

McFarlane still had his half-full champagne flute in his hand. He didn't like champagne much, but he drank it anyway. He set the glass down on the carpet by the wall.

In these first moments of silence and calm for some time, he asked himself what on earth he was doing. He was heading to a hotel room with a woman he'd met only half an hour ago. Oh, she was pretty, and she smelled nice, and he was sure he would enjoy her young body but... *Christ Almighty... What about Emily? What about Sandra?* Well, actually, he didn't care for Sandra so much any more. It was a shame, really, how it had worked out. And quite amusing that Sophie had guessed correctly. Sandra was a bit posh, and these days, she preferred spending time with her horses rather than her husband.

But Sophie? *Well*, he thought. *Why not? Why not?*

Three minutes passed, and he wondered what had been taking her so long. After five, he knocked on the door. "Sophie— Are you okay, Sophie?"

No reply. As no one had entered or come out of the ladies' toilet while he'd been waiting, he felt justified in pushing the door open slowly. "Sophie?" he called again. "Sophie?"

The ladies' room was completely empty. There were three cubicles. The door of each open with no one inside. "Sophie, where are you?" he called out, more loudly. But the place was empty. There were no windows, no fire escape, no hidden doors or trapdoors. And no Sophie.

McFarlane stepped back out into the corridor. He was getting agitated again. What the hell was going on? The only pattern he could see in his experience of the past couple of hours was that of thwarted expectations. And horror.

Someone was playing games with him, he was sure. That was the only explanation. He crossed the corridor and pressed the call button for the elevator.

By the time it arrived, Sophie had still not emerged from the ladies' room. Nor could she, because she wasn't there. McFarlane didn't know how, but she'd disappeared and would not reappear. The elevator doors opened, and he stepped inside. There was no R level on offer, so he pressed for the ground floor.

As the doors began to close, he saw Sophie come out of the ladies' room. He caught the words, "I'm so sorry—" as she looked round for him; then the doors snapped shut. He tried to stop the elevator by stabbing at the *Open Door* button, but it was too late. He thought about hitting the buttons for intermediate floors, but the elevator seemed to have picked up speed. He arrived at the ground floor in seconds. As the doors opened, he thought of pressing again for the fifth— *Was it the fifth?*—to rejoin Sophie but he knew she wouldn't be there. No, she wouldn't be there.

He stepped out of the elevator into the foyer.

The sight of the red carpet was reassuring, and there was the Greek column next to where Emily had been standing when she'd waved to him earlier. But the lighting was subdued, and there didn't seem to be anyone around. *The conference, the opening session, that is, couldn't be finished already, surely*. He looked at his watch, which told him it was 1:03 am.

"1:03? No, no, no." His breathing had picked up again and he tried to master it. "It's after one in the morning? Impossible…" It felt as if it should be no later than 9:30 pm.

He looked round the foyer. The only bright light he could see was above the reception desk. And there was someone there, a man in a dark red jacket and top hat. Probably the night porter. McFarlane made his way over to him and said, "Good evening."

The floor behind the desk was higher than the foyer level, so the night porter seemed quite tall. He looked down at McFarlane and said, "I believe *good morning* might be more appropriate, sir." He smiled.

McFarlane said, "Could you tell me what the time is, exactly?"

The night porter removed his top hat and laid it to one side. McFarlane could see he was about fifty years old, with thinning grey hair and a nose that reminded him of the young boy, the hall porter he'd met earlier. Perhaps this was his father.

The consultation of the watch involved the movement of an elegant or perhaps pretentious nature. The porter was wearing white gloves. He stretched his left arm out straight so that the sleeve of his dark red jacket rode up over his wrist to reveal his watch. Bending his arm, he took hold of the watch delicately with the thumb and forefinger of his gloved right hand. "It's one oh four precisely, sir," he said.

"I see." McFarlane glanced at his watch to confirm this. "So I've missed everybody," he said.

"It would appear so, sir, yes."

"I thought some of my colleagues might still be hanging around. You know, in the bars and so on."

"Which party are you with, sir?"

"I'm one of the delegates at the conference."

"Conference?"

"Yes."

"Which conference is that, sir?"

Looking up at the porter's smiling face, McFarlane experienced again that moment of disquiet that he'd felt two or three times already this evening or morning or whatever it was. On each occasion, this faint sensation of unease had led to further, deeper moments of trauma. "The Belvart Conference," he said.

The night porter repeated the words slowly, "The Belvart Conference." Then he said, "Belvart. You know, that name does ring a bell."

"Well, I should hope so," McFarlane said. "Your hotel is full of delegates. And I'm... I'm the principal speaker."

"Are you, sir?"

"Yes."

"At the Belvart Conference?"

"Yes!" McFarlane allowed his impatience to show. "The Belvart Conference! That's why I'm here!"

"Sir, please. Please calm down."

"I'm sorry," McFarlane said, his irritation disappearing as quickly as it had arrived. "I'm sorry, it's just that I've had quite a trying day... extraordinary, in fact, and I just need to get to my room... I'm on level R. Which elevator do I take?"

"Level R," the night porter said. "That would be elevator number three. Over there." He pointed.

"Thank you." McFarlane turned to go. Then he asked, "When are we booked for breakfast?"

"Breakfast is from eight to nine-thirty, sir."

"I think we've got a group booking, actually. I know the first session starts at eight."

"A group booking?"

"For the conference delegates. Christ, what have we just been talking about!"

"Please don't shout, sir."

McFarlane sighed. "I'm sorry. No, really, I'm sorry. I'm just… I'm just a bit over-tired."

"There's no conference taking place in the hotel at this time, sir," the night porter said.

"What?"

"There's no conference, sir."

"But I'm… I'm booked in, I'm here to speak… I'm the principal speaker…"

"So you said, sir, but I can assure you, there's no conference taking place here."

"No, I don't believe it."

"You said the Belvart Conference?"

"Yes."

"Now, I do remember that one. But just because it was here when I started at the hotel. Quite a while ago now, as I think you'll appreciate. I was sixteen. I joined from school, and this has been my only job. Yes…" He smiled at the memory. "The Belvart Conference. That did keep me busy. But they canceled it the following year and I think that was that. No more Belvart."

"What are you talking about?" McFarlane felt a bit dizzy. He held on to the front edge of the reception desk. "What on earth are you talking about?"

"Well, sir, if you've come here for the Belvart Conference, I'm afraid you're about thirty-five years too late."

McFarlane was shaking now, still holding on to the reception desk but shaking. *This isn't happening,* he told himself. *No, this can't be happening.* "I don't… I don't understand."

"Perhaps a good night's sleep will help, sir."

"I'm not drunk if that's what you mean."

"No, that's certainly not what I mean. It's just that, by your own admission you've had a stressful day. Perhaps things will seem clearer in the morning."

McFarlane nodded. "Maybe, but I doubt it." Then he said, "Okay, here's a puzzle for you. I'm thirty-eight years old. If, as you say, the Belvart Conference stopped thirty-five years ago, what possible reason could I have for being here, saying I'm going to a conference that last took place when I was three?"

"That's a very good question, sir," the night porter admitted. "I'm afraid I don't know the answer."

"In that case, I'll say goodnight." McFarlane turned and set off across the foyer toward elevator number three.

"Good morning, sir," the night porter called after him.

Once inside the elevator, McFarlane spotted the button for level R straight away. As he pressed it, he saw the night porter come from behind his desk and run toward him. "Sir! Excuse me, sir!" But McFarlane had the satisfaction of watching the elevator doors close well before the night porter could reach him. And then the elevator began to rise.

Level R, McFarlane saw, was right at the top of the floor indicator, above floor fifteen. *Does R stand for Roof?* he wondered. There were no stops at the intermediate floors, so the elevator rose swiftly. The doors opened at level R.

He stepped out into the air, which was very cold indeed. He took a couple of paces forward on a white carpet that turned out to be snow. Without a doubt, he had arrived on the flat roof of the building, outside in freezing temperatures. He turned to get back into the elevator, but the doors had already closed and no matter how many times he pushed the call button, the elevator continued to plunge until it illuminated the lowest button, which was negative three, and stayed there. McFarlane, shivering now, continued to press the call button for a couple minutes but the elevator did not move. In fact, the negative three button lost its light and there was a great gust of wind up the elevator shaft as if the whole mechanism were giving a huge sigh before expiring. No more sound or light came from the elevator and the call button appeared to be dead.

McFarlane's teeth chattered. He was only wearing a shirt and a lightweight suit. He hugged himself in an effort to imbue his body with heat. This procedure was largely a failure.

The only light available was the night-time city glow and a full moon almost directly overhead. He decided to explore two small structures that stood on the roof, but just as he approached the first of these, crunching across three or four inches of snow, he noticed there was a fire a little way ahead. It looked like a small campfire and as he got closer, saw there were two people—a man and a woman—huddled around it. Attracted more by the potential for heat than light, he walked quickly forward and pushed his hands close to the flames.

"Hi!" he said.

The man looked up momentarily and then concentrated on the flames again. He was about sixty, McFarlane reckoned. It was difficult to be sure because of the poor light, but he appeared to be wearing good quality clothes that were just worn out. He was sitting on a low stool, or it might have been an up-turned bucket or a paint tin, a low seat anyway. His elbows rested on his knees, and his bare palms were thrust toward the flames.

The man said, "Warm yourself up."

"Thank you," McFarlane replied.

"You're not a regular, are you?"

"No. Yourself?"

"Been here for twenty-five years, on and off, I guess."

"Twenty-five years? That's a hell of a long time."

"I suppose it is."

"Up here?" McFarlane said. He was rubbing his hands together above the flames, but he was still cold. "Not actually up here all that time, surely."

"I sneak down occasionally."

"I go down to get food," the woman said. She was about the same age as the man, maybe a bit younger. She was wearing a very old and very dirty hooded jacket. Some of her pale grey, wiry hair could be seen escaping from the sides of the hood. Her face was wrinkled; there was some dirt high on her cheekbones. "Grab yourself a chair," she said to McFarlane and then laughed. "Look, there's one over there." She pointed to a small wooden crate.

McFarlane swept the snow off the top of the crate and pulled it in closer to the fire.

"Don't get too comfy," the man said. "You might get to like it up here, and that would never do."

"But you don't actually *live* up here, do you?" McFarlane asked.

"Oh yes," the man replied. "See that hut over there?" He pointed. "That's home."

"Only thing is," the woman explained, "in this kind of weather, it is colder in there than it is out here. So here we are."

"But how do you survive?"

"Oh, there's one or two of the staff that sneak us up some food from time to time."

"And what…" McFarlane began. "What exactly…"

"What do we do about toilets and so on? That's what you want to know, isn't it?" the woman asked.

"Well, yes, that did cross my mind."

"Just don't ask," the man said, smiling. McFarlane could see his face clearly now in the light from the fire. He'd been good-looking at one time. Possibly. There was, actually, something familiar about his face. It was the shape of his nose, perhaps, or was it his chin?

"When did you begin?" McFarlane asked.

"Begin?"

"When did all this begin, I mean. After all, you must have done something before this, surely."

"Oh yes, we were very active," the woman said. "Very active."

"Extremely active," the man added.

McFarlane was warming up a little, though his back was still cold. He became aware of an unpleasant stale odor and reckoned it came from one or other of his two new companions. Perhaps both. He pushed his crate back a little, away from the fire.

"I was in the theater," the man said.

"Really?"

"Oh yes. Producer and director rather than actor. Very unusual stuff. Very experimental."

"Too experimental," the woman added. "That was the problem."

"The public are fickle," the man explained. "They get tired and move on."

"And were you in the theater, also?" McFarlane asked the woman.

"Not directly, no. Though I suppose I was, in a way. No, I was a whore."

McFarlane wasn't sure how to respond to this, so he said nothing.

"Shocked you, have I?" she asked. She pulled her hood down to reveal her thick grey hair, streaked with dirt. "What a beauty!" she said and laughed.

McFarlane stood up.

"Going so soon?" the man asked. "Company not quite convivial enough for you?"

"I'm going to try and get the elevator," McFarlane said.

"It comes eventually," the woman said. "Hit the call button quite hard three times. That usually does it. Oh, and when you get to reception, tell Mr. Upnall—he's the night porter—tell him that Steve and Sophie are hungry."

McFarlane's heart started banging in his chest. "Steve?" he said.

"That's me," the man said.

"Which, by process of elimination," the woman said, "will lead you to conclude that I'm Sophie, which is correct."

"Steve and Sophie," McFarlane said quietly. "Christ…"

"No, he's not here," Steve said and laughed.

"Not been here yet, anyway," Sophie added.

"Just say Steve and Sophie," Steve went on. "Don't mention anybody else, all right?"

"You mean there's more of you?"

"Just one," Sophie said with distaste and pointed. "Over there."

McFarlane could see another fire farther along the roof. He hadn't noticed this before but became aware of it now and saw, also, that there was a figure hunched over it, much as Steve and Sophie were leaning over theirs.

"Stuck up bitch," Sophie said, with some passion. "Thinks she's so much better than us, but she's just an old whore too."

"What's her name?" McFarlane asked.

"Now, you're not going to mention this to Mr. Upnall," Steve said. "He gets very upset."

"Fine. I won't"

"It's Emily," Sophie said.

"Emily?"

"Yes."

"Emily Stranton?"

"No idea," Sophie said. "We don't do surnames up here. Call her Stranton if you like. I don't think she'll mind. Probably forgotten. Sometimes, I struggle to remember my own name."

McFarlane turned and began to make his way hesitantly toward the figure by the second fire. Behind him, he heard Sophie call out, "Oh, don't bother to say goodbye!"

He began to feel nervous—understandable, certainly, but he was more nervous than he'd felt at any time during the past… during the past *what?* Twenty-four hours? Thirty-five years? Nothing seemed quantifiable any more. He'd lost all ability to keep anything constant. He began to breathe quickly in short, shallow breaths. When he reached the woman crouched by the fire—he was behind her and slightly to her left—he reckoned she hadn't heard his approach, so it was still quite possible for him to turn and leave. But he couldn't do it. There was an opportunity he felt he shouldn't let pass, an opportunity for… for what exactly?

"Emily," he said quietly. Then, when there was no response, not even movement, he said, in a louder voice, "Is that you, Emily?"

Her head turned slowly, and she said, "Might be. Who wants to know?"

She had thick grey hair, similar to Sophie's. It tumbled loosely over the shoulders of her heavy brown overcoat, which had patched elbows and frayed cuffs. The hands she held out to the fire were wrinkled and dirty; her fingernails were uneven and chipped. McFarlane struggled to recognize the Emily he knew in the features of this old woman.

"It's Richard," he said. "Richard McFarlane."

She shook her head, shrugged, said nothing.

"Are you Emily Stranton?" he asked.

"What makes you think I'm the best person to ask?"

He waited for a few moments and then said, "Do you remember the Belvart Conference?"

"Conference? Do I look as though I go to conferences?"

"No, well… it was a long time ago."

"A lot of things were a long time ago."

"But it was here," he went on. "Here in this hotel. We were together…"

"Really?" she said but her voice was dismissive, uninterested.

"The last time I saw you, you were in the foyer. I had to go up to my room. I said I'd only be a few minutes…"

"Ten minutes," she said.

"Yes, yes, that's right." McFarlane's voice rose. "Yes, ten minutes! So you do remember…"

She smiled and shook her head again. "No. If I had a quid for every time someone told me they'd be back in ten minutes… well, I'd be rich. I wouldn't be here, that's for sure."

"But you *must* remember me," McFarlane said, allowing his frustration to define the tone of his voice. "You must remember me!"

"Why should I remember you?" she asked.

McFarlane stepped back. He hadn't gone anywhere near the fire, so he began to shiver again. "I'm sorry," he said, "I truly am." He got no response.

He made his way back to the square structure that housed the elevator. Sophie shouted across to him, "Don't forget to speak to Mr. Upnall! We're hungry! But just the two of us, okay? Sophie and Steve." McFarlane slipped and slid on the melting snow until he arrived at the silvered doors. He struck the call button three times. He was shivering uncontrollably now, shaking with the cold. Still, he was heartened by the sound of the returning elevator, the illumination running quickly up the column of floor buttons until the R flashed before him and the elevator doors opened.

4.

He almost fell inside but immediately realized the elevator was not empty. The night porter was there in his red uniform and top hat.

"I'm so glad I found you, sir," he said as he pressed the button for the ground floor.

"You must be Mr. Upnall," McFarlane said.

"Ah, I take it you've met some of our unofficial guests."

"Yes. Steve and Sophie want you to know they're hungry."

"Thank you, sir. Information noted. However, you won't be surprised to know I've never had a message from them saying they're *not* hungry. But they haven't starved to death yet."

"Clearly not, no. But I believe there's someone else up there, too. Is that right?"

"Emily. Yes, a very sad case indeed. Very sad."

"So what do you know about her, if I may ask."

"Only that she's been here a very long time, sir. Had some sort of mental breakdown."

"Did she?"

"Yes. She keeps saying she used to be a professor, but… well, I've no idea if that's true or not."

They descended three or four floors in silence, and then McFarlane said, "It's a bit odd, don't you think, having down-and-outs living on the roof of the hotel?"

"Oh, I've got used to it now, sir."

"Yes, but why are they here? I mean, who allows them to stay? Or is it all a big secret?"

"Oh, it's no secret, sir. No, the owner of the hotel is fully aware of the situation. In fact, he's the one who was instrumental in allowing them to stay. I believe he knew them many years ago, and when they got down on their luck, he tried to help them. I don't think they would be able to live anywhere else."

"I see. He sounds like a very philanthropic gentleman."

"Oh, he certainly is."

"And who is the owner?"

"Lord Bratley, sir."

"Bratley?"

"Yes. Now there's someone who definitely is a professor. Or was. I believe he retired from academic life some years ago."

"Lord Archibald Bratley?"

"That's right. Do you know him, sir?"

McFarlane paused before replying, "I think I met him some time ago."

"Well, I can assure you he's an excellent employer."

"Is he?"

"A very decent man. Ah, here we are."

They had reached the ground floor. As they left the elevator, Upnall said, "If you'll just come with me for a moment, sir."

"Certainly."

Upnall led him across the foyer to reception.

"I realized, just as you left, that there must be some mistake with your reservation."

"Mistake?"

"When you said you wanted level R. Of course, level R is… well, it's as you saw it. It just… didn't register with me at that moment."

"Well, level R is what my key says," McFarlane said. He took the key from his pocket and handed it to Upnall, who examined it carefully.

"My word!" Upnall said. "I haven't seen one of these in years. This system went out—oh, a long time ago. Where on earth did you get this from, sir?"

McFarlane struggled to think of a reply. If everything had actually shifted thirty-five years or so, what could he say that made any sense? He said, "How old do you think I am?"

"Actually, sir, you told me earlier."

"Did I?"

"Yes. You said you were thirty-eight."

"Did I? Well, actually, I'm seventy-three."

Upnall laughed.

"You think I'm joking?"

"I'm sure you are, sir."

"Well, you're right, of course. But, getting back to the key, I can't remember the details. I thought I got it last night when I arrived here, but I could be wrong."

"Well, let me just check your reservation, sir," Upnall said as he consulted his computer screen behind the reception desk. "Could you remind me of your name, sir, please?"

Knowing that any reply he might offer would be useless, McFarlane said, "To myself, I answer to McFarlane, but I've got no faith in that name anymore."

"McFarlane… let me see…" Upnall consulted on-screen lists and then did a search on the name. He shook his head. "No, I'm afraid we don't have a booking in the name of McFarlane."

"No?"

"No, I'm afraid not. Ah… tell me, did you book yesterday, sir?"

"Well, my secretary would have made the booking."

"At what time, sir?"

McFarlane's powers of invention, as he would admit, were not great. "No idea. Probably in the afternoon."

"The afternoon… let me see." Upnall stared intently at the information before him. "Not in the morning?"

"Could have been the morning."

"We had some difficulties with our booking system in the morning, sir."

"Really? Well, that's probably it."

"Yes, now it's very unlikely but possible your booking was lost." He looked at McFarlane. "Which would be most unfortunate, sir."

"Most unfortunate," McFarlane agreed. "But, putting that aside, do you have a room free for me right now?"

"Well, I think you're in luck, sir, yes. We have a room free on the fifth floor. Just for one night, though. How long had you intended to stay?"

"No more than thirty-five years," McFarlane said. Then, seeing Upnall's confusion, added, "Let's leave that problem till the morning, shall we? Or later in the morning, I should say."

"Quite alright, sir. Now, I'm afraid there is one other tiny problem."

"Which is?"

"You don't have any luggage with you, do you, sir?"

"I'm afraid not. Lost in transit. Has anyone phoned from the airport yet?"

"No, sir, not so far."

McFarlane shook his head. "Typical. Oh, and to pre-empt your next question, no, I'm afraid I can't."

"Pay in advance?"

"Correct. All my valuables are in my suitcase, including my credit cards."

"Credit cards?"

"Yes."

Upnall's blank look continued.

"Oh, it's just an old-fashioned expression I use to cover various… payment systems. Now, a man called…" He thought hard. The letter *E* came to mind. *Yes, Etherington, there was a good name.* "A man called Etherington said he'd call."

"Etherington?"

"From the airport. He was terribly apologetic when they couldn't find my luggage. Said he'd call right away when they found it." He looked at his watch. "Bit late now, though."

"Would you excuse me for a moment, sir?"

"Certainly."

The night porter went to an office at the rear of the reception desk, separated by a glass wall. McFarlane could see Upnall inside, talking on the telephone. He knew that his immediate future well-being would be decided by the conversation he was having. There were only two calls he could be making—either to internal security or the police. Neither option offered McFarlane any comfort.

Upnall returned to the desk. His expression was gloomy. "I'm really very sorry, sir," he began.

McFarlane had grown to like the night porter insofar as fondness could develop in so short a time. He said, "Look, don't worry, Mr. Upnall, it's hardly your fault, after all."

"No, no, but it *is* my fault, most certainly my fault, Professor McFarlane." He began searching behind the desk. "Yes, most certainly my fault."

"I'm not sure that I understand you," McFarlane said.

"Well, it's quite simple really, sir…" He was still looking for something. "Ah! Here we are." He drew out a small suitcase, lifted it up, and placed it on the desk. He turned it around so that the handle faced McFarlane. "This is yours, I believe, sir."

McFarlane recognized the case immediately and was astonished. "Well, yes, it is, but how on Earth did you find it?"

"With Mr. Etherington's help, sir."

"Who?"

"Mr. Etherington, at the airport. You said yourself that he was searching for it."

"Ah, ah… Mr. Etherington. Yes."

"I happen to know Mr. Etherington. Unfortunately, from previous mishaps of this nature, but he's always very helpful. He assured me your suitcase had been delivered earlier in the evening, so it really was my fault for not checking that it was here."

"Well, look, don't get upset, Mr. Upnall—"

"It's unforgivable, sir, unforgivable."

"Oh, don't be ridiculous," McFarlane said, perhaps more sharply than he'd intended. "It's not unforgivable at all. It's entirely forgivable, and I forgive you." Realizing that all this sounded a bit lame, he added, "Not that you need to be forgiven in the first place. As I hope I've made perfectly clear." He decided to stop speaking at this point.

"I'll take you to your room, sir," Upnall declared.

"You will not!" McFarlane said forcefully. "You've already had to leave your desk because of me once, and I'm quite able to manage. So, just give me the key, please."

"Well, you're very understanding." Upnall handed over a key. "It is room thirty-one on the fifth. Take elevator number one, sir."

"Excellent. Then I'll say goodnight."

"Well… goodnight, sir. And again, I'm really awfully sorry."

McFarlane waved this apology away. When he reached elevator number one, he pressed the call button, and the doors opened immediately. He stepped inside and selected the fifth floor.

Given that his experience so far with elevators and with attempts to reach room thirty-one on the fifth floor had not been good, McFarlane was surprised he felt in such buoyant mood. He had no idea how he'd managed to secure a room—that business with Etherington was most peculiar—but at least he had somewhere to stay and the prospect of a decent night's sleep. The night, of course, was already much reduced; he looked at his watch and saw that it was already 1:30

am—but he could sleep till eight or even nine o'clock, now that he knew his presence was not required at the conference.

No, he had no idea about what was happening to him. The theatrical performance, Steve and Sophie, Emily... Remembering Emily gave him a shock. Should he go back to level R and talk to her? No, that would be a mistake, he was sure. But this business of the conference, of its disappearance, of his sudden release from powerful constraints... he had to admit to a sense of liberation. And one result of this was that he could not bring himself to worry about tomorrow. His influence over what was happening to him was clearly zero, so why worry about anything?

He stepped out of the elevator on the fifth floor. He glanced at his key: room thirty-one. He shook his head. Room thirty-one on the fifth floor. Just as it was a couple of hours or maybe thirty-five years ago. Thirty-five years? No. Ridiculous. There had to be some simple explanation. The room indicator told him to turn right. Within seconds, he was standing outside room thirty-one.

As he raised his key to the lock, his attention was caught by bright lights to his left. Not just lights but activity. He could hear soft music and voices. He pocketed his key, left his suitcase by the door to his room, and went to investigate.

At the end of the corridor, there was what appeared to be a bar lounge. McFarlane thought it was unusual for a bar to be located so close to the guest rooms because of the potential for noise and consequent sleep disturbance, but then nothing really surprised him about this hotel anymore. He walked into the bar.

The room was very large, with a low ceiling. The emphasis was on comfort, tending toward luxury. There was a deep pile carpet in dark blue and groups of sofas and armchairs around low, circular, glass-topped tables. The bar itself, though McFarlane couldn't see the other side of it, appeared to be a circular island in the center of the room. Wine glasses hung from the ceiling, and behind the bar were bottles of wine and spirits that McFarlane had never seen before, bottles of all shapes and sizes, decanters in colored glass and cut crystal, all glinting in the low lighting.

"Good evening, sir."

McFarlane, concentrating on a survey of the room, had failed to notice one of the bar staff—the only one he could now see—who approached him from his right, returning from delivering a drink to a customer at a far table. The man was wearing a white jacket and reminded McFarlane of a steward on a ship.

"Good evening," McFarlane said. "Or should that be good morning?"

The barman lifted a flap on the bar counter and entered the service area. He placed the tray he'd been carrying on the bar counter itself.

"As it's approaching two am, sir, I suppose morning is more accurate than evening, yes."

"I was following the example set by your Mr. Upnall," McFarlane said.

"Mr. Upnall?"

"The night porter. A little earlier, he corrected me when I mistakenly wished him a good evening."

"Oh, I see, yes. Mr.… Upnall, did you say?"

"Yes."

"No… I don't think I know him."

"Really? Well, that's…" *Very odd*, he was about to say but didn't. Instead, he said, "Could I have an orange juice, please?"

"Certainly, sir. Take a seat, and I'll bring it over."

"Thanks." McFarlane turned to go but then said, "Have you been working here long?"

"Five years now, sir."

"And you don't know Mr. Upnall?"

"Possibly before my time, sir."

"I see. And what about Sophie and Steve and Emily?"

The barman's expression was not encouraging.

"On level R," McFarlane continued.

"Level R, sir?"

"Yes."

"There's no such thing as level R, not that I'm aware of, anyway. Ah, but this gentleman might be able to help you." He turned to smile at a new arrival. "Good evening, my Lord."

McFarlane twisted round to see that the barman had addressed an elderly gentleman in a green tweed suit who was slowly making his way toward the bar.

"Good evening, Torrington," the elderly gentleman said. "Or should that be good morning?"

"You know, this gentleman said the very same thing only a moment ago."

"Did he now?" He looked at McFarlane. "Very perceptive. And you are, sir?"

McFarlane said, "Oh, just another guest in the hotel."

"Hotel, you say? Well, a compliment indeed. Of course, I've modeled everything on the best hotels. It's the only way, really. The very best." Then he stuck his hand out and said, "Bratley."

"Bratley?" McFarlane repeated quietly. "Bratley… you mean—"

"I mean, my name is Bratley. What's yours?"

"Oh, I'm sorry—" McFarlane took the proffered hand which had remained extended for longer than usually necessary. "McFarlane. Pleased to meet you." They shook hands vigorously. "Would I be right in saying Lord Bratley? Lord Archibald Bratley?"

"That's right, yes. Have we met?"

"I think… I think we may have," McFarlane said, "but it was quite a long time ago."

"I see. How long ago, do you reckon?"

"Well, let me see, you were a professor at the University of Central London, Department of Polypragmatics, I believe."

"Oh, ancient history," Bratley said. "I left academia decades ago."

"Yes, but do you remember the Belvart Conference?"

"Belvart? Well, yes, of course I do. The name, anyway. The last one was… well, before I left the university."

"The last one," McFarlane said. "Yes, that was the last time we met."

The old man gave McFarlane a quizzical look. Then he said to the barman, "Perhaps I could have a glass of my usual, please."

"Certainly, my lord."

Nothing more was said until a glass of orange juice was set on the bar in front of McFarlane, and a glass of brandy was presented to Lord Bratley. Then Bratley said, "So, Mr. McFarlane, the last time we met was before you were born, I take it?"

"Before I was born? Oh, I see. No, no, I know it's hard to explain—"

"How old are you, Mr. McFarlane?"

"Thirty-eight."

"Right. Well, I'm eighty-seven. Oh, difficult to believe, I know, but not as difficult to believe as your story. The last Belvart Conference took place at least forty-five years ago."

"No, not forty-five years ago. It can't be."

"Oh yes, and even if it was only thirty-five or twenty-five I think the likelihood of our meeting there would be, very approximately, zero." He drank his brandy in one swallow and set the empty glass on the bar. "I'll bid you a goodnight, Mr. McFarlane. Or rather, good morning. And I suggest you take to your room soon as we're due for a storm shortly." With a nod to the barman, he turned and walked slowly toward the bar exit.

McFarlane called after him, "What about level R? What about Sophie and Steve and Emily?"

Bratley stopped and half-turned. "Now *that* is quite interesting. Not very interesting, obviously, but quite interesting." He walked back to the bar and stood beside McFarlane. "Level R, and Steve, and Sophie and… what was the other one called again?"

"Emily."

"Emily. Yes, that's right. So how do you know about them?"

"Upnall told me."

"Who?"

"Upnall, your night porter."

"Oh yes. Upnall. Good grief. Yes, I remember him. Strange old fellow. Worked for me for years. But he struggled with the transition, though."

"The transition?"

"To cruise ships. He much preferred the hotels. Didn't like the water, you see. Well, didn't like huge expanses of it on every side. Had to retire him in the end."

"Retire him?" McFarlane said. "Retire him? But…"

"But what, Mr. McFarlane?"

But McFarlane didn't know what to say other than, "Yes, yes… he was a very nice fellow, wasn't he."

"Oh, my view entirely. Worth his weight in gold. Anyway, I gave him a very good retirement package, and he's doing well. The last I heard, he'd bought a place in the Seychelles. Having rather a good time, I imagine."

"But…" McFarlane began again. Then he fell silent.

"But what, Mr. McFarlane?"

"What about Sophie and Steve and Emily?"

"Oh, sad cases, all of them. I suppose you knew them in an earlier life, too, didn't you? Just like Upnall." He smiled.

"Well," McFarlane said, "something like that. But you helped them, didn't you? Level R and everything. Now why did you do that?"

"And why do you want to know?"

McFarlane realized that his question had been abrupt and inquisitorial. "I'm sorry," he said. "I didn't mean to be rude. It's just that I know what Steve,

Sophie, and Emily became. The difficulties they found themselves in. And I know they owed a great deal to your intervention in their welfare. Did you know them before their decline?"

Mollified by McFarlane's softer tone, Bratley summoned Torrington who had moved away to a discreet distance. When he drew near, Bratley said, "Give me another one, will you? Very small this time." He turned to McFarlane. "Emily was the one I knew first. She'd been a colleague of mine—quite bright, too, as I remember—but she had a mental breakdown, I think, because of some affair she'd had that didn't work out. I don't know the details and never asked her about it. Anyway, she wound up on the streets. Difficult to believe, I know, but she did. And I tried to get her into various places for rehabilitation and so on, but it never worked. And then I lost track of her for a while. I came into a lot of money, inherited all those hotels, and so on, and I found her begging in the street one day. I think she'd already hooked up with the other two by that point. So, I decided to invent level R. It was a solution of sorts. Oh there were quite a few others over the years, but Steve, Sophie, and Emily were there the longest."

The barman slid another small brandy across the bar toward Bratley's hand. Bratley turned to thank him.

McFarlane said, "Sophie and Steve, were their stories similar?"

"Yes. Well, actually, no. The story of how they came to be in a similar situation to Emily was no doubt different, but the end result was pretty much the same."

"I see." McFarlane took a sip of his orange juice. "So what happened to them, if I may ask?"

"Oh, they lived on into ripe old age—not as ripe as mine, obviously—and then they died."

"They died?"

"Yes."

McFarlane picked up his glass of orange juice, put it to his lips but then replaced it on the bar without drinking.

Bratley said, "Oh, don't get upset. It was years ago."

"Does that make it better?"

"Of course not, no. Might ease the pain slightly, that's all."

After a few moment, McFarlane said, "Possibly."

"I had to make other arrangements for those few who remained, of course, when I eventually sold the hotels and level R disappeared."

"You sold the hotels?"

"Yes."

"Including this one?"

Bratley picked up his brandy glass, swirled around the spirit inside it, and drank it down in one. "Goodnight, Mr. McFarlane," he said as he replaced the glass on the bar.

"But look, I really don't understand," McFarlane said.

"No, obviously not, but look here, you've tried my patience several times already this evening—met me before you were born, got information from Upnall who couldn't possibly have met you, and so on. You're just trying to make a fool of me and I won't have it. No, I won't have it."

"Please! I promise you I'm not making fun of you. Certainly not. It's just that I'm… I'm rather confused…."

"How much did you drink before you started on the orange juice cure?"

"I'm *not* drunk. I'm *not* drunk!"

"Maybe not, but you are shouting, Mr. McFarlane."

"I'm sorry, yes, you're quite right," McFarlane said more quietly. "I apologize. There's no need for shouting. It's just that very strange things seem to be happening to me, and I'm trying to make sense of them."

"And failing, obviously."

"Yes."

"Well, look," Bratley said, "I can see you're upset, and I can see you're not drunk, but I really don't know how I can help you."

"You don't remember me?" McFarlane said, his voice breaking.

"How could I possibly remember you?"

"But we came here… now I know it sounds ridiculous, but we came here together for the Belvart Conference… we did. Really, we did…"

"Look, Mr. McFarlane, apart from the fact that, as we've already established, the last Belvart Conference took place before you were born, it certainly didn't occur here."

"Oh, it was here. I'm quite certain of that."

"No, no, no," Bratley said. "Quite impossible."

"Impossible, dear?"

The two men turned toward the source of this new voice. An elderly lady had joined them. She was perhaps younger than Lord Bratley, but it was difficult to tell. She had short white hair that was rendered even whiter by her skin, which was dark but more likely a result of tanning than ethnicity. She was wearing a silver evening gown. "Is everything all right, dear?" she asked.

"Oh yes, yes. I was just talking to Mr. McFarlane here. This is my wife, Sandra."

The old lady held out a thin hand. "Mr. McFarlane. How nice to meet you."

"Sandra?" McFarlane said. He appeared to be in shock.

"Are you all right?" Bratley asked.

McFarlane held on to the old lady's hand. "Sandra?" he repeated.

"Yes, that's right." She smiled at him. "Have we met?"

"Your maiden name… was it by any chance Duncannon?"

"Why yes, it was. How ever did you know?"

"Well," McFarlane began, "It's because… because…" He was shaking again and his voice was fading, becoming tremulous.

"Yes?" Lady Bratley said.

"Because… you'll find this hard to believe, I know…"

"I'm sure we will," Lord Bratley said.

"Do sit down, Mr. McFarlane," Lady Bratley said. "You don't seem well."

But McFarlane was determined to make his point, even if they all found it quite ridiculous. He put one hand on the bar to steady himself. "It's because we used to be married," he said. Then he collapsed.

A short time later—or so McFarlane believed, though his understanding of time was clearly not what it used to be—he was stretched out on one of the sofas being tended to by a small group of concerned people: Lord and Lady Bratley, the barman, and a fourth person, a man in a pale grey suit who was conducting medical checks. He held McFarlane's wrist and said, "Quite high." Then he lay his right hand on McFarlane's forehead. "Well, he's a bit feverish but I can't find anything major wrong with him. We'll need to keep him under observation of course, for twenty-four hours at least. You say he seemed confused?"

"Oh, completely." This was Bratley's voice. "Coming out with all kinds of nonsense about meeting me forty-odd years ago and even once being married to Sandra here."

"Really?"

"Yes. Very odd."

"But he managed to tell me my maiden name," Lady Bratley said. "And I doubt that many people know that."

"Oh, it's a matter of public record, my dear. In *Who's Who,* for one thing."

"Is it?"

"Oh, quite definitely."

"All the same…"

McFarlane felt comfortable on the sofa. He was very, very tired but comfortable. He decided it would be nice just to go to sleep. Right there. Upnall was right. A good night's sleep was what he needed. But first—

He managed to find his voice. "Can someone tell me…"

"Yes?"

"Can someone please tell me where I am exactly?"

"You're in the lounge bar," Bratley said.

"Yes, but where's the lounge bar?"

"On E deck."

"What?"

"On E deck."

"But where… *where*…"

"Oh, lord…" This from Bratley who was beginning to lose patience again.

"Now, darling, remember the poor man is confused. We need to help him as much as we can. He clearly needs a full explanation," Lady Bratley said.

"Oh, a full explanation," McFarlane said. "That would be good. That would be very good."

"Well, young man, you're in the lounge bar on E deck on the cruise ship *Himalaya*. And right now, we're more or less in mid-Atlantic."

5.

McFarlane woke up a few hours later. He became aware that he was lying in a small white room. He felt tired and weak but quite comfortable, though he soon became disconcerted by the fact that the bed was moving. It was rising and falling gently in a constant rhythm. He began to feel queasy and decided to try and sit up.

An alarm sounded as he drew his right arm out from under the crisp white sheet. It wasn't particularly loud but continued in a series of high-pitched beeps. He got the impression that his movement had triggered the sound, but he couldn't be sure. Nevertheless, the alarm stopped after half a minute or so and four people entered the room and stood around his bed.

There were three women and one man. Two of the women were nurses in pale blue uniforms and butterfly hats. The third woman, McFarlane guessed, was a doctor. She was wearing a white coat and had a stethoscope around her neck. The man was the only one not in uniform. He was wearing a grey tweed jacket and a white shirt with no tie. He was about forty, McFarlane guessed. He appeared to be the one in charge. It was this man who spoke first.

"How are you feeling, Mr. McFarlane?"

"Oh, I'm fine," he replied. "Well, actually, I'm feeling a little bit sick. Queasy, that is. I mean, it's the bed. It keeps moving."

"The bed is moving?"

"Up and down, all the time."

"Ah."

"Can you stop it?"

"No, I'm afraid not, Mr. McFarlane. There's quite a heavy swell at the moment, and I'm told it's probably going to get worse. But there's no need to worry."

"A swell, did you say? A heavy swell?"

"Yes, that's right."

"Ah, yes," McFarlane said. Despite the fact that the details were fuzzy, he could remember some of the last conversation he'd had before his collapse. "The *Himalaya*, is that right?"

"The *Himalaya*?" the man repeated.

"Yes, the…" He paused and looked round at the four faces which were regarding him carefully, as if he were a specimen in a museum. "Yes, that's… what's the name of this ship again?"

"This is the *Hindu Kush*."

"The Hindu…?"

"*Hindu Kush*."

McFarlane shook his head and smiled. "Yes, the *Hindu Kush*. How silly of me to forget."

The doctor said, "Did you say the *Himalaya*, Mr. McFarlane?"

"I'm not sure. Did I say that?"

"The *Himalaya* was the forerunner of this vessel."

"Yes, of course."

"It sank."

"It sank?"

"Yes. Oh, a decade ago, at least. Tragic."

"Yes, I remember, of course," McFarlane said. "It belonged to the Bratleys, didn't it? Lord and Lady Bratley. Whatever happened to them?"

"They were on the ship when it went down."

"Oh, so they drowned. Is that what you're telling me?"

"I'm afraid so, yes."

"Well, I knew that, of course," McFarlane said. For a few moments, he thought of Sandra, whom he'd loved. Well, he'd loved her for a while, at least. But then, maybe he hadn't loved her at all; maybe he'd just convinced himself of it.

"Did you know the Bratleys?" the female doctor asked.

"Yes," he said. Then he added, "Slightly."

"Can I ask a question?" the man said.

"Of course, yes."

"It's just that we don't have any records of you. Obviously, I've been trying to locate your medical history but I can't. And you're not registered as a passenger on this cruise. So… so can you tell me how you came to be here?"

"Not really, no."

"You see, you've got no papers, no passport…"

"Everything's in my suitcase."

"And where's that?"

"Outside room thirty-one on the fifth floor."

"You mean cabin thirty-one on deck five."

"No, I mean room thirty-one on the fifth floor of a hotel that may or may not be connected to the cruise liner *Himalaya*."

"That doesn't really make a lot of sense, Mr. McFarlane."

"Oh, I'm well aware of that."

"Are you sure your name is McFarlane?"

"No. Let's say that I used to be sure, but I'm learning the merit of doubt these days. About everything."

"I see."

The four of them left the room shortly after this last exchange. McFarlane was glad of the peace and quiet, though still a little disturbed by the movement of his bed, which seemed to be increasing in distance of rise and abruptness of fall. *A bigger swell*, he reckoned.

Then, the doctor returned. She introduced herself as Dr. Coventry. McFarlane looked at her more closely. She had a pure complexion, and he found her very attractive. Her short red hair reminded him of Emily at twenty-five, before she had completed her doctorate. "Is your name Emily?" It was a silly question, he knew, but he asked it anyway.

"No," she said. "Alice."

"Dr. Alice Coventry."

"That's right. Now, I've returned because I'd like to ask you a few questions, if that's okay."

"Of course."

She drew up a chair to sit by the side of his bed. "You see, we're very concerned about you."

"Are you?"

"Yes, because we can't trace you at all. We've no idea how you came to be here so it's a question of… of trying to establish your identity. Do you understand?"

"Perfectly."

"So… well, can I say first of all that it's really very important that you answer my questions truthfully. Can you promise you'll do that for me?"

McFarlane considered calling her a patronizing bitch, but instead said, "I promise on one condition."

"What's that?"

"Well, you want me to answer truthfully, so you have to supply me with a definition of truth."

She smiled, but it wasn't a warm smile; it was a smile of uncertainty. "Whatever do you mean?"

"What kind of truth do you require? That's the question."

"There's only one kind of truth, Mr. McFarlane."

"Really? Well, I have to inform you that you're wrong. And this interview is over." He leaned back into his pillows and closed his eyes.

"Mr. McFarlane? Mr. McFarlane?"

But McFarlane didn't speak or even move. He waited, feigning sleep, until he heard her pushing back her chair and closing the door behind her as she left. All in all, he felt, this little interaction had gone rather well. And he fell asleep.

Immediately, he was under attack from words and images, but mostly words, with names at first—Belvart, Emily, Bratley, Sophie, Steve, Upnall, Bratley again, and Sandra, Torrington, Himalaya, Hindu Kush, Coventry, Alice Coventry, Emily Coventry, yes, Dr. Emily Coventry… Can I ask you to do that for me? … That's a very good question … There's no level R … What a stuck-up bitch that one is … Conference? What conference? … That's a very good question … Mid-Atlantic … I'll only be a moment, wait for me … Look, I'm in a hell of a hurry … Can't you? … It's him! It's him! … Wait for me, won't you? … Will this take me to the foyer? … That's a very good question … So why shouldn't I kill you? … That's a very good question, and I'm afraid I don't know the answer …

Even before he woke up, he began to feel sick, and when he woke, he realized immediately that the bed was bucking underneath him. He gripped the edges of the mattress to stabilize himself. An alarm began to sound. This wasn't the earlier restrained *beep, beep, beep* within the room but a loud caterwauling scream of an alarm that threatened to render him both deaf and blind. In between bursts of this alarm, he heard shouting outside his room, and there were calls of panic as the ship threw itself about in violent spasm.

McFarlane was tipped out of bed onto the floor which, to his horror, was wet. He pulled open the door and saw that waves of seawater were breaking toward him down the corridor. He splashed his way forward to the nearest staircase down which more water was cascading. He realized he was wearing pajamas and was barefoot, but there was no question about returning to his room.

He reached the foot of the flight of stairs going up but was immediately pushed aside by a group of young men heading for the safety of the upper decks. He managed to scramble up the stairs after them. By this time, he was soaked. His pajamas clung to him like rags applied with wallpaper paste. He felt cold. He had no time to feel cold! He got to the next deck. There were more people. Some children were screaming. He thrust them out of the way and continued climbing.

He reached a level where he could step out onto the outer deck and look at the sea which was huge, grey, belligerent. The white tops of the waves were stretched out horizontally by the wind. Below him, lifeboats were already in the water. They rose against the ship's side then plunged into the trough of a great wave, which then threw them back again to smash against the side of the ship. He saw the boats overturned and people spilled across the grey water like rice grains from a punctured sack.

He flung himself back from the rail and grabbed ahold of the door he'd come out. He forced himself back inside. He found the stairs again and moved higher, up the internal slopes of the ship. The alarm still sounded, but there were no people there, none at all. *How many had reached the lifeboats? How many had already drowned?*

He began to run, inasmuch as he was able to run, along the corridors of the upper structure of the ship. Now and then, he pushed open a door, but he encountered no one. On this particular level, he was completely alone. He went higher. Still no people. He reached the top of the ship, the highest point, close to the bridge, and he stepped outside again, holding tight to the rail as the ship shuddered under the impact of colossal waves. He could see, to the rear of the ship, detritus in the water, shattered lifeboats and human flotsam, rising and falling, rising and falling.

But the ship wasn't rising and falling anymore, or at least not to the extent it had been earlier. It was wallowing in the water; it was sluggish; it was filling with water. It was sinking.

The wind eased slightly. McFarlane held onto the rail. He began to shout. He screamed. Words came from him that he could not hear above the hooting of the alarm and the rush of wind and sea. He shouted and he screamed and he ranted against powers he didn't understand. He was shivering. He was cold and terrified, and all he could do was wait until the first wave reached him.

6.

"How are you spelling that?"
"B-E-L-V-A-R-T"
"Belvart?"
"That's right. Archibald Bratley Belvart."
"Right. Good. So, how are you feeling today, Mr. Belvart?"
"Fine. Absolutely fine."
"You're lucky to be alive, you know."
"Am I? I'm not so sure about that, actually."
"Oh, but you are. You're the only survivor. Didn't they tell you that?"
"No."
"Well, there you are. The only one out of two thousand people. Imagine that. Plucked from the sea half-dead…"
"Only half?"
"Oh, come along, Mr. Belvart, you're a lucky man. I'd call it a miracle myself. Do you believe in God?"
"No."
"What about fate? Do you believe in fate?"
"No. I don't believe in anything. You can only believe in something that's constant. I mean, something fixed that you can rely on. No such thing exists."
"No?"
"No. And hasn't ever existed. And I reckon the prospects for the future are pretty slim, too."
"Well, I'd say that sounds rather cynical, Mr. Belvart."
"Does it? Well, I'm not a cynic; I'm a realist."

The two men were in McFarlane's hotel room. The bed was to one side; they were sitting at a small round table close to a drinks cabinet. The questioner was a man of thirty or thirty-five with short-cropped blonde hair. He was wearing a charcoal-grey suit and had an identification badge clipped to his top pocket. This badge declared him to be Dr. P. P. Stratford.

McFarlane was wearing clothes designed for someone else. His grey trousers were too long, but the dark green jacket was too small—tight around the shoulders, and the sleeves too short. When he'd said he was feeling fine, he was telling the truth; when he said his name was Archibald Bratley Belvart, he was not. For he'd reached the stage when he wasn't so much taking everything one day at a time, but he was taking things minute by minute. In the recent past—whether this was a few days or decades didn't matter—he'd found the name McFarlane didn't really advance his cause, so he decided to change it. (The name, that is, not the cause.) But then, what exactly was his cause? He wasn't sure. All he could say for certain was that he was having a serious problem with definitions. For the moment, however—for the next minute at least—things were looking quite good. After a couple of days in the hospital, he'd wound up in this hotel, and it was very comfortable, too. He supposed he would be staying here until it was decided what was to be done with him. The next minute, then, was assured.

"Who should I call?" Dr. Stratford asked.

"Call?"

"On your behalf. I mean, here you are with only the clothes you're wearing, with no documentation and no money."

"There's no one," McFarlane said.

"No one at all?"

"No."

"Belvart," Dr. Stratford said. "It's an unusual name, but I'm sure we can find some relatives for you. Let's take a look, shall we?"

There was a small laptop on the table. Stratford opened it up and began typing.

"I'm sure you won't find anything," McFarlane said.

"Are you sure, Mr. Belvart? Absolutely certain?"

"Yes," McFarlane said, though the resolution in his tone was more to convince himself than Stratford. "I'm quite certain," he added.

"Well," Stratford said, and he continued typing. "You might very well be wrong." He looked up and smiled. "Or right. I mean, it's just possible…" He looked at the screen again. "Well, I've found you, anyway."

"What?"

"Archibald Bratley Belvart. It's just the register of the *Hindu Kush*. You were bound to be listed there, after all."

"I'm on the ship's register as Archibald Bratley Belvart?"

"Well, yes. Who else would you be registered as? I mean, that is your name, isn't it?"

"Well, it must be," McFarlane said, "if it's on the ship's register, don't you think?"

"Exactly. They never get these things wrong. Now let's see…" He continued to search. "Well," he said after half a minute or so. "I'm getting some responses to Archibald Bratley and a few to Belvart, but apart from the ship's register, there is nothing else for all three names together. Which is odd."

"Is it?"

"Yes. You're not a ghost, after all. You're bound to pop up all over the place."

"I like to keep myself to myself."

"Obviously."

"So what does it say about Belvart?" McFarlane asked.

"It's the name of some conference or other that took place last century."

"Does it say when the last conference was?"

"Let's see… Yes, yes, it was seventy… no, seventy-two years ago."

"Really? Well, I'm getting older and older."

"What?"

"I'm a hundred and ten now." McFarlane allowed himself a smug smile.

"What on earth are you talking about?"

"Oh, just a little joke. What does it say about Bratley?"

"Bratley… Okay… Yes, here we are… Distinguished professor of polypragmatics." He looked up from the screen. "What on Earth is polypragmatics?"

McFarlane said, "No idea. I bet it's pretty, though."

"What?"

"Never mind."

Stratford consulted his screen again. "Left academia and became an entrepreneur, it says. Owned a chain of hotels and then some cruise ships."

"And died in a shipwreck."

"That's right."

"Just like myself. Only I didn't."

"That's right, Mr. Belvart, you didn't. So, anyway, to repeat my question: who should I call? I mean, there must be *someone*, surely."

McFarlane shook his head. "No."

"No one at all?"

"None."

Stratford said, "You know this is very difficult."

"Well, I'm sorry," McFarlane said, allowing a note of exasperation into his voice. "I'm sorry this is hard for you, but look at it from my perspective. There's no one left who knows who I am. I mean, I'm not completely sure who I am myself. All I know right now is that I'm wearing clothes that don't fit, and I'm sitting in a hotel room talking to you. These are the only certainties in my life, and even that could stretch the definition of certainty quite some way."

Stratford considered this statement for a few moments and said, "I see." He waited a few seconds more before continuing, "Well, of course I realize it's difficult for you, Mr. Belvart, of course I do. There's no doubt about that." He paused again, then went on, "Were you traveling alone on the ship?"

"Yes, I was."

"Did you get to know any of the other passengers?"

"Not really, no. And anyway, what good would that be since they're all dead?"

"Well, I suppose you're right. But anyway… you mean you didn't even speak to anyone?"

"Well, obviously, I spoke to one or two—"

"Can you give me a name?"

"Well, if it makes you happy, but this really is a waste of time, you know."

"Just give me a name, Mr. Belvart."

McFarlane noticed a new edge to Stratford's tone. It was harder, not yet aggressive, but heading in that direction.

"Well, I can give you one name."

"And that is?"

"McFarlane."

"McFarlane. Okay, let's see." Stratford consulted his laptop again. "McFarlane… Yes… R. R. McFarlane?" He looked up.

McFarlane began to feel uneasy again. He tried to will his heart to calm down, to stick to the regular, steady beat that was the product of quiet living, but it wouldn't obey. "That's right," he said. "But I don't see how he could be on the list. Impossible."

"Of course he's on the list. You said yourself you met him on board. So he's got to be on the list, and he is."

McFarlane struggled to turn his confusion into sense but found he couldn't do it. He decided to smile instead. So he smiled. "Well, you're right, of course. He was on the ship; therefore, he must be on the list."

"Oh, and I'll tell you something else, too…" Stratford was looking hard at the screen again. "My god, that's impossible!"

"Now you're at it," McFarlane said.

"No, no, this is… well, it's most peculiar… amazing in fact—"

"What is?"

"Well, there's been a mistake, you see." He looked up from the screen. "Yes, they've changed the data. It seems that you *weren't* the only survivor."

"What?"

"There was another one."

McFarlane's unease moved swiftly toward discomfort as he prepared himself for another revelation. "Don't tell me," he said. "McFarlane survived as well."

"Yes! Isn't that great!"

"Well, it's a surprise, certainly."

"And do you know what's even better?"

McFarlane's discomfort grew. "I'm sure you're going to tell me."

Stratford stood, closed his laptop, then leaned over the table toward McFarlane. In confidential tones, he said, "McFarlane's here."

"Here? What do you mean *here?*"

"In this hotel."

"No," McFarlane said. "It's not possible." But he knew, and Stratford probably knew, too, that the words were to convince himself of their veracity.

"Possible and actual, Mr. Belvart. Now come with me." He stepped over to the door.

"Where are we going?"

"To see Mr. McFarlane, of course."

"Oh, I don't think so," McFarlane said. "No. Maybe another time."

Again, Stratford's lively, enthusiastic tones disappeared. As if issuing a command to an inferior, he said, "We're going to see Mr. McFarlane, and we're going now." He opened the door and held it open.

"This way," Stratford said, and he set off briskly. McFarlane followed.

Soon they reached a elevator. When Stratford touched the call button, the doors opened immediately. When they were inside, he pressed for the fifth floor.

"The fifth?" McFarlane said.

"Yes."

"I thought it might be. And tell me, it's room number thirty-one, isn't it?"

"How did you know that?"

"Oh, I only had a few hundred to choose from. It was easy."

When they reached the fifth floor, they walked along a corridor and arrived at a viewing point. From a wide, curved window that stretched from floor to ceiling, McFarlane could see the city before them in all its early summer colors. The sky was very close to them; it was blue and cloudless. A mile or so distant was the port with ships arranged in rows like kindling laid out to dry.

"This is the fifth?" McFarlane said. "Surely we're a lot higher."

"Things are a bit different in this hotel," Stratford said. "This is the fifth from the top. Rather a refreshing change, don't you think?"

"Oh, certainly."

They walked on. At the next corner, Stratford said, "It's down there on the left." He pointed. "I'll wait for you back in your room."

"You're not coming with me, then?"

"No." He turned and began walking back the way they'd come.

"I might not go in," McFarlane called after him.

Stratford didn't slow down. "Oh, you will," he said. Then he was around the corner and gone.

McFarlane stood in the corridor, unable to move. Then he decided just to go back to his room. The whole thing was preposterous. Why should he allow this… this Stratford fellow order him about? Absolutely mad. No, he'd just go back to his room and to hell with it. He took a few hesitant steps in the direction Stratford had taken and then stopped. *No, no, no!* He stood in the middle of the corridor, unmoving, until he realized there was a danger that he would start crying. And then he did cry. A few tears anyway. Not of self-pity, he assured himself, but of frustration. That was it, frustration. Think of everything he'd been through, after all. *No, best not think about it, actually.* He took a handkerchief from his pocket and wiped his eyes. Then he blew his nose. Then he turned around.

He walked resolutely forward until he reached room thirty-one. He felt calmer now but couldn't stop himself from shaking as he raised his hand and knocked on the door three times. About half a minute passed before he saw the doorknob turn. There was a tiny click, and then the door swung open.

Buy or be Bought.

YOU CAN'T STOP
YOU CAN'T GO BACK
YOU CAN'T OPT OUT

To his surprise, Ellis found he had only nine Declines left. He had to pay for Declines so that he was allowed to not buy anything. He never liked his Declines reducing to single figures, so he brought up his account on his phone to buy more. The message was already there: *How many do you wish to purchase?* He tapped in *100*. He reckoned that would see him through the weekend. He slipped the phone into his pocket and carried on walking.

He was crossing the Thames on "The Bridge of the Top Adviser." Ellis was approaching the center of the bridge when his phone beeped. He took it from his pocket and saw the message: *Transaction denied.*

Curious.

He stepped off the walkway and into one of the several viewing areas. These were large glass bubbles reaching out over the Thames. A small crowd of tourists already occupied this one. They were checking out the sights on offer and photographing them: St Paul's Cathedral, the Gherkin, the Zahra Tower. In Ellis's opinion, this was one of the great views of London, but right now he wasn't interested. He pulled up the full message on his phone: *Transaction denied. Standing Charge of £1,000 required before purchase of more Declines.*

There was clearly some mistake. He'd paid a thousand only— He flicked through his accounts calendar. Yes, he'd paid his last thousand on— there it was, the seventh of April, only three months ago. There must be some problem with the system. At that moment, another message came through: *Declines remaining: 5.*

No, no, no. That couldn't be right either. It suggested he'd used up four Declines in... in, what was it... two minutes? He went back to the other message and sent a reply: *£1,000 paid 7 April. Problem?*

Almost immediately came the response: *Received with thanks. Next installment due today.*

Seventh of July? No, no. He could see the simple error the system had made.

Next install due 7 April next year. Charge annual.
Incorrect. Charge quarterly.
Since when?
All customers informed.
I was not informed.
Message sent.
Not received.
Incorrect. Message sent and received.
NO. MESSAGE NOT RECEIVED.
Incorrect. Message sent and received.
Shit!

He willed himself to remain calm, but it was difficult. He had to think carefully about this. Could he have received the message but not noticed it? Or deleted it by accident? He checked his main message box. No, nothing there. He checked Junk 1 and Junk 2. Nothing. Then he saw Junk 3, a folder he didn't even know he had. There was one message in it: *Decline Standing Charge held at £1,000. Quarterly.*

Quarterly. Right. He shook his head. He had to make an effort to fight the frustration and anger he felt. He looked at the time and date stamp on the message and saw he'd been given fully twenty-three minutes' notice of the change. He slipped the phone back in his pocket.

He breathed deeply a few times and approached the edge of the viewing area. The glass wall rose from floor level to a few meters above his head, where it met the curve of the glass roof. He stepped up close to the edge so that his nose was almost touching the glass. The blue water of the Thames rippled below him. The first group of tourists had moved on, rejoining the walkway to be whisked off to the South Bank. They'd been replaced by a group of a dozen teenagers with orange rucksacks that bore the message BUY NOW! in large blue capitals.

Ellis took out his phone again. *Agreed*, he responded. *Message received.*

Then the next message: *Do you wish to pay? Declines remaining: 1.*

Only one left? Something really strange was happening. That meant that nine had been used up in as many minutes. No, no, no.

Do you wish to pay?

No, he bloody well didn't want to pay! It was completely crazy. How could they just… just quadruple the charge with… with… with just twenty-three minutes' notice? No, he damn well—

Another message arrived: *Declines remaining: 0.*

Shit!

He switched back to the other message and made his reply: *Yes, I wish to pay.*

Thank you.

He said "Shit," again, but this time it was more resigned than angry. He switched off the phone and put it back in his pocket.

The young man leading the teenagers with the orange rucksacks was telling them about the Great Fire of London and pointing to St Paul's. He also had an orange rucksack, a much bigger one. He set it at his feet and extracted from it a screenpad on which he displayed some historical data. Two of the teenagers had already wandered off. "Mike, Alice, could you get back here, please!" he called after them. Reluctantly, they returned. "So, any questions?" he said to the group.

"Why's the water so blue?" one of them asked.

Ellis thought that was a bloody good question. But he was distracted from hearing the answer by his phone, which vibrated in his pocket. He took it out and read the message: *Transaction denied.*

What?

Transaction denied. Insufficient funds in target account. Insert funds immediately. Currently required: Standing Charge £1,000; fine £500.

This time, he didn't exclaim. No angry expletive came from him. Not even a resigned sigh—his mood had dwindled beyond resignation toward a feeling of hopelessness. As the blue Thames passed beneath him, he transferred £5,000 from his savings account, paid his £1,000 Standing Charge and the £500 fine. Then he bought two hundred Declines for £5 each.

It was too late, of course. Declines could not be invoked retrospectively. He checked his account. Seven Accepts had gone through before his hundred Declines arrived. The total bill for these seven items that he'd bought, whatever they were, was £568.93. An expensive afternoon so far and it was only two o'clock! In all, he'd spent £3,068.93 in order to purchase nothing. And he'd failed.

•••

Ellis wondered if there was any link between these financial difficulties and the events of earlier in the day at the office where he worked. Or rather, at the office where he *used* to work.

On leaving university at the age of twenty-two, he got a job in the Department of Post-Philately. This was an ever-diminishing section of the ever-growing Ministry of Further Information. As the rise in information technologies ensured the decline, almost to extinction, of the physical letter, the need for postage stamps had dwindled. Nevertheless, Ellis still designed stamps. This difficult situation was further complicated by his latest design for a stamp to commemorate the recent "blueing" of the River Thames.

"It's a fish," his boss Downbridge had said to him that morning. He pointed to the design proofs of the stamp that lay on the desktop between them.

"That's right," Ellis said.

"It's a dead fish."

Ellis nodded. "It's a statement."

"It's a dead statement."

"It's a dead fish statement."

Downbridge sighed. "It's always a statement with you, isn't it, Ellis."

"Technically," Ellis replied, "everything *is* a statement. Even a statement that states it's not a statement is a statement, though a futile one."

"Is it really."

"Yep."

"You know, I hate all this statement nonsense."

"As you've stated several times."

"Okay, okay. Look—" He stood up. Then, to Ellis's surprise, he smiled. "Would you like a cup of coffee?" He stepped over to the corner of his office, where a coffee maker was on a table with a small fridge beside it.

Ellis declined. This was the first time Downbridge had offered him a coffee, so he knew that things were either very good or really very bad. Almost certainly the latter.

Downbridge returned to the desk with his own cup of coffee. "Why's the fish dead?" he asked.

"Why's the Thames blue?" Ellis countered.

"You've never liked that, have you?"

"Correct. I've never liked it."

"Why not?"

"Well, apart from the fact that the Thames isn't the sea—which is rarely blue anyway, and never that particular shade of blue—there's the little matter of the deaths of thousands of fish."

"There's no evidence," Downbridge said, "that it was the dye that killed the fish."

"Oh, please tell me you don't believe that," Ellis said. "The day after the dye was introduced, they were picking up dead fish from Putney to Greenwich."

"Okay, but let's put it this way…" He pointed to the design documents. "We can't celebrate a dead fish."

"Oh, I agree entirely," Ellis said.

"I mean… actually, I like the idea of using a picture of a fish but not one that's…" He leaned over the design proofs to get a better look. "…not one that's half rotten and hasn't got any eyes."

"Okay, no problem. You find me a live fish in the Thames, and I'll redo the design, and you'll have the liveliest, bluest, Thamesiest piscine philatelic celebration ever."

Downbridge shook his head, then took a sip of coffee. For a few moments, there was silence in the room.

Downbridge said, "I'm going to have to let you go."

"Ah." That was a surprise, certainly, but then Ellis smiled. "Decruitment?" he offered. "Or is this downsizing or rightsizing? Smartsizing? Capsizing?"

Downbridge said nothing.

Ellis went on, "Lay-off? Pay-off? Day off? No, can't be a day off. Rest of your life off?"

"Ellis—"

"Oh, wait a minute… you're freeing me up to enable me to pursue my wholeness unimpeded by future employment in the Department of Post-Philately—"

"Please be quiet, Ellis."

Ellis was quiet.

"Don't you ever take anything seriously?" Downbridge asked.

"I take dead fish seriously."

"Right. Okay." Downbridge opened a drawer in his desk and took out a green envelope which he passed across to Ellis.

"It's green," Ellis said. "Shouldn't it be brown?"

"You're objecting to the color of the envelope?"

"Well, green is more positive, I can see that," Ellis said. "You know, green shoots, spring, new beginnings, and so on. Now brown—"

"Will you please be quiet—"

"—just reminds everyone that what they're being handed is—"

"Shut up!"

"—shit."

•••

When he got back to his apartment, Ellis found eight packages waiting for him. There were seven in his basket, and one stuck in his in-chute. The in-chute indicated its anger at this inconvenience by beeping loudly as Ellis walked in the door. He released the package, which slid down to bounce on top of the other seven items. So, eight packages in all, but why eight, not just seven?

All of them were wrapped in orange paper with the motif TA stamped all over in blue. Seven of them also had a label indicating the contents. The eighth, however, had an extra-large label that occupied one entire side of the parcel and proclaimed:

> Your free gift from
> our Top Adviser who
> loves you.

He set this package to one side.

The first of the others that he picked up was a Megaband Expander. On the side, next to the label, there was a picture of what looked like a plastic tube. Ellis had no idea what a Megaband Expander was, nor did he wish to find out. He looked at the others. There was a pair of non-slip slippers that glowed in the dark so that you could save on stair lighting at night. There was a Multi-Crevice Cleanser. From the illustration it appeared that this was something you could slip over the top of an ornamental statuette to clean all those awkward corners and cavities. Perfect, so he was informed, for putting a real shine on your Rolls Royce Flying Lady. There was also a single-touch dimmer table lamp. He thought he would probably prefer a single-touch brighter table lamp, but he hadn't received one of these.

He couldn't be bothered looking at the others. He took all seven to the kitchen area and dumped them, unopened, into the recycle chute. The chute complained about the sudden influx of large objects, but he told it to shut up, and it did.

In general, Ellis was quite happy with his apartment. He had a place to sleep and a place to sit. The food dispenser was a basic model but he wasn't bothered about that. His entertainment area with its surround HoloTV was more than adequate for his needs, but he rarely used it. He received, but declined, regular invitations to upgrade.

The only thing he really wanted to change was the relative position of the in-chute and the recycle chute. If he could place the first directly over the second, then there would be no need for any mediation between the two. All the piles of junk that arrived every day could go straight out again without him knowing anything about it. But this was one change he knew he wouldn't be allowed to make.

He turned his attention to his free gift. As he was opening it, he realized what it was going to be. It was the gift that accompanied the first order of more than five items. For the past four years since the introduction of NonStopShop, he'd bought nothing through the system, so he'd never received one. He'd never even *seen* one up close. He opened the package and tore away the wrapping to reveal a plastic figurine, about half a meter high, of our Top Adviser herself. He was impressed by how tacky it was. Nevertheless, this was his first direct encounter with Top Adviser, whatever her name was—it'd never been made public—the CEO of the most powerful company in the country, Greatest Shopping.

Ellis shook his head and smiled. He turned the statuette over in his hands. It wasn't just the product of the grossest vanity and in the poorest of taste, it was badly made as well. When he set it on the table, it fell over because there was some excess plastic on the circular pedestal. Yet it was oddly fascinating. He'd intended to chuck it down the recycle chute to follow the other rubbish he'd already disposed of, but now he thought he might keep it after all. He would trim the pedestal so the thing could stand upright. Then maybe he could paint it. Paint it white? Yes, why not. An indication of the angelicism of this wonderful person.

He laid the statuette on its side on the kitchen table and went out to meet his friend Dave.

●●●

Y"ou got fired?"

"Oh, come on, Dave, nobody gets fired anymore. I was… I was *released* to pursue my career within another employmentary context."

"A what context?"

"Employmentary."

"Is that a word?"

"It is now."

"Christ. Well… I'm sorry, El. I mean… did they give you any money?"

"Two months' pay."

"That's not much."

"Oh, I don't know. Should last me… well, at my current rate, about twelve hours."

"What are you talking about?" Dave asked.

"You been having any trouble with your Declines Account?"

"Not that I know of, no."

"But you know they've shifted the charge from annual to quarterly, don't you?"

"Have they?"

"Check it out."

Dave took out his phone and brought up his Declines Account. "Let's see… Next payment due… September. There you are. Annual."

"Well, mine's now quarterly," Ellis said.

"That's because they don't like you."

"Well, that's clear enough. So I pay a thousand a quarter, and you pay a thousand a year."

"I pay eight hundred, actually."

"Eight hundred?"

"Yes. Well, I do buy some stuff, you see. What I pay for is what they call a 'Moderate Decline Account.' In total, I actually spend less money than you do in a 'Total Decline Account.'"

"I don't want to buy anything," Ellis said. "Which means they really don't like me. Well, anyway, when I asked why it'd gone up by four hundred percent, I just kept getting the message *Incorrect*."

"Well, so it is, technically."

"What?"

"From a thousand to four thousand is a three hundred percent rise, not four hundred."

"Is it?"

"Yes."

"You know, that doesn't really make me feel much better."

They were sitting in Ellis's favorite café, Café Lipp. It was his favorite for two reasons. First, it was different from the norm. There were open tables rather than the individual or dual cubicles preferred by the newer café chains. The coffee did not appear from a dispenser in a cubicle wall; it was brought to the table by a smiling waitress. The smiling waitress was the second reason Ellis liked the place. She was the owner of the café, and she was known as Mat. This was short for Matilda, a name she hated. She'd thought of Tilda or Til or just Da but finally settled for Mat. She had a warm disposition, a lightness of presence that Ellis found very attractive.

Mat was at their table now, offering them more coffee.

"Refill, gentlemen?"

Dave looked at her as if this was a profoundly odd offer. "No thanks," he said. "I'm fine."

"I'll be happy to take some more," Ellis said.

"Great. Here you are." She poured more coffee from a large jug into Ellis's cup. "Plenty more," she said as she moved away.

Dave said, "This place is weird."

"You think so?"

"Yes."

"So you don't like the coffee then?"

"No, no. The coffee… well, the coffee's pretty good, actually. But why don't they use paper cups like everyone else?"

"Too expensive."

For a few moments, they drank their coffee in silence. Dave looked around the café. The walls were decorated with large square highly-colored canvases. "Are these paintings?" he asked. "I mean, by actual people?"

"By actual people," Ellis confirmed.

"Weird." Then he added, "You need to buy stuff, El."

"But I do buy stuff."

"Okay, but not through NonStopShop."

"Correct. I refuse."

"But that's why you're in so much trouble."

"So I'm in trouble now, am I?"

"Sure you are. If two months' pay doesn't last two months, you're in trouble. Look, what they're doing is sending you more and more stuff so they can charge you more and more for not buying it. They're targeting you. Can't you see that? Well, not you specifically, just people like you. They need to make it more expensive for you not to shop than to shop."

"So that I'll start buying stuff."

"Sure. That's what they want. And they particularly dislike people who set up permanent automatic Declines. I mean, you don't even look at any of the offers, do you? You just decline everything."

"Yeah, but I'm allowed to do that if I want to, surely?"

"Well…" Dave hesitated for a few moments. "I'm not convinced, actually."

"What do you mean?"

"I mean… Well, maybe you should think about buying stuff now and then. Just a few things. You know, just sometimes."

"You're saying I've got a duty to buy stuff?"

"Well, yes. Sort of."

"A duty to who?"

"Well, right now, to yourself. I mean, it would get them off your back, make life a bit easier for you."

Ellis shook his head. "I don't like it," he said. "Anyway, I did actually buy a few things today."

"You did?"

"Before I sorted out my account and bought more Declines, I'm afraid a few Accepts went through."

"Really? So what did you get?"

"Oh, a pile of complete crap."

"You have to be selective."

"Well, I didn't have the option, did I? I wound up with a something something Expander, for example. Just a bit of plastic, it looked like. And, let's see… I got a special thing for cleaning ornaments. Gets into all the little crevices and so on. Very good for Rolls Royce Flying Ladies, apparently."

"Very useful."

"Well, exactly. As for the rest, I didn't even bother looking. Just dumped the lot, unopened."

"What do you mean, *dumped*?"

"Just threw everything down the chute."

"Really? And you're saying you didn't even open them?"

"That's right."

"I see. Well…" He picked up his cup and drank the remaining coffee. He put the cup back in its saucer. "You know, El, I don't think that was such a good idea."

•••

When he got back home he received a phone call.

"Is that Mr. Ellis Bennington?"

"Possibly. Who's calling?"

"I'm calling on behalf of our Top Adviser."

"Really? And you are?"

"My identity is not relevant to this conversation."

"Oh, I don't know," Ellis said. "I'm always keen to know who I'm talking to, so your identity is relevant to me."

"I believe otherwise."

"You are not me."

"That is correct."

"Excellent. At least we've established something."

"Mr. Bennington…"

"Look, I'm sorry, but I'm going to have to establish your identity first."

"My identity is not relevant to this conversation."

"So you've said. But I disagree. And I'm going to have to ask you a few questions. Can you tell me your mother's maiden name, please."

"My mother's identity is not relevant to this conversation."

"You know, I rather thought you might say that, but look, could you at least tell me if your mother has a name or merely a model number?"

"My mother's identity is not relevant to this conversation."

"Well, I think that makes it all perfectly clear. And now I'm going to say goodbye. Goodbye!"

He cut the call and switched off his phone. It began to ring immediately. Curious. He checked the phone status. Definitely off. But it was ringing. He accepted the call.

"Hello."

"That was imprudent, Mr. Bennington."

"What? Oh, it's you again. How did you do that?"

"Do what, Mr. Bennington?"

"Renew the call. My phone was switched off. I mean, it's not possible."

"The methods underlying the resumption of the call are irrelevant to this conversation."

"Really? Well now, I should have known that, shouldn't I. So, look, I'm just curious… Tell me, what is relevant to this conversation?"

"The fact that our Top Adviser is very upset."

"Is she? Well, I'm sure we all have our off days. Do give her my very best wishes."

"I detect, Mr. Bennington, a note of levity in your voice—"

"Well done!"

"—and I should advise you that this is not in keeping with the gravity of your situation."

"Gravity of my situation? But it's our Top Adviser that's upset. Or so you said."

"Yes, Mr. Bennington. Precisely. She's upset with you."

Ellis experienced a moment of unease and said nothing for several seconds. Of course, he was talking to a computer, but a very intelligent one who could make decisions and implement them. It was much superior to the drudge he'd argued with earlier about the Decline payments. A computer that could detect humor and even irony! This represented a major advance, possibly toward considerable danger.

He said, "I'm listening."

"I know you are, Mr. Bennington. Now, the problem is that earlier today, you threw away no fewer than seven purchases—"

"How the hell do you know that?"

"—all of them unopened. This is most unusual behavior. Was this done in error, Mr. Bennington?"

"No, it wasn't."

"Do you mean to say you deliberately placed them in the recycling chute?"

"That's correct, yes."

"You didn't want them?"

"No, I didn't."

"Then why did you buy them?"

"I'm sure you know the answer to that."

"I do not wish to prejudge your position through my preconceptions."

"Well, that's very fair of you, I must say. Anyway, as you know, I had no option. I didn't have any Declines left in my account."

"It is very remiss of you to let your account lapse to such an extent. I'm sure I don't have to remind you of that."

"You don't have to remind me of that."

"Good."

"But tell me," Ellis went on. "Now that Declines are so expensive—and just for me, it seems—what happens when I can't afford anything, and I can't afford to buy Declines either?"

"You must work harder, Mr. Bennington."

"I've just lost my job."

"That is indeed most unfortunate. You must find another one quickly. You must work hard to earn more money so you can have more choice."

"Suppose I want less choice, not more?"

"That is not possible."

"No? Why not?"

A short silence followed, and then came the reply: "More choice does not include the choice of less choice."

"I see."

Another silence, then: "There is something that works in your favor, Mr. Bennington."

"Well, that is good news! I'm in favor!"

"No, that is not the case. The fact that something has worked to your advantage does not imply any wider benefit to your overall situation or that you are in favor."

"Well, that's a pity."

"I refer merely to your free gift. You did not place that in the recycle chute."

"Certainly not! Heaven forbid that I should act so disrespectfully toward our Top Adviser!"

"As you are doing now."

"What on earth do you mean?"

"I mean the tone of sarcasm you bring to bear on matters of great importance."

"They're not important to me."

"Oh, I assure you they are. Now, let me give you a piece of advice, Mr. Bennington."

"Well, interesting. Advice from a computer. This should be good."

"Buy or be bought, Mr. Bennington."

"Buy or be bought? What does that mean?"

"It is my fervent wish that you do not have to find out. Goodbye."

"Hold on! Hold on! Hello?"

The connection was dead. Ellis tried to reconnect, but his phone would not allow it. He asked for the number of the caller, but access was denied.

●●●

When Ellis woke up the next morning, he found he'd been sweating during the night. This often happened when he'd been dreaming, and there had been dreams, certainly, but he couldn't remember the details. All he could be sure of was no horror had been involved, no slashing of flesh or breaking of bones, no decapitation. Oh, he sometimes had those dreams, too, but last night's dreams were, in a way, worse. They were full of uncertainty and ambiguity; they were unsettling, disturbing, like a queasiness in the stomach that didn't quite make you vomit but didn't go away either.

He stripped his bed and put the bedclothes, as well as the tee shirt and shorts he'd worn during the night, into the laundry chute. He showered and picked out his favorite clothes which, his wardrobe reminded him, were very old and needed replacing.

"Replace now?" his wardrobe asked.

"No."

He said no to breakfast as well, noting as he did so that this cost him two Declines. Ten pounds! For the honor of having no breakfast!

It was Saturday morning. Normally, he'd be at work earning some extra money to spend not shopping. On this Saturday, however, he decided to walk to Café Lipp and buy breakfast there. There was good food and the added attraction of meeting Mat.

Unfortunately, this morning Mat informed him that the café would soon be closing down.

"Closing down? But why?"

"Can't afford to keep running the place."

"But it's so popular. I mean, look…" Ellis gestured around the room. There were nine tables in all. Only one was unoccupied.

"I know, I know, but that's not how it works."

"Put your prices up."

She shook her head. "No. I mean, lots of people are paying Declines to eat here in the first place."

Ellis shrugged. "I know."

"You too?"

"Fraid so. Yes."

"Well, there you are. And anyway, there's all the equipment we've got here, the cookers and all the stuff in the kitchen, the coffee machine…"

"The coffee machine looks fine to me," Ellis said.

"Well, it is. But it's old."

"Ah."

"It still works okay, but there's always pressure to buy a new one. I mean, I've spent so much on Declines not to buy new stuff that now I can't afford to buy the new stuff anyway. Whole system's just… crazy."

"Certainly is," Ellis agreed.

"How did we end up like this?" Mat asked.

"We must have wanted it, I suppose. Well, not you and me, but most of the population."

"Probably the people who sell, not the people who buy."

Ellis took a sip of his coffee. Mat was standing by his table, glancing around occasionally at the other customers.

"So what are you going to do?" he asked.

"No idea." Mat brought her attention back to her most regular customer. "I'll register for nonprov straight away. That'll give me a couple of weeks, and it'll stop them trying to sell me any more catering equipment."

"But then what?"

"As I said, I really don't know right now. I suppose I could always get a job in a Top Adviser Café."

"Ah, she's got a café chain, has she? Might have a little problem there," Ellis said.

"Really?"

"Your skill at making coffee."

She looked at him in silence for a moment. "What exactly do you mean?"

"I mean, you're very good at it. Very good indeed. You wouldn't want your new colleagues getting resentful, would you?"

She shrugged.

"Learn to make bad coffee," Ellis suggested.

"Maybe that's what I'll have to do."

"But not today, please. Not today."

•••

When Ellis got back to his apartment, he was feeling quite depressed. He'd lost his job, he was paying huge sums now for the privilege of not buying anything, and his favorite café was about to close down. He would probably lose touch with Mat whom he really liked, which left only Dave, really, as his closest friend. He'd made no close friends at work even after six years. None of his former colleagues had been in touch since he'd been fired yesterday.

He met Dave for lunch.

Dave's choice of venue was a new diner called Regulations, which was in the City, close to where he worked. Ellis wasn't exactly sure what Dave, whom he'd met at university, actually did for a living. He worked in the Ministry of Monetary Kinetics and his current title was Pre-Trajectory Information Manager. Dave had told him once that it was "mostly PR stuff," but there was no further explanation.

As far as Ellis could see, Regulations was very much like any other restaurant, only more expensive. He and Dave sat in a double cubicle and ordered via a touchscreen menu on the wall. The food appeared almost immediately through hatches adjacent to each place setting. Dave enjoyed this instant service; Ellis did not.

"What happened to settling in, browsing the menu, making a choice, and then talking for a few minutes while the meal's prepared?" he asked.

"Too slow," Dave said.

"I like slow."

"Well, you like a lot of weird things. Here it's important to get to the eating bit as quickly as possible. That's the idea, anyway."

"Whose idea?"

Dave ignored this question. He went on, "Speed—nothing reckless, you understand—efficiency. A clean-cut, direct, focused experience. It's all about the pace of the zeitgeist."

"God, you're beginning to sound like me, only you're sincere, and I'm not."

"How's your steak?" Dave asked.

"Haven't started yet."

"Well, get a move on, El. We've only got thirteen minutes left." He pointed to a digital clock above one of the serving hatches. It was counting back from… whatever these courses allowed, a figure Ellis couldn't remember. But now it registered 12:52… 12:51… 12:50…

"If we order dessert," Ellis asked, "do we get extra time for that?"

"Of course we do."

"Okay. In that case, I suggest we wait till there's one second to go and then order strawberry mousse."

"Not possible," Dave said in a tone of finality.

"It's on the menu," Ellis responded.

"Yes, yes, I know that. No, what I mean is that you're not allowed to order like that. You've got to order at least five minutes before the time of your first course runs out."

"Okay, so we wait till it reaches five oh one."

"I'll be ready before that."

"Will you?"

"Sure." Dave placed a forkful of steak in his mouth. Then he mumbled, "Please get started, El."

Ellis cut into the meat on his plate. "I got a phone call from our Top Adviser last night," he said.

"No kidding? And what did she have to say to you?"

"Oh, it wasn't our Top Adviser herself, you understand."

"Thought not. One of her Sophisticates, perhaps?"

"Is that what they're called?"

"Yep. Try to keep up, El."

"I don't want to keep up."

"Your problem in a nutshell."

"You think I've got a problem?"

"I know you've got a problem. And you know it, too. If the Top Adviser is calling you, then of course you've got a problem. She wasn't calling to congratulate you, was she?"

"Not exactly, no."

"It was about yesterday, wasn't it? I mean, all that stuff you threw away."

"Yes."

Dave shook his head. "I told you that was a bad idea. I mean, unopened and all…"

"But how did they know that?"

"Chute sensors. You've heard about them, surely."

"Can't say I have, no."

"Well, they were brought in a few months ago. They check everything that goes down. You know, just in case…"

"Just in case what?"

"Oh, terrorism, bombs… that kind of thing."

"And anti-Top Adviser behavior?"

"Well, it seems like it, doesn't it?"

"But why are they getting so upset about me? I mean, I'm not a revolutionary or anything; I just don't like what's going on much. I want to be left alone."

"You're probably the kind that worries them most—ordinary guys who just don't want to fit in. Too many of them around, and there's a problem."

"I find that hard to believe."

"Well, it's true. Anyway, tell me more about the call."

"Oh, it was mostly… you know… intellectual jousting."

"You mean a logical argument from them and sarcasm from you."

"More or less, yes. But then, right at the end, I got a kind of warning. Well, it sounded like a warning, anyway. 'Buy or be bought.' That was the message. Any idea what it means?"

Dave said nothing for a few seconds. Then he said, "Not good."

"Really? Not good or actually very bad?"

Dave shook his head slowly. He wasn't saying no, just indicating a feeling of considerable concern.

Ellis said, "So, not so much 'Buy or be bought,' more like, 'Bite or be bitten.' What do you reckon?"

"Look, El," Dave said, "You've just got to start buying stuff. You really, really, *really* have to start doing that. And it actually doesn't have to be lots of things, just a few bits and pieces occasionally. Keep them happy. You want a quiet life, right?"

"Of course I do."

"Okay. So just keep a low profile. Buy the odd thing. It's when you refuse to buy anything at all that they get twitchy. Just a little compromise, that's what's needed."

"I don't like it."

"Just think about it. Please. It's for your own good."

"Is it?"

Dave allowed his exasperation to show. "Yes, yes. For Christ's sake... I mean, look, your Standing Charge for Declines is now what? Four thousand a year, something like that?"

"Well, it was yesterday."

"That was yesterday. And it might go up even more. But if you started buying stuff, the charge would come down, I'll bet you. I mean, mine's only eight hundred because I buy stuff. Not lots, you understand. Just average amounts. It's not that difficult."

"Sure. Okay. You buy stuff, but more than you actually need, right?"

"Yes. I suppose... I suppose that's true, to an extent."

"So what do you do with it? I mean, the stuff that you really don't need?"

"I recycle it."

"Well, exactly!"

"But not straight away. That's the whole point. I keep hold of it for a while, and then I chuck it. And I always open the packets. Christ, El, that was really dumb... chucking them away still unwrapped."

"It's more honest than what you do."

"Honest?" Dave's exasperation was reduced to resignation. He relaxed back into his seat. "You just don't get it, do you, El?" he said quietly.

"Obviously not."

"Look, in one respect, you could say it's just a game—"

"A game?"

"Yes, it's a game, but you refuse to play it. That's why they're so pissed off with you. So, look... just think of it that way. It's a game that you've got to play. Please, El, please, please, *please* play it."

●●●

Ellis was feeling even more miserable when he got back to his apartment. He felt that he was heading toward a crisis, and the speed at which he was approaching it was ever-accelerating. He got confirmation of this when he checked his messages and found: *Declines remaining: 10*. Usually, a hundred Declines would last him three days, but he'd used up a hundred and ninety in less than twenty-four hours. Not only had his Declines Standing Charge been raised to a ridiculous level, but he was being bombarded with offers so that his Declines would be used up more quickly.

But he would not give in; he would not buy piles of junk he didn't need. He wouldn't even buy one thing. Not even one. He would buy only Declines. He requested fifty more and noticed, with more alarm than surprise, that this cost him two thousand five hundred pounds. The price—his price—per Decline was now fifty pounds, up from five the previous day.

It was clear that he couldn"t possibly win. The Standing Charge would go up again; the price per Decline would rise and rise until his entire life savings—or what was left—would not even buy a single Decline. He had a moment of doubt. Should he take Dave's advice and buy one or two things? After all, there might be a few items on offer that he actually needed or, at least, would derive some benefit from. He picked up his phone and, for the first time ever, switched off Automatic Decline.

An offer came through immediately. It was for a silver-plated rocking horse money box. *Buy now!* he was instructed. He declined. Straight away he was asked to buy a Mega Bubble Maker with two liters of Mega Bubble Mix. He declined. Then there was a Multifunctional fully DZ compatible Pocket Triceptor (waterproof). He had no idea what this might be. Declined. Next came a Sewing Thread Organiser Box with 150 Skeins of Embroidery Floss, then a model Happland Lift-Off Rocket, including Two Astronauts, a Space Dog, Alien, Moon Buggy and Crater, a Thermowhite Wrapover Toilet Seat calibrated to a constant temperature of twenty degrees, an Over-Sink Kitchen Tidy with… *No! No! No!* He declined all these, and before the next offer arrived, he reinstated Automatic Decline.

He placed his phone on the table next to the statuette of the Top Adviser, and then he went out. He was aware that going out 'raw'—without your phone—was against the law. Nobody had paid much notice to this change, which had been introduced a few months before. Since everyone was already required to have a phone, what was the problem about taking it with you at all times?

He found that walking the streets without the constant presence of the phone in his pocket was a liberating experience. Though he often had it switched off while he was out, that wasn't quite the same. There was the knowledge that at any time, it could alert him to the arrival of a call or a message. Then he realized, as he passed so many people, phone to ear, talking intently about everything and nothing, that the next logical step was to make it illegal to have your phone switched off.

In twenty minutes, he'd reached Café Lipp. The place was empty. There was just Mat cleaning the tables.

"Not quite sure why I'm doing this," she said.

"Closing up early?" Ellis asked.

"Closing up and closing down."

"Today? So soon?"

Her gesture was one of resignation. "Yep, I'm afraid it's today. Got to be out of here in an hour."

"I'm really sorry." He stepped up to her side and put a hand on her shoulder. "It's rotten for you."

"Yes, but..." She shrugged. "What can I do?"

"Well..."

"I can make you a coffee," she said, smiling through her disappointment. "Last one." She left the cloth on the table she'd been cleaning and went to the coffee machine behind the counter. "Machine's still on. Take a seat. Anywhere you like."

Ellis sat. "So what's this place going to turn into?" he called over to her.

"A TotalTopShop."

"Well, we do need a few more of them, don't we."

"Oh, we do, we do."

Mat made two cups of coffee and brought them over to where Ellis was sitting. She placed a cup before him and then sat opposite him. "Enjoy," she said. "It's good coffee, and it's free."

"Free?"

"I got notice to quit at about two o'clock," she said. "Since then, everything's been free. Your friend Dave was in about an hour ago and he was surprised, too. That his coffee was free, I mean. He wanted to pay, but I said no."

"Did he drink the coffee or not?"

"Oh, he did."

"So nobody paid, but they all drank the coffee? Well, I hope you'll be okay in that case."

"What do you mean?"

"You could be arrested for not charging them."

"Really?"

"Well, yes. The government won't get any purchase tax for free coffee."

Mat took a sip. "You know, I really don't care," she said. "Tomorrow, I'll be starting in a Top Adviser Café, and I probably won't last ten minutes, and I don't care about that either."

"I'd like to keep in touch with you," Ellis said. "Maybe we could meet up sometime."

"I'd like that," she said. "Yes, I'd like that." She took her phone from her pocket. "What's your number?"

Ellis was about to reach for his phone when he remembered he didn't have it with him. "You know, I left it at home," he said.

"Really? You mean deliberately?"

"Yes."

"Wow. Well now..." She drank some more coffee. "I'd say that was dangerous."

"No more dangerous than giving people free coffee."

• • •

Ten minutes later, Ellis was on his way home. Once more, he had this unsettling feeling of being separate. As he followed this logic, he decided the people he could see pursuing private conversations so very publicly were themselves the instigators of this separation, cutting each other off by their constant need to communicate.

When he arrived at his apartment, he could hardly get the door open. His in-chute basket overflowed with packages that had begun to spill over the floor. The pile immediately above the basket was so high it impeded new packages from arriving down the chute. Realizing he was now in serious trouble, Ellis began to laugh. He carefully stepped over the scattered parcels and pulled the basket away beneath the in-chute. This cleared the blockage, and four or five packages fell to the floor. Then new ones began arriving at thirty-second intervals. He threw everything from the basket directly into the recycling. One package fell to the side.

He picked it up and found that he'd bought a Mega Bubble Maker, after all, with two liters of Mega Bubble Mix. Into the recycle chute.

He managed to clear some space on the floor but noticed that the basket was filling up again. He picked out a long thin package and found that he'd bought an Extendable Pre-corded Metal Curtain Track. This was an awkward length for the recycle chute, so he threw it into a corner. The next package to land—JZ Nicer Dicer and Splicer—was much smaller and easily disposable, as was the Multi-Function Silver Finish Tilt Bracket (Self-Assembly).

But there was little time to read the contents of these packages because the speed of their arrival was increasing. The delivery of one every thirty seconds was reduced to one every fifteen seconds, ten seconds, then five. He couldn't recycle the packages quickly enough. Soon they arrived in clusters of three or four, then in a steady stream until there was nothing less than an avalanche of objects, all neatly wrapped in orange and bearing the blue legend: "Our Top Adviser Loves You."

Then the recycle chute gave up. Something had stuck further down, or maybe the entire building system was clogged with items. Ellis took his phone from the table and with the statuette of the Top Adviser in the other hand he stumbled through the drifts of packages to a free corner and sat on the floor in wonder at what was happening. He placed the statuette on the floor beside him and checked his phone. There were hundreds of messages. He ignored these and flipped to his target purchase account, which was dwindling fast. He had only a few hundred pounds left. The Declines had run out half an hour ago, and since then, he'd bought more than two hundred and fifty items.

He looked up at the in-chute. Nothing more was coming in because the pile beneath the chute now reached up to the vent in the ceiling. Packages were choking the in-chute and stacking up inside the vent. For a moment or two, there was silence. Then his phone began to beep. Not only that, it started to flash red. He'd never seen that before. In fact, he didn't know it was possible. But it was flashing and beeping and, unbidden, it took him to his target purchase account, where he found his balance was zero. *Please add funds* was the instruction, followed quickly by *Add funds now!* followed by *Situation critical! Funds required now!*

He placed the phone on the floor. From where he was sitting, he could read the contents list on the side of some of the nearest packages. What about a Vitri-Sendan Bonnet Hood Dryer with Detachable Palm Overflow and Concentrator Nozzle? Probably no use for what he wanted to do. A Double-Size Chocolate Bedspread with Cream Piping? No, what he needed was something hard. A Water Hyacinth Rectangular Lidded Storage Basket (Stackable)? Unlikely. Then he remembered the statuette, the Top Adviser. Yes, she was reasonably sized and made of solid, heavy plastic. He caught her around the waist and used the pedestal to smash into his phone on the floor. Three or four blows ensured the thing was broken, but that wasn't enough. He brought the Top Adviser down harder and harder onto the disintegrating phone and then turned his attention to the fragments themselves. Apart from the metal casing, all the glass, plastic, and tiny circuit boards were smashed into smaller and smaller pieces until he felt his arm heavy and tired from the effort. He put the Top Adviser down, thanking her for her excellent work.

By this time, the silence had ended. He heard alarms going off in the street, in the building, and even in the apartment itself. A red light started flashing from the choked in-chute, pulsing to the same rhythm as the alarm from the recycle chute. Ellis remained where he was, sitting on the floor in a corner, broken pieces of phone on his right-hand side and in front of him the scattered products of his indiscriminate buying.

He settled down to wait for unpleasant people to arrive.

Eden Rich.

1.

Victor Pelling said, "Ask him something."

"What sort of thing?"

"Try history. Ask him anything about any historical period you're interested in." Pelling turned to look at his son. "You know everything about history, don't you, Jim?"

Jim said, "Yes."

Pelling turned to Paul Leverson again and said, "He's completely confident. And I am, too. So just ask him."

Paul Leverson was considered to be a leader in the field of corporate management mainly because, at the age of twenty-six, he was already a billionaire. His company, Leverson Idiosyncratics, specializing in personalized computer applications, was among the top ten most successful companies in the FTSE 100. He'd been invited by an experimental scientist, Victor Pelling, to witness the results of a recent experiment. The subject was Pelling's son, Jim, who was sitting directly opposite Leverson, with a large coffee table between them. All three were in a big, luxurious office on the thirty-sixth floor of the Unity Power Building in the city. Victor Pelling, aged thirty-one, tall, slim, with a manner that could be described as forceful, resilient, was standing to one side of the coffee table, looking intently at his son.

"Things have really moved forward in the past week, haven't they, Jim?" Pelling said.

Jim said, "Yes."

To Leverson, the little boy looked not exactly sad but forlorn, as if he was struggling to understand the situation he was in. This was more than likely, given that he was only about eight years old, or so Leverson guessed. Jim was sitting on the edge of his seat, elbows on knees, a posture betraying a certain anxiety, though the expression on his young face denied this, suggesting that he was calm, impassive, and distant. His hair was thick, black, shoulder-length, with a fringe at his forehead, which reached down to touch the upper edge of the black frame of his spectacles.

"How old are you, Jim?" Leverson asked.

With no change to his expression, Jim said, "Seven years, eleven months, thirty days, six hours, and forty-eight minutes."

"Really?"

"And a few seconds."

"Right. Well…" Leverson gave this some thought. "So it's your birthday tomorrow, is it? Going to be eight?"

"That's right, yes."

"Only eight years old," Pelling said. "You'll be astonished at the level of his knowledge. Go on, try him…"

"Okay, history… let's see… in what year was the battle of the Somme?"

Immediately, Pelling laughed and shook his head.

"Something wrong?" Leverson asked.

"Too easy," Pelling said. "Anyway, you might as well give us the answer, Jim."

Jim said, "Nineteen sixteen—"

"Well, that's correct."

"—started on July the first and continued till November the eighteenth."

"Right." Leverson nodded.

"Something more obscure," Pelling suggested. "Give it a go."

"Okay, okay…" Leverson thought for a moment and then, concentrating on the boy sitting opposite him, said, "Can you tell me any of the events that occurred in the year thirteen sixty-eight?"

"Well, there were lots of things. Could you narrow it down? Give me a country, perhaps?"

"What about China?"

"Well, the Ming Dynasty was established on January twenty-third by Zhu Yuanzhang, who was the Hongwu Emperor—"

"Amazing," Leverson said, smiling.

"I bet what he said is correct," Pelling said.

"Well, I know it is, actually. I studied Medieval History, and I had a special interest in thirteen sixty-eight. Interesting year. Yes, start of the Ming Dynasty."

Jim added, "As far as we know."

"Well, of course."

"There's a study going on right now. They've found some interesting things in an archeological dig in Wuchang. It could be that the dynasty started earlier, and January the twenty-third was just taken as the official starting date."

Pelling grinned at Leverson. "Already way ahead of you, eh? Try him with another question if you like."

"No, I think you've made your point," Leverson said. "Right now, I'd…" He paused as he noticed Jim's left eye beginning to twitch. Just a flicker at first but then rapid opening and closing of the eyelid. "Are you okay?"

Jim said nothing. He appeared to be approaching some kind of bodily event, perhaps an unpleasant one.

And so it proved. He leaned forward quickly, pulled a plastic basin toward him from underneath the coffee table, and vomited into it. As he did this, his hair shifted. It was revealed to be a wig that fell off and landed on the coffee table, along with his spectacles. Jim was completely bald with a single tiny scar above his left temple.

"Christ, are you okay?" Leverson stood up and began to step around the table, reaching for Jim as he did so.

Pelling waved him back. "He's fine. No, really. We've had one or two minor issues—and I really do mean minor issues—but they're being addressed." He turned to his son. "Jim—"

Jim sat back up. From the coffee table, he retrieved his spectacles but not his wig. Then he took a tissue from his pocket and wiped his mouth. "I'm okay."

"Are you sure?" This from Leverson, whose need to be convinced was clearly greater than the boy's father.

Jim said, "I'm fine. Really." He began to roll up the left sleeve of his shirt to reveal a cannula had been injected into his forearm. He looked up at his father. "Maybe a little extra…"

"Sure, sure," his father said. "Go on through. I'll tell Alice. Are you sure you're okay?" he asked him quietly.

Jim looked at him, his expression blank as it had been the whole time. The pupils in his eyes, Leverson noted, were tiny. He realized that though Jim's speech hadn't been affected, he was probably under the influence of powerful drugs. "I'm fine," Jim said.

On his phone, Pelling said, "Alice, could you come in, please."

A few seconds later, Alice arrived. She was a woman in her mid-twenties.

"Give Jim a hand, will you," Pelling said. "Needs a bit of light medication and maybe a short nap."

Alice efficiently picked up the plastic basin, suggesting this was a regular occurrence. Then she and Jim left the room slowly, Jim leaning into her, his left hand pulling down on her right elbow, his thick black wig dangling from his right hand. Leverson heard her whispering, "Don't worry, Jimmy, you'll be fine. I'll sort you out."

When the door closed behind them, Pelling stepped across the room and sat down in the chair that his son had vacated. "Don't you think it's amazing," he said and he wasn't so much smiling as beaming. "The extent of his knowledge is incredible."

"He doesn't look very well, though, does he?" Leverson asked.

"Oh…" Pelling waved this comment away. "He'll be fine. I mean, I said before that we've had a few tiny side-effects, but they've all been sorted."

"All of them?"

"Absolutely. We're aware of the one you've just witnessed, and we've fixed it. I'm quite sure that's the last time Jim'll have that problem."

"Pretty disturbing, nevertheless," Leverson said.

"Look, do you think I'd put my child at risk?" Pelling said. He leaned forward and his voice became more assertive, close to aggressive. "My own child?" he repeated. "Considering the enormous strides we've taken with this new technology, the side effects are tiny, negligible. And we've tackled each one successfully. The aim is to have this product ready for sale next year with absolutely no downside. Zero complications. After all, that's the only way we can sell it. It's got to be totally risk-free, and it will be."

Leverson said nothing.

Pelling gave a brief, irritated smile. "Still haven't convinced you, have I?"

"What happened to his head?" Leverson asked. "Looked pretty bad to me. What's that little scar that he has?"

"That's where we placed the inject. It's tiny, and the chance of biorejection is one in a billion. But it got to Jim, and in a way, that's a *good* thing because it gave us the chance to examine it in detail, which we did, and come up with a solution, which we did."

"We don't want sick kids, though, do we?" Leverson asked.

"Of course not." Once more, Pelling's voice took on a tone of managed irritation. "We don't want sick kids and won't have any. I believe in science, and I'm sure you do, too. Science has the answer. No doubt about that."

"Tell me how the product works," Leverson said.

"Well, you've read about the basic principles, haven't you?"

"Yes, but an explanation from the inventor himself would be good."

"Okay, so… it's basically a question of how do we convert electronic data into some kind of thought stream and then introduce it to the neurons in the brain. After that, the data has to be transferred to the hippocampus, which is where the brain stores long-term memories."

"Put like that, it doesn't sound too difficult."

"Describing the process is easy," Pelling said. "Actually *doing it* is bloody difficult. Neurons are very diverse, which creates problems, but there are about a hundred billion of them with maybe a hundred trillion interconnections. So there's a bit of scope for experimentation. We did one hundred and ninety-seven experiments on our first volunteer before we had success, and during that time we accessed naught point three-five percent of his brain. All the history data that Jim's got now probably occupies less than a tenth of one percent of his brain capacity."

"The brain's pretty much fully mapped now, isn't it?"

"Yes, it is. We've got what we call *cranial pockets*, which are associated with specific types of memory. You know, language, music, mathematics, history, geography—all of them."

"And how many cranial pockets are there?"

"Oh, somewhere between eight and ten million. It varies from individual to individual."

Leverson smiled. "Got names for all of these, have you?"

Pelling ignored the smile. "Of course we do. It's all hierarchical, a bit like a filing system. Obviously, I can't name them all, but the taxonomy's in place. Let's put it this way: Can you name all the species of insects on the planet?"

Leverson shrugged. "No, I can't. But I imagine there are a few hundred thousand species."

"The latest estimate is nine point three million. And that's around about the number of cranial pockets in a single brain. Amazing, isn't it?"

"Well, I can't argue with that," Leverson said. "But what about that scar on Jim's head? You're going to sort that out, aren't you?"

"As I said, that's where we put the inject. It's really very small. A tiny globe, two millimeters in diameter. It's a thought stream dispersion device. Receives the transmitted data and sends it to the appropriate cranial pocket, usually in the hippocampus."

"You mean you actually have to put something into the brain? I mean, a physical piece of equipment."

"Inside the cranium, next to the brain. There's quite a bit of space between lobes and so on. Anyway, as I said, it's tiny, not much bigger than a pinhead. And it works. You've witnessed that just now. It really works."

"And what about Jim's hair?"

Pelling shrugged. "It'll grow back. No problem."

As he spoke, Pelling's voice rose as his passion for the subject increased. "The world's going to change; I mean, think of the implications!"

"Well, I can think of one or two—"

But Pelling was in full flow. "All information about everything can be added directly to everyone's brain. No more schools. No more universities. No need for education. Well, what I mean is that *traditional* forms of education are now obsolete. You don't need to learn anything because it's already implanted in your brain. You don't need to refer to an external source like a database or an encyclopedia because it's already inside your head. You think of the question, and the answer's right there, just like that." He snapped his fingers. "Fantastic!"

"Probably the right word, yes," Leverson said.

Pelling smiled, a taunting, semi-aggressive smile. Then he shook his head. "Not convinced, are you?"

"I need to think through the potential effects of this," Leverson said. "If what you're proposing is actually implemented worldwide, then we're talking about major societal changes."

"Of course we are. I mean, everyone could be educated to PhD level. *Instantly*. Imagine that."

"I'd rather not," Leverson said. "What about manual labor? What about cleaners, waiters, people at checkouts in supermarkets? What about drivers? We'll still need people to do things like that, won't we?"

"Everyone can have the level of education they want. There'll be apprenticeship modules for skilled labor jobs and stuff like that. We're not talking specifically about employment here…"

"No? I'm looking at it more pragmatically than you are."

"Well, I don't think so. I'm being realistic, too. Let me give you an example. Do you know how many languages there are in the world?"

"A few hundred?"

"About six thousand nine hundred. And the top ten, in terms of the number of native speakers, account for about forty percent of the world's population. So just think of it. You don't need to learn languages any more; you just, well, it's like uploading a file directly into your brain. You don't learn a new language; you just know it. It's there to use. Get all ten of them, and that accounts for less than one percent of your brain capacity. Communication difficulties between different ethnic groups? Gone! In an instant!"

"World peace?" Leverson said with more than a hint of cynicism.

Pelling shrugged. "Why not? It'll certainly make it easier."

There was a short pause, after which Leverson said, "So why did you ask me over here to tell me all of this?"

"Because I need a partner who can market the product. I've created and developed it, but I need someone with expertise in product presentation, marketing, and selling. Right now, you're number one in the world."

"And I imagine you need someone with a lot of money to invest in it."

"That's right. And that's you, too."

Leverson stood up. "Thank you for the demonstration. Fascinating stuff. And I hope Jim gets better."

"Oh, he will," Pelling said. "No doubt about that."

"Good. Well, I hope so. Anyway, give me two days. I'll be in touch."

•••

Leverson didn't get involved. He was only twenty-six, but he was already tired. He'd worked hard for eight years, starting with nothing and then compiling a fortune. He didn't want to jeopardize his wealth by investing in something that might not work long-term. He decided that what he wanted was a quiet life of luxury. Two months after his meeting with Victor Pelling, he sold Leverson Idiosyncratics for a sum of money that allowed him to retire on his twenty-seventh birthday. He bought an enormous yacht and sailed it, with professional help, to the Caribbean, where he planned to spend the rest of his life.

And that's what he did, mainly because there wasn't very much of his life left. At the age of twenty-seven and one month, he fell overboard and drowned.

He never knew that Victor Pelling had gone on with what he called cranial florescence experiments and found a partner who was willing to invest in the product. Leverson never knew either that Pelling's son, Jim, died three months after they'd met. His age was eight years, three months, six days, twelve hours, five minutes and twenty-eight point three seconds, to be precise.

2.1.

Twenty years later.

The site in Inject City that particularly attracted the Eden Rich Corporation was right next to a station. Following a major donation by ERC to the local council, it was agreed that there could be an entrance to the new ERC Tower directly from the station. ERC employees arriving by an underground line did not need to exit the station to the street; they could go directly to a basement reception area within the tower.

However, Mark Ridgeway came by taxi. He made his way up the steps of the twenty-five-meter-wide granite stairway leading to the ERC Tower's main entrance. It was Mark's first day at work for ERC. He was nineteen years old.

The enormous glass doors of the tower's main entrance were open, and revealed an atrium that spread upwards for ten floors. Inside, glass-fronted corridors could be seen at all levels to the right and left with a huge statue, eight floors high, sitting at the rear of the atrium, looking down on everyone who entered the building. The statue was a copy of Michelangelo's David, about twenty times taller than the original.

Mark could see all this even while he was still outside with twenty meters to go to the entrance. At this point, the granite concourse became covered by plastic sheeting decorated as the Ardabil Carpet, duplicated many times. When he stepped onto this carpet-like structure, Mark immediately heard a voice in his ear saying, "Good morning, Mr. Ridgeway. Welcome to the Eden Rich Corporation. Please approach security guard number seventeen."

Interesting. Mark realized the carpet coincided with the security monitoring area. No doubt his clothes, briefcase, shoes—pretty much everything—had been checked, but... well, his instruction to go to one of the guards suggested that there was something about him that needed further investigation. As he crossed the threshold of the building and looked around for guard number seventeen, he had an idea of what that object might be.

"Mr. Mark Ridgeway." Guard 17 smiled at him. He was a young man in a dark blue uniform with *ERC* embroidered in gold on the lapel of his jacket. "Can I take a look at that thing tied to your wrist, please."

"Sure." Mark held up his left hand and pulled his sleeve back to reveal one of the watches his grandfather had given him about fourteen years ago, just before he died. "It's a watch," he said.

"A watch? Yes, I've heard some people still wear these things..."

"A family heirloom," Mark said. "It's over a hundred years old. I wear it sometimes as a kind of good luck charm."

"I'm afraid I have to ask you to leave it here for further investigation. I promise it'll be quite safe, and you can pick it up when you leave."

Mark managed to hide the fact this requirement annoyed him. An examination of technology that was over a hundred years old? He loosened the wrist band and gave the watch to the security guard, who said, "It'll be quite safe here. Really." On the wall behind him, there was an array of small deposit boxes. He opened one and placed the watch carefully inside. "My name's Malcolm. When you leave here later today, just ask for me, and I'll return it to you."

Then he handed Mark an ID card on a necklace loop. "Please wear this at all times. You must wear it during your first two weeks of employment here, then you'll receive an inject in your lower arm. Don't worry, quite painless." He smiled. "But while you've got this badge, it must never be further than two meters away from your head, otherwise an alarm will sound. Please acknowledge that you understand this instruction."

"Understood," Mark said.

"Fine. Can I ask you, then, to put it on now so that I can activate it?"

"No problem." Mark slipped the cord over his head and positioned the ID card on his chest.

"Excellent. Thank you. Now, I've been asked to tell you that your first meeting today is with Mr. Alex Duro—one of our senior managers—in room 487 on the forty-eighth floor. The quickest way to get there is to take elevator D up to floor fifty and then elevator L down two floors." He smiled again. "Ms. Melissa

Mortimer, Mr. Duro's office manager, will meet you at the elevator on floor forty-eight. So…" He pointed across the foyer. "Elevator D's over there. Welcome to Eden Rich."

Elevator D took less than two minutes to reach floor fifty, where elevator L welcomed him and announced that Ms. Melissa Mortimer was waiting for him on floor forty-eight and that they would meet in eleven seconds.

Which they did.

As the elevator doors opened—Mark was the only passenger—Melissa Mortimer said, "Welcome to Eden Rich, Mr. Ridgeway." She was standing before him with a small screen held to her chest. A woman of about thirty-three with short hair of a color somewhere between chestnut and blonde.

"Please call me Mark," he said.

"Well, I'll be happy to, and please call me Melissa. This way, please."

As she led him down the corridor, she said, "Oh, by the way, there's one person who's always referred to by his surname. It's Mr. Pelling."

They reached a door with *A. Duro* embossed on a small plaque at eye level. Melissa knocked on the door and, after a couple seconds, was invited in.

"You must be Mark Ridgeway," Alex Duro said from the far side of the room as Mark entered.

"Yes, and you're Mr. Duro."

Mark heard the office door close behind him. Melissa Mortimer had left.

Alex Duro stepped across the floor of his office and extended his hand. Mark took hold of it. A firm handshake. "It's Alex," Duro said. "We're all on first names here. Except—"

"Mr. Pelling."

"That's right, yes." He smiled and then said, "I've heard quite a lot about you from our recruitment team." He gestured to an area of the office where there were three armchairs around a low coffee table. Mark saw that the office appeared to be divided into two parts, one associated with business—a desk, a conference table with six upright chairs, and a conference screen—and the other which offered a more casual, informal tone, the area which he now approached. He sat on one of the pale blue armchairs. Duro sat adjacent to him, not opposite.

"I hope what they said was positive," Mark said.

"Well, if it had been negative, we wouldn't have offered you a job, would we? I mean, it was also very interesting. You've had nineteen injects, am I right?"

"Yes."

"And all the relevant updates?"

"Two hundred and forty-three in total."

Duro smiled again. "Very impressive. And what's more remarkable is that you seem to have retained very nearly all of the inject data."

"As far as I can tell, yes."

"So the question is…" Duro paused for a moment and then asked, "Would you like some coffee?"

"That would be great, yes."

Duro leaned forward and touched the edge of the coffee table. A small screen appeared on the table's surface. He touched several icons and then sat back again. He said, "It always seemed to me that calling this table a *coffee table* was a bit of a waste of time unless it could actually supply you with coffee. What do you reckon?"

"Sounds good," Mark said. He watched as a circular area in the center of the table flipped open, and a cup of coffee rose from the interior, and was pushed gently toward him. Then another coffee appeared and was sent toward Duro, who raised his cup and said, "Cheers."

Mark's research had found that Alex Duro was thirty-eight years old, although he did look a little older. He was beginning to go bald and was at least five kilos overweight. Despite his obvious ability to smile, his general expression was one of someone whose life experience had been successful but testing.

"Coffee okay?" Duro asked.

"Perfect," Mark said.

"Actually perfect or just close to perfect?"

"Well, to give it an actual score, I'd say nine point seven."

"Nine point seven? Sounds good."

"Nine point seven eight, to be more precise," Mark said. "For me, anything over nine point seven five enters the perfect zone."

"We did a nutritional analysis of you," Duro said. "Well, we do that with most of our employees. It's relatively easy these days. You know, based on your medical. Anyway, we examined your stomach contents and noticed you drink coffee. Then we were able to determine what kind of coffee you really like. Reckon it's this one." He pointed to Mark's cup.

"Spot on," Mark said.

"Well…" Duro leaned forward and placed his cup on the table. "I can't agree. You see, the systems we have here are based on the idea of perfection, and perfection, for me, on a gauge going up to ten, is ten. Now, I accept that it's in your interest to be positive and sociable, particularly on your first day at your new job, but for me, nine point seven eight is not perfection." He picked up his coffee cup again. "Any comment?"

Mark thought about this for a few seconds. He took another sip of his near-perfect coffee. He said, "It's been sixteen days, two hours, and four minutes since I last had a cup of coffee which I rated above nine point seven five, so this is fine. Excellent coffee."

"But you see what I'm getting at, don't you?" Duro said.

"Yes. I imagine the message is that ERC aims for absolute perfection in all things, and a score of ninety-seven point eight percent isn't good enough."

"Correct. For example, there's something in the region of a hundred and twenty million items that make up the hydroelectronic environment constructed on Mars. If two point two percent of them were to fail, then everybody on Mars would be dead, wouldn't they?"

Mark nodded.

"I accept that the situation with coffee is different," Duro said with a smile. "No potential fatalities involved, but the aim of everything we do here at ERC is perfection, and by that, I mean ten out of ten or at least closer to ten than nine point seven eight. See what I mean?"

"Yes," Mark said. "Yes, I do."

"And that's why we decided to hire you. That's why we chose you out of the two hundred and fifty candidates who applied for this position. You've had all the injects and updates and retained more of the knowledge you gained than anyone else. Your scores on your entry exams… well, what do you think your average was?"

Mark said, "Ninety-nine point nine six."

Duro nodded. "Exactly. Now look, don't let that make you feel superior. No arrogance allowed—"

"No, not at all."

"—but it means you can help us with future inject developments, help us more than the others because we need to know what qualities your body and your brain have that brought you to within… within a micro-millimeter of perfection. Are you happy to help us do that?"

"Certainly," Mark said. "Certainly."

Duro stood up. "Well, Mark," he said, and he extended his hand. Mark stood up and took it. "I look forward to you working for us."

"Thank you," Mark said. "I'm fully committed to what you require me to do."

They shook hands.

"Excellent, excellent," Duro said. He pointed to the door. "Now Melissa will take you to Peter Roundhill's office. He's your direct boss. Welcome to Eden Rich."

●●●

A few minutes later, Mark was in the office of Peter Roundhill. This was on the thirty-first floor. Mark would soon learn that the higher ERC personnel reached on the management scale, the higher their office was in the tower. Peter Roundhill clearly had some way to go. He learned, too, that Alex Duro was a much higher manager than his floor forty-eight office suggested. He was a close confidant of CEO Victor Pelling and had another office on floor ninety-eight.

Roundhill was older than Duro—forty-three, as Mark had found out by examining ERC on-data—but he was in better shape. He was slim, had a full head of dark hair greying at the temples, and was tall. His welcome to Mark was different from Alex Duro's, more enthusiastic, less investigative.

"I believe you met Alex Duro," Roundhill said when the initial welcoming was over. They were seated by one of the windows in Roundhill's office, looking out over Inject City. There were buildings close to them that rose further and disappeared up into the clouds.

"I did, yes."

"And you got the coffee test?"

Mark smiled. "Yes, I got the coffee test."

"Well, I'm sure you did fine. By the way, I need to tell you that every conversation in every office in the entire building is recorded."

"Sound only?"

Roundhill smiled. "No. Cameras everywhere. You'll get used to it."

"And why…" Mark began but then stopped, wondering if he should be asking such questions on his first day. Yes, he should. "Why is it felt to be necessary?" he asked.

"Security," Roundhill said.

"You've had security problems?"

"Not since we introduced total monitoring. Now, just look around this office."

Mark did so, moving his head slowly around, away from the window.

"Is there anything you particularly notice?" Roundhill asked. "Things that you see, things that you don't see?"

"Well, I…" He thought hard. The office was large, similar in size to Alex Duro's with an obvious work area— desk, screens, small conference table with six chairs—and what could be termed a leisure area, where he was sitting now—armchairs, a low table, sideboard with a coffee machine, a kettle… The walls, as in Alex Duro's office, were painted a silver grey color and were bare. The work area, if not the whole room, was rather clinical in tone.

"No personal items," Mark said.

"Correct. With total monitoring, it was decided there should be no personal items in this building, no family photos, no ornaments, nothing like that…"

"No plants?"

"No. But the major conference rooms are quite different. There's nothing personal in there, of course—they don't house particular staff members—but there's lots of potted plants, wonderful decoration and… well, I'd describe them as *art galleries*. Some great paintings. Mr. Pelling's very keen on early twenty-first-century stuff. So we've got works by Kumar, Bould, Worrall, Eden—"

"Eden?"

Roundhill laughed. "Well, yes. But not just for the name. She's a great painter. That group was very good. *The Hornsey Five,* I think they were called."

"Who was the fifth one?"

Roundhill shook his head. "Can't remember, I'm afraid."

"Can I ask about my watch," Mark said.

"Your watch?"

"Yes. I had to hand it to security when I arrived. It was a present from my grandfather, just before he died. Can't I wear it?"

"Ah. No, I'm afraid not. Seems a bit odd, I agree, but we don't allow anything that could be classified as jewelry."

"Really? What about items such as wedding rings, for example?"

"Not allowed."

"Bit of a surprise, that," Mark said.

"Agreed, and people do get a bit upset about it at first, but then it's fine. Nobody complains now. Phones are the only… what can I say… the only *semi-personal* items allowed. Essential for business, of course."

"Can I have a photo on my phone?" Mark asked.

"Not recommended," Roundhill said, but he was smiling. "Well, of course, that's where nearly everyone has their photos."

Mark shrugged. "No problem. That rule about personal items is fine for me, but can you tell me why it was brought in?"

"Very simple," Roundhill said. "We had a case a couple years ago in which a display of particular personal items led to conflict between two employees and… well, it was a very messy business."

"Does everyone have access to streaming from all the offices?"

"No, only top management—which doesn't include me, by the way," Roundhill said, smiling. "But today, Alex Duro actually wanted me to watch your meeting with him, so he arranged it. Just one more thing, your ID card—"

"The security guard who gave it to me told me all about it," Mark said. "Got to wear it at all times."

"That's right. Alarms will go off if it's over two meters from your head for more than fifteen seconds."

"I understand, yes."

"But, don't worry, people get used to it. And you only need to wear it for two weeks, then you'll have a tiny inject in your forearm."

"I look forward to that."

"Good. I think that in the past couple of years, we've only had one alarm go off, and we've got close to ten thousand people working in this building."

"Nine thousand six hundred and five," Mark said.

"Done your research, then."

"Yes. Of course, that was yesterday's figure. Today, it's nine thousand six hundred and six." He smiled.

"Well, of course it is. Okay, look… you're going to be working with me. By the way, I prefer to say working *with* me, not *for* me, because we need a close association, interdependence, and so on."

"Sounds good."

"Our main job is to assess new injects, see if they're worth it or not. And we need to check if anything in the new stuff is inconsistent with what's gone before. Now, we could do a similarity check against the base data, but we reckon the best way to do it is… well, I imagine you've already figured that out, haven't you?"

"Inject someone with it," Mark said. "So they can review it against the previous inject."

"That's right. But of course, that means that we need someone who's managed to retain all the data they've been injected with. Most injectees lose some. The average retention rate is seventy-two percent, but yours... well, you know what it is, don't you?"

Mark nodded. "Ninety-nine point nine six."

Later, when he left the building, Mark was walking down the steps when he heard his name called. "Mr. Ridgeway! Mr. Ridgeway!" He turned and saw one of the security guards approaching him at speed.

"Mr. Ridgeway," the guard repeated when he reached Mark. "Please..." He took in a breath. "You..."

Mark recognized him. "Malcolm, is that right?"

"Yes." Malcolm raised his right hand, holding Mark's watch. "You forgot this."

"So I did." Mark took it and slipped the band over his wrist. He pulled it tight and gave a gesture of display. "Thanks for remembering. Nice, isn't it."

"It's really beautiful," the security guard said.

"Belonged to my grandfather. He gave it to me on his deathbed."

"Oh, I'm so sorry—"

"Gave me two, actually. Anyway, thank you very much. See you tomorrow."

"Yes, see you tomorrow."

Mark watched as Malcolm, the security guard, made his way back up the steps and re-entered the building. He checked the time on his watch. He liked doing that, although, of course, it was no longer necessary. He'd had the time inject. Time, like everything else, was already inside his head.

2.2.

Victor Pelling, now fifty-one years old, was sitting in front of a screen in his office on floor one-hundred of the ERC Tower. He was aware that, in keeping with the culture that had developed within ERC, he should really have an office on the top floor, number one-hundred-twenty. Top man, top floor. In fact, he *did* have an office there, not just an office but a suite of rooms that occupied the entire space. He used the suite to entertain guests. Occasionally, he would spend the night there. Occasionally, he would spend the night there with a female guest. In this suite of rooms, he allowed himself to possess personal objects.

The office on floor one-hundred was similar in style to Duro's and Roundhill's, but larger. There were several screens attached to the walls, the actual number changing every two or three weeks. Currently there were six, ranging in size from the largest, which was three meters by two meters, to the smallest, about one-meter square.

There was one other difference. Pelling's prohibition of personal items within offices did, in theory, apply to all members of the corporation, including himself, but he broke the rule. However, his misdemeanor was limited to one thing only, something that was never seen by anyone who visited his office. In one of his desks—there were three—he had a drawer with only one item in it. The drawer was opened by thumbprint recognition, so there was no chance it could be opened by anyone else. The object inside was a photograph.

Pelling stood before one of the screens and said, "Alex Duro." The screen split into two images. On the left, occupying a quarter of the screen, there was a representation of the ERC Tower with a bright red dot on one floor. Next to it was a small text box containing the words, "A Duro, floor 48." To the right was a CCTV shot of Alex Duro in his office, seated at his desk. He appeared to be doing some sort of calculation on a small tablet type of device. Pelling said, "Magnify," and the view enlarged. Duro's left shoulder and his hands obscured Pelling's view of what was on Duro's device, making him wonder if Duro was aware of the positioning of the cameras in his office. *Almost certainly.* "Switch camera," Pelling said, and was offered another view which also failed, even under magnification, to reveal the detail of Duro's activity. Pelling smiled and quietly said, "Clever bastard." Then, to the screen, he said, "Peter Roundhill."

Peter Roundhill appeared on screen with the ERC Tower diagram, noting that he was on floor thirty-one. He was in conversation with a very young-looking man Pelling didn't recognize. "Sound," he said and he started to listen to the coversation.

"—couple of years, we've only had one alarm go off, and we've got close to ten thousand people working in this building."

"Nine thousand six hundred and five."

"Done your research, then."

"Yes. Of course, that was yesterday's figure. Today, it's nine thousand six hundred and six."

"Well, of course it is. Okay, look—"

Pelling said, "Identify speakers."

"Peter Roundhill, Mark Ridgeway."

"Information on Mark Ridgeway. CV and personal data."

The screen went blank for a moment, and then a photograph of Mark Ridgeway was displayed, along with some basic details such as date of birth, address, blood group, health statistics, etc. Pelling said, "Next" and got a breakdown of Mark's education—all his injects, all the relevant updates. He studied this for several seconds and then said, "Back to the conversation."

"—lose some data. The average retention rate is seventy-two percent, but yours… well, you know what it is, don't you?"

"Ninety-nine point nine six."

Pelling said, "Close down," and the screen went blank. He stayed in his seat for a few seconds and then got up. He walked across to the main window of his office, which looked over to Archibald Meadway's office. As he walked the four or five meters to the window, he saw his reflection, which didn't exactly *disturb* him but gave him a little cause for concern. He was a bit overweight. Not much, only two or three kilos, but the slight bulge of his stomach meant he always had to unbutton the front of his jacket when he sat, otherwise there would be an inordinate strain on the suit material.

When he reached the window, he stood right up against it. It was a floor-to-ceiling thick pane of reinforced glass, and he knew it was solid, unbreakable, and totally secure. But he was aware that emotional reaction could easily overturn intellectual understanding and pure logic. When he'd first moved into the office, he'd been unable to approach the window at all, and he'd had a false interior wall put in place, a light, wooden panel about a meter and a half high along the full extent of the window. He needed confidence to get close to it, and the wall—despite its obvious flimsiness—helped him overcome his fear. Then he'd had the wall removed. Time to tackle this obstacle and overturn these pathetic feelings of vertigo with pure mental determination. It took him a couple months, but he succeeded. These days, he was able to approach the window, as he was doing now, and press his body against it, touch the glass with his forehead, and look down at the street, which was about half a mile below. Yes, he still had tinglings of vertigo, but he dismissed them as minor contingencies.

He turned away from the window and walked back toward the screen he'd been interacting with earlier. He said, "Victor Pelling," and there he was, V Pelling, floor one-hundred, standing in front of the screen. Such was the positioning of the camera that he was looking at himself, hundreds of images or, more likely, an infinite number, diminishing in size and fading down to a distant single pixel. He stepped aside and said, "Alex Duro," and there was Duro, standing in a small room, yes, an elevator, and moving up the building: floor fifty-five… floor sixty…

Pelling said, "Now switch off all recording, sound and vision. Understood?"

The screen responded, "Understood," and went blank.

Two minutes later, Pelling and Duro were seated at a low table close to the window.

"I've got a paper version," Duro said.

"Good."

Duro handed over a document made up of two sheets of A4 paper.

"First thing," Pelling began, "is that it's too long. I can say that without even reading it. Not suggesting it's your fault—"

"Big font," Duro said.

"That's true, but… well, let's take a look." Pelling skimmed the two pages quickly and then concentrated on page one. Duro waited as, silently, Pelling read both pages slowly and then put the document on the table. "Not bad. Actually, no. Quite good. Would you be persuaded?"

"Well, there's actually a bit of me in there," Duro said. "More in the presentation than the content, but yes, I think it's pretty good all around."

"Ten points is too many, I think," Pelling said.

"Really? Ten commandments? No?"

Pelling smiled. "Very funny," he said. "Anyway, get rid of... let's see... number six and number ten. Then reduce the font so that it can all appear on a single sheet."

"Six and ten?" Duro picked up the document and checked the items. "Tax issues and immigration."

"Important stuff, I know," Pelling said.

"Well, immigration particularly," Duro said. "I'd say that most people would agree that we need to reduce the overall population. And maybe not just by lowering immigration."

"Oh, I take that point. Probably not a good idea to raise it in the manifesto, though. I mean, major statements on immigration later on. And tax."

Duro nodded. "Okay, so... we've got education at number one. You're going to reduce the costs—"

"Yes, maybe even make it free for a while. We'll see."

"—and number two, increase the size of the police force."

"Yes."

"By how much?"

"Don't know. What do you reckon? Double it?"

"At least."

"Let's say double, for the moment."

"Fine. So... number three, bring back the death penalty."

"Yes, we'll keep that one in."

Duro said, "Yes. Lots of support for that, I'm sure. And four... reduce the number of homeless to zero." He smiled. "You're not thinking of a big house-building program, are you?"

"Not necessarily, no. Just give the aim right now. Not the method."

"Right. Five. Reorganisation of government structure."

"Yes, essential."

"Well, sure, but Victor—you don't even have a political party, do you?"

Pelling shrugged. "Don't need one."

"Really?"

"When I'm elected, I'll be elected by a huge majority. I'll have the power to do all this."

"Victor, I— I'm sorry, but I find all this a bit weird."

Pelling smiled. "Good," he said.

"Good? I mean, are you serious about this?"

"Utterly serious."

"But the election's next week. You're going to announce tomorrow your aim to be president?"

"Yes."

"But that means you've got a campaign lasting only six days. No time to organize anything."

"Not required."

"No speeches?" Duro asked. "No air-time? No organized campaign?"

"No, none of that's necessary."

"What are you going to say at your press conference?"

"Nothing," Pelling said. "I won't be there. I want you to handle it."

"You want me—"

"Alex, you arrange the press conference for tomorrow at a time that suits you. All I want you to do is announce my candidacy. That's it. Don't even take any questions."

"Just hand out copies of this?" He pointed to the document on the table.

"No. Just announce my candidacy and tell them my manifesto will be available—let's see—make it the day before the election. So, just make the announcement and leave. No questions. Shouldn't take more than twenty-five seconds, twenty-eight at the most." Pelling smiled.

Duro sat back in his chair. He smiled too, but it was a wry, confused smile. "Just a stunt then, is it?" he asked. "A little bit of publicity? No campaign, no speeches, just an announcement that lasts half a minute?"

"I think we agreed on twenty-eight seconds max," Pelling said, smiling.

Duro laughed. "Okay, right, but—"

"I'll make a prediction," Pelling said. "As I said, I'm going to win. I'm going to be the next president. Landslide victory."

Duro looked at Pelling, the man he'd known for eleven years. Yes, he seemed entirely serious. "Okay, but how are you going to do it?"

"Alex, just think about it. There're strategies open to me that aren't available to other people."

2.3.

Half an hour later, Peter Roundhill was summoned to floor one-hundred. "You've got a new recruit," Pelling said. He was sitting opposite Roundhill with the low table between them. "Mark Ridgeway, correct?"
"That's right, yes," Roundhill said.
"Tell me about him."
"Very interesting character," Roundhill said. "Very young…"
"Nineteen, is that right?"
"Yes, but the main thing about him is he's the only person that we know of who's had every inject we've ever issued, plus all the relevant updates. But more impressive is that he seems to have retained all the data he's been injected with."
"All of it?"
"Well, ninety-nine point nine six percent."
"Interesting figure," Pelling said.
"Certainly is. I mean, we tested two hundred and fifty applicants, and his score was seven percent higher than the highest of the rest."
"That's impressive. But… obviously, you didn't test him on *every* single datapoint?"
"No, but the level of testing is very high so that the result is guaranteed to be within one-tenth of a percent of actuality."
Pelling nodded. "Still pretty good. So what's the average retention rate in the general population?"
"At the last estimate, seventy-two point three eight percent."
Pelling thought about this for a few seconds. "Okay, so, any clues as to why this Ridgeway fellow can retain so much?"

"We've done a couple brain scans and the structure of his brain does seem to be a little unusual."

"In what way?"

"Certain areas—the hippocampus, for example—are slightly larger than normal which suggests greater capacity. There might even be duplication of certain cranial pockets which would suggest potentially quicker access to certain data."

"In that case, how are we going to benefit from Mr. Ridgeway's expertise, do you reckon?"

"Give him every new update so that he can do a check against the previous one and we can be sure there aren't any inconsistencies."

Pelling nodded. "Sounds good."

"Obviously we can do computational checks on thought stream data but I've calculated that it'll actually be quicker to use Mark Ridgeway's brain." Roundhill smiled.

As did Pelling. Then he said, "Religion."

"Yes, that's the next update."

"To be approached with caution."

"Certainly…"

"But I'd like it to be ready for release tomorrow."

"Tomorrow?"

"Earlier than originally scheduled, I know," Pelling said. "But I'd like to speed up delivery over the next few months. Lots of updates coming along."

"Tomorrow," Roundhill said. "What time?"

"Doesn't matter that much. Evening would be okay. How long does Ridgeway need to make his assessment, do you reckon?"

"This'll be the first time," Roundhill said. "So we can't be sure of exactly how long it'll take."

"Yes, of course, I understand that. So, look, give me a call tomorrow morning—let's say ten thirty—and let me know how things are going. Okay?"

Roundhill stood up. "Certainly, Mr. Pelling."

Two minutes later, Roundhill met up with Mark Ridgeway and said, "Work starts now. Get ready for an inject."

2.4.

When Mark arrived at the Eden Rich Tower on his second day, he went first to the security area and looked for the guard he'd spoken to the previous day, the one called Malcolm. Luckily, Malcolm's shift had just started, so he was there.

"Handing in your watch again, Mr. Ridgeway?"

"No," Mark said, but there was a watch in his right hand. He held it out toward Malcolm.

"So what… but you do have a watch…"

"Yes, but it's not mine. It's yours."

Malcolm's moment of surprise deprived him of speech.

"I told you I had two," Mark said. "No point in having one in a cupboard at home all the time, is there? Especially when there's someone who likes these things." He pressed the watch forward, and Malcolm eventually took hold of it. He whispered, "Wow," and looked hard at the watch. "This is… well…" He looked up at Mark. "Are you serious? I mean, are you really giving this to me?"

"I am. Not a loan, a gift."

"Well, thank you very much… I really—"

"Just enjoy it," Mark said, and before Malcolm could say anything else, he set off toward the elevators.

•••

So it's okay, then, is it?" Peter Roundhill asked. He was talking about the latest religion update. Mark had received the inject the previous afternoon.

"It's fine," Mark said.

"You've been through the checklist?"

"Yes." Mark brought the list up on his screen. He skimmed through the items. "No changed data without explanation. All controversies given full, unbiased consideration."

"What about item ten?"

"Ten? Let's see. No specific religion was promoted. Yes, that's all fine."

"You look really tired," Roundhill said.

"It's a big update, lots to check out, and you said Mr. Pelling needs to know about it this morning—"

"How long did it take you to review it?"

"Well—"

"Did you get *any* sleep at all last night?"

"Actually..." Mark managed a rather tired smile. "Not much, no."

"How much? I'd like to know exactly."

"None. I didn't sleep at all. But it doesn't really matter..."

"Well, it does," Roundhill said. "I know you want to be positive about everything, but I've got to consider your welfare, too. So I want you to go home and get some sleep."

"Really, I don't need to go home—"

"I want you to leave now," Roundhill said in an assertive rather than an aggressive tone. "We need you to be in good health, so go home now, and we'll see you tomorrow."

Mark looked exhausted and disappointed, but he accepted that he couldn't complete work of any value in his present condition. "Okay. See you tomorrow, then," he said as he headed for the door. "I'll be here early."

● ● ●

As Mark left the ERC Tower and headed back home, Alex Duro was meeting Victor Pelling on floor one-hundred-twenty. They were sitting in armchairs that were more adjacent than opposite each other. There were side tables. On each of these sat a plate of cakes and a cup of coffee. The room they were in was relatively small and windowless. There were no microphones, no cameras, no recording devices of any kind.

"Come on, Alex, you must've figured it out by now."

"How you're going to win the election?"

"Yes."

"I think maybe I have," Duro said.

"So?"

"Some kind of subliminal message in one of the injects?"

"Exactly, yes. You got it."

"I'd say it's very risky."

"You don't think it'll work?"

"That's not what I mean," Duro said. "If I can figure it out, somebody else will and that'll mess the whole thing up. Let's be clear—that could lead to the demise of the company. I'm serious."

Pelling shook his head. "I think you're wrong there," he said as he reached for his coffee. "No one understands the system as well as you do, and the people out there… well, they won't know. That's what subliminal means, isn't it? You don't know you're being told to do something, you just do it."

"Who else knows about this?" Duro asked.

"Nobody. Just you."

"And how are you going to add it to an inject?"

"Easy. I've got the base configuration for the next update—"

"Politics," Duro said, smiling. "Good choice."

"Yes. Anyway, I'll add the message myself."

"You can do that?"

"Christ almighty, Alex, I invented this product, remember? Of course I can do it. Still got the technical ability."

After a few moments of silence, Duro said, "There's something we need to sort out—only you and me know about this, but our new guy, Mark Ridgeway… well, he may be able to figure it out. We'll need to make sure he doesn't get the inject."

"Good. I'm glad you thought of that."

There was a short silence. Then Duro said, "Well, best of luck, Victor. It'd be great if you win the election and become our president." He took a slice of ginger cake from the plate on his side table. "But tell me," he went on, before he bit into the cake, "how are you going to manage everything if you win?"

"What do you mean *if I win*? I'm going to win. I'm certain of that."

"Okay, but how are you going to… I mean, you'll need a big team of people to… well, for one thing, to implement what you promise in your manifesto. You'll have to appoint people to interact with all the institutions and so on. You're taking on a huge task, an enormous task."

"Yes, I know that. But you know me, Alex, I'm good at delegating, and sure, I'll need help, but I'll be relying a lot on my deputy."

"You mean your Vice-President?" Duro tried to restrain himself from smiling but failed.

"That's right. Vice President Alexander Duro."

Duro laughed. "Very funny," he said.

"That's not a joke, Alex."

"What?"

"I mean it. I want you to be my running mate. Imagine it, the two of us organizing this country."

"Christ."

"Alex, your strength is knowing how to get things moving, knowing who to contact about every issue, knowing how to motivate people."

"Sure, but that's what I do within the business—"

"Oh, come on, Alex. Politics is just another form of business."

"You think so?"

"I know so. And anyway, if it isn't totally a business, I'll make it one. Just think about it, will you? Hand over all your current projects to one of your deputies and concentrate on this from now on. Do your research. Make a plan. We can work together to determine who will oversee all the areas you mentioned. Sure, we'll need a lot of help, but plenty of people want to get in on the game."

"Business or game?" Duro asked.

"Oh, same thing, really. And by the way, I'll double your salary. And… well, maybe you need some time to think about this, so you have till tomorrow morning to decide whether you want to do it or not. I'll tell you now that your answer is *yes*. Okay?"

•••

Peter Roundhill contacted Pelling at 10:30 as requested.

"So, the religion update okay?" Pelling asked.

"Yes," Roundhill said. "Fully checked and verified."

"Do you trust this new man, Ridgeway?"

Rather surprised at the question, Roundhill said, "Well, yes, of course I do."

"Look, I'm not suggesting he'd do anything wrong, I just mean are you sure that he hasn't made any mistakes or missed anything?"

"I'm quite sure."

"But he's very new, isn't he?"

"That's right, but I've got complete faith in the screening system. He passed every test with top marks and I don't mean just within the recent group of candidates but the highest marks we've ever recorded in the company."

"Really? That's impressive. Can I have a word with him?"

"Actually, he's not here," Roundhill said. "I've sent him home because it took him approximately sixteen hours to complete the review of the update. He was injected at four o'clock yesterday afternoon, and he finished his review at eight this morning. He didn't have any sleep, so after he got here and told me what he'd done, I sent him home."

"Well," Pelling said. "You did the right thing. So… could you get in touch with the network people and tell them to set up the religion update for broadcast at nine tonight."

"Of course I can do that, Mr. Pelling, but we usually have a few days of advertising beforehand, don't we?"

"Yes, we do, but not necessary this time. This update's free."

"Free?"

"Yes. It's a gift from the corporation to celebrate our first fifteen years."

"That's very generous…"

"Agreed. But sometimes being generous is good for business. So the next one, Politics, that'll be free, too."

"Fine. We'll get started on the Politics update straight away."

"Actually, no. I'd like you to skip that one. No need to check it out."

"Really?"

"Yes. I'll give you two reasons. First, I've taken a look at the update data myself, and I'm sure it's perfectly okay. By that, I mean there aren't many additions, so it doesn't need any more checking. And the other thing is what you said yourself about this Ridgeway fellow—"

"Mark."

"Yes, Mark. He needs a break. All that activity in his brain for such a long time… really not good. Now, I'm not blaming you, Peter. After all, this is a new experience and you couldn't have known how long it would take—"

"Well, that's right…"

"But clearly this man is a valuable asset to the company and we need to take good care of him. So tell him not to have the Politics inject, okay?"

"But if it's free he'll get it automatically, won't he?"

"Good point. Make sure he's de-registered."

"Okay, I'll do that straight away."

2.5.

"Sorry to keep you waiting," Alex Duro said as he entered his office, where Peter Roundhill was already sitting with a cup of tea.

"No problem."

"How's the tea?" Duro came over and sat down opposite Roundhill.

"Excellent," Roundhill said. "A well-trained table."

"I'm late because I've just been at a press conference that was supposed to last twenty-eight seconds, but I think it ran to twenty-nine."

"A press conference? About the next two injects?"

"No, not that," Duro said. "Some news that'll almost certainly surprise you. You see, Mr. Pelling—"

"Is he okay?"

"Oh yes, he's fine. It's… well he's decided he wants to stand for the presidency, and he asked me to make the announcement."

Roundhill looked shocked. "He wants to be president?"

"Yes. So that's what the press conference was about. Oh, I know; I found it hard to believe, too. But then anyone who wants to can stand for president. Fancy having a go yourself?"

Roundhill smiled. "Not remotely. Well, not this time if Mr. Pelling's going for it."

"Wise decision."

"So what did he say at the press conference?"

"He wasn't there. Just me. I made the announcement. I know, it's all a bit odd—"

"And very late," Roundhill said. "The election's next week."

"Yes. All a bit bizarre, but I'm sure Mr. Pelling has thought things through, and… well, anyway, I wanted to see you about something else—I just want to make sure that you know that Mark Ridgeway mustn't be given the next inject. The politics one."

"Yes, Mr. Pelling's already told me about that."

"Has he? Good. So… that inject doesn't need to be checked, and, more importantly, as I'm sure Mr. Pelling said to you, we're concerned that Mark might get ill if he's given this second inject so soon after the first one. Now, I don't think he'll get ill, but he might get exhausted. In fact, and this is a further instruction from Mr. Pelling himself, don't let Mark have any new injects until further notice. Is that clear?"

"Well, I understand that, of course, but remember that inject reviewing is what we decided to employ him for."

"Oh, I agree, but I'm sure that for the moment, he can help you out in other ways. Let's just say we'll review the situation in a couple of weeks' time. Okay?"

"Fine," Roundhill said." He'll be disappointed, particularly as I've had to de-register him."

"You've already done that? Good. Make sure it lasts for a fortnight, and then we'll talk again. Okay?"

"No problem," Roundhill said. "Understood."

•••

When he got back to his office, Roundhill sat down and thought for a while. He thought about the coffee and tea-serving table that Alex Duro had in his office. Really good. Maybe he could get one, too. But more importantly…

He stepped out into the corridor and tapped on the door of Mark's office, which was right next to his own. All ERC system employees working in Peter Roundhill's department had their own offices, primarily to allow them some seclusion for the intense work they were involved in. The offices were relatively small—four meters by four meters—but crammed with various types of equipment.

Mark opened the door.

"Just a quick word," Roundhill said.

"Sure, come in."

Roundhill entered the office and said, "I won't stay long. Just to let you know that I've had an instruction from Mr. Pelling himself—"

"Really?"

"Yes. He knows about your involvement with checking the injects, but he doesn't want you to get any more until further notice."

Mark's expression was a mixture of shock and confusion. "No more injects?"

"That's right. We'll review the situation in a fortnight."

"But… well, checking injects is what I'm here for, isn't it?"

"Oh, I agree, and I've made that clear to both Alex Duro and Mr. Pelling himself." Roundhill's tone edged toward disappointment.

"What reason did they give?" Mark asked.

"Well, there's one reason I do understand: they both know how your first inject review completely exhausted you. But for me, that just covers the next inject—"

"Politics."

"Yes. Maybe they're just being very cautious. I don't know. Anyway…"

"A bit disappointing," Mark said. "But in the meantime, there's quite a lot of other stuff I can get on with, I suppose."

"Yes, do a stats review. I think there are more ways to examine what we do, and I'd like you to develop some new ideas."

"Well, I'll give it a go."

"And I need to tell you that I've had to de-register you from inject issues. Just for two weeks. Had to do it because the politics one is free, so you'd get it automatically."

"Yes, I realized that. It's going out tomorrow, right?"

"Correct."

"Any link, do you reckon, between the politics inject and Mr. Pelling's candidacy for the presidency?"

Roundhill shook his head. "Absolutely not."

●●●

Back in his office, Roundhill sat down in an armchair near the main window. He could see buildings—high, silver, and shiny—and, looking up, there were clouds. A muddling level of grey covering the upper stories of many of the Inject City buildings. There was a low table in front of him. He reached forward, tapped the edge, and watched it carefully as nothing happened. No tea. He grinned. *Not standard issue then. Pity.*

Against one wall, there was a sideboard with a kettle on it and a few mugs. Not many employees went for this old-fashioned method of creating hot drinks, but all those who did had this type of kettle. Standard company issue. Roundhill would have liked to supply his own kettle—a different make which he much preferred—but that would have been a personal item, and thus not allowed.

Using this lesser-liked but fully adequate kettle, he made himself a cup of tea, adding milk from a bottle taken from a small fridge inside the sideboard.

He took his mug over to a desk where he had a couple of personalized devices with standard screens. He then spent nearly two hours making his way into several secure areas until he could place, side by side on one screen, the pre-translated neuron epi-language versions of two injects. This meant that each inject, in the format he was examining, filled over one hundred terabytes of data. Even the titles—written in the highly symbolized epi-language—filled four screen pages. He highlighted these and converted them into English text. Yes, he had the correct injects: *Politics updates 17 and 18*. Good. Then he did a size check and found that update 18 was fourteen terabytes larger than update 17. Now why was that if, as Alex Duro had assured him, the difference between the two updates was very small? He set up a difference search but was told that this would take forty-two hours to complete, so he abandoned the idea.

He reached for his mug of tea, still half-full but cold. He made another mug.

Unsure what to do next, he took his tea and sat by the window again. He looked out over the City, the dark sky now full of office lights, vertical and horizontal patterns. Someone knocked at his door. It was Mark. They had a brief chat about the day's work, then Mark left for home.

Roundhill began again, but he was still not sure how to progress his investigation. He decided to search for neuron epi-language differences within each inject. Update 17 had a total of 125 epi-languages while update 18 had 126. Interesting. He knew that these languages were updated all the time, so did the two injects have 125 languages in common? The answer was yes. Good, so there was one addition, admittedly very large. When he asked for this additional language to be identified, he was given the name *puro-dimit-pleth-grand-worklay 2148.79*. Of course he didn't know the names of all the epi-languages—there were hundreds of them—but he did know the taxonomical system used to classify them, and this name did not fit.

Puro-dimit-pleth-grand... Yes, that was fine. But the rest? *worklay*? No idea what that was, and then a seven-character digital identifier (seven, including the decimal point)? No, this didn't comply with the standard taxonomy. He asked for the first example of this epi-language in update 18 to be displayed. When it appeared, it was presented in rows of symbols, only a few of which he recognized.

Odd.

He asked for a translation into English text. That took seventeen minutes, so he went to the toilet, came back, made himself another mug of tea, sat down, and waited. When the English text appeared on the screen, he found himself in a state of shock.

Vote! Vote! Vote! Vote!
Vote for Victor Pelling!
Vote for Victor Pelling!
Vote! Vote! Vote! Vote!
Vote for Victor Pelling!
Vote for Victor Pelling!

Further investigation revealed that this subliminal message appeared in update 18 no fewer than 2,374 times.

3.1.

The following day, Brian Lymington was at his desk on floor twenty-eight of the ERC Tower at 5:30 am. On days when a new inject or update was about to be issued he liked to be in the office early—5:30 am was good. But this was only half an hour earlier than his regular arrival time at work. He was wedded to work and, as a result, no longer wedded to his wife, who'd left him three years ago. Holidays had to be forced on him. He might enjoy a few days off, but soon would be overtaken by a craving to return to work. On his one sick day in five years, his doctor had told him to slow down, or he might die before he reached thirty-five. That was three years ago, shortly after his wife left him. Now Lymington was thirty-four years and eleven months old, and he was convinced that his method of enjoying life even more was to work harder.

On this particular day, he wished he'd got to work at 4:30, not 5:30, because he'd discovered something very odd in the first half hour. Very odd indeed. It was something that needed to be reported urgently. Unfortunately, he had to wait nearly two hours before he could contact Melissa Mortimer, Alex Duro's PA, and ask her to get in touch with Duro straight away. "Code five," he said to her.

"Code five?" she asked. "Are you quite sure?"

"I'm quite sure," he said.

At 7:42 am, Lymington was in Duro's office. Duro waved at the ceiling and said, "Everything's switched off, okay? No recording of any sort. So just tell me exactly what the problem is."

Lymington was clearly nervous. A tall man, and at least ten kilos overweight, he looked closer to forty-four than thirty-four. His eyes—perhaps as the result of years of staring at screens—were partially closed, as if the intensity of their focus extended beyond computing devices to… well, just about everything. The result was that wrinkles had gathered above, below, and to the side of his eyes. Similar lines afflicted the bridge of his nose. What he'd discovered was something that had never happened before, and this was the first time he'd invoked code five, which related to major breaches of security.

"This morning," he began. "I discovered that late last night someone got through the security barriers and took a look at the Politics update that's due for release today."

"What do you mean *took a look?*"

"Did a number of searches through the epi-languages. Spent several hours on it."

"Really? What kind of searches?"

"They appear to be random dips into the data. It's difficult to see a pattern—well, not yet, anyway. I'm still investigating it."

"So somebody hacked into one of our systems?"

"Yes."

"Can you locate this hacker?"

"I should be able to do that, yes. But he's very clever. I mean, he's managed to cover his tracks well, though not perfectly."

"So you'll be able to identify him?"

"I'm pretty sure I can do it, yes. But there's one thing I can tell you already."

"Oh? What's that?"

"It's somebody from inside this building."

"Ah." Duro said nothing for a few seconds. Then he said, "Maybe we should sit down."

Both men had been standing not far from the office door up to this point. Now, they stepped toward the window and sat opposite one another with the coffee table in between.

Lymington was beginning to feel even more nervous, perhaps because Duro seemed more relaxed.

"Someone in the company, then?" Duro asked.

"It would seem so, yes."

"And you can you find out who it is?"

"Almost certainly, once I've got a few of the other guys on it."

"Hold on. Who knows about this so far?"

"Nobody. I mean, just you and me."

"What about Melissa?"

"I just told her it was code five. I didn't give her any details."

"And you're the only person working on it?"

"So far, yes."

"Good, good. Just one more thing, though. Is it possible anyone else in your department will get suspicious? Spot something?"

"Not unless I tell them to, no. I was just double-checking a few things. The rest of the team are already working on the next inject. Busy time right now."

"Well, it is, yes. So..." Duro looked across at Lymington intently. "An important question. Would you... would you like a cup of tea? Maybe a coffee?"

After a tiny moment of shock and confusion, Lymington said, "A coffee... yes, thank you. I'd love a cup of coffee."

"Fine. Put your hand flat in the middle of that circle there." Duro pointed to a circle outlined in white on Lymington's side of the table. "Nothing sinister," he added when Lymington looked a little unsure. "It'll just check your internal chemical assets to determine what coffee you like best. Do you drink a lot of coffee?"

"I do, yes." Lymington leaned forward and placed his hand in the circle.

"Good. Always makes it easier. Your coffee'll be ready in... oh, about thirty-five seconds. I think I'll have tea, myself." He activated the table screen, tapped a few icons, and then leaned back in his chair. "Right. First of all, thank you very much indeed, Brian, for raising this issue with me. Absolutely the right thing to do."

"Well, I was just following the rules."

"Good. So, just to recap, you haven't mentioned this to anyone else?"

"No. You and I are the only ones who know about it."

"Good. Well..."

At that moment, a flap in the coffee table rose. A cup of coffee emerged and was slowly moved toward Lymington. Duro gestured toward it. "Clever little thing, isn't it? I'd be prepared to make a bet that it's the best coffee you've ever had."

Lymington, his hands trembling slightly, picked up the cup and took a sip. "It's very good," he said as he replaced the cup in its saucer. "Really excellent." For a moment, he looked almost comfortable.

Duro smiled as his tea arrived. "Now, you said you'd be able to identify the hacker more quickly if you got a couple of your team involved."

"That's right, yes. Probably another hour, hour and a half—"

"And if you just did it by yourself?"

"Difficult to say. Maybe three hours."

"Okay. Then, this is what I want you to do, and please, I want you to follow these instructions exactly."

"Of course."

"Right. First, no one else is to be involved. No one at all. No mention of it to anyone. Okay?"

"Fine. Agreed."

"Good. Now, I know it might take longer with you working on it alone, but an hour here or there doesn't matter that much. We're the only people who know about this, you and me, and that's how it's going to stay. Is that clear?"

"Perfectly clear."

"Fine. So first, see if you can identify the hacker, and when you find out who it is, come and tell me in person. Don't phone me, just contact Melissa and she'll make arrangements. Also, obviously, I need to know what the hacker's done. If he's changed anything in the update, then we'll need to postpone it."

"I'm pretty sure that'll be relatively easy to check."

"Good."

"Actually," Lymington said, "I'm fairly sure already that he didn't change anything. All the basic dimensions—size, cognitive speed, and so on—they're all the same as before. I'll double-check, of course."

"Good." Duro stood up. "One more thing, though."

"Yes?" Lymington got to his feet quickly.

"Can you do this work pretty much anywhere in the building? I mean, is all the specialist equipment you need… is it portable?"

"Well, it is, yes. I can hook up to databases almost anywhere."

"Okay," Duro said. "Go to your office, pick up what you need and come back here. There's an empty office along the corridor. I'll get Melissa to sort it out for you. I'd like you to work there."

Lymington shrugged in agreement. "Fine."

"Don't mention any of this to your team. Tell them you've been asked to give me some help just for the day. Tell them that dragging people in for some specialist work is my usual routine." Duro smiled. "Not far from the truth, actually."

3.2.

Mark Ridgeway got to the office at seven twenty. He began the day by looking through the inject schedule for the next three months. The Politics update, which he was to be denied himself, was due to be released later that day. Then there was one on Palaeontology, followed by Ethics, Quantum Mechanics, Originaria, Dridothermatics... A list of quite obscure subjects, he reckoned, but he was aware that the purpose of Eden Rich was to offer education to all, no matter how many or how few were interested in a particular subject. Then, just as he was scrolling down through the list, the screen went blank. For a moment, he wondered if there had been a power blip, but the screen returned within two or three seconds. The words ***Inject Update*** appeared in the middle of the screen and then the inject list returned. Now, however, the next few releases would be very different. After Politics came Basic Mathematics update 23, Accounting update 35, Basic Computing update 27, Great People in History update 15... This sudden reorganization was a shift toward the more popular subjects. Strange.

At 8 am, Mark got a phone call from Peter Roundhill.

"Mark? Peter here. I'm afraid I won't be at the office today. Well, not this morning, anyway. Feeling a bit rough."

"Sorry to hear that, Peter—"

"Oh, it's nothing serious. Just a recurrence of something I get occasionally. Seeing my doctor at ten, and I'll be in touch sometime after that."

"Well, I hope it all goes well."

"Oh, it'll be fine. So... something I'd like you to do. Draw up a list of the next ten updates and categorize them by size, implementation issues, etc. Check the change in size from the previous update. Okay?"

"Sure. I—"

"Bye for now."

Mark then began reviewing the schedule of injects. He drew up a list of the previous updates for the same subjects and checked the indices. Nothing extraordinary there. He took a short break and then returned to do further comparisons. At about 9:30 he spotted that the new Politics update, due to be released that evening, was just over fourteen terabytes larger than the previous one. That seemed quite a lot, considering that Alex Duro made it clear that the new update—18—was only marginally different from update 17.

He stood up and took a few steps across the office which was too small for anything resembling thoughtful walking. Then he left the office, walked to the end of the corridor and onto a fully enclosed balcony from which he got a good view of the city, despite being only on the thirty-first floor. He loved heights and wanted to be higher. He stood by the balcony window and thought through the information he'd just discovered.

Could the increase in size of the update just be the result of more subject data? No. What about an increase in implementation infrastructure? Again, unlikely. So, some kind of new introduction or guide to the system? Almost certainly not. Mark knew that the current standard guide was less than one terabyte and even if there'd been a plan to change it, the increase would never be as big as fourteen terabytes. An advertisement, perhaps? A schedule of all the up and coming injects and updates? Again, no. Advertising not allowed. So, nothing to do now until he could discuss it with Peter Roundhill.

He went back to his office and reviewed his own response to his findings. Why was his reaction one of suspicion? *Lighten up!* he told himself. *Lighten up!* It could be something very simple he'd never thought about.

Time for an early lunch.

• • •

At about the same time Mark left for lunch, Brian Lymington was entering Alex Duro's office. Once again, he and Duro stood by the door and waited for Melissa Mortimer to leave.

"You've got an answer then, have you?" Duro said.

"I have, yes," Lymington said.

"And?"

"Well, the person who got through the security barriers—actually there's a little bit of a problem there…"

"Just tell me who it is."

"Well…" Lymington looked uncomfortable. He raised his right hand and rubbed his chin. "I've done three checks on this because it seemed very odd… clearly some kind of disguised infiltration, an impersonation sort of thing—"

"Please," Duro said, interrupting. "Forget all that for the moment and just tell me, who does it all point to?"

Lymington took a deep breath. "It points to you."

For the first time for a long time Duro found himself speech free. For several moments only breathing was possible. Then his early irritation gone, he said, "You know, I think we should sit down."

When they were both seated in the armchairs, just as they had been at twenty to eight that morning, Duro said, "Are you saying that whoever hacked into the system used my security details to get there?"

"That's right, yes."

"Which security details?"

"Well, pretty much all of them. There's your employee ID and password, your workplace access card and PIN…"

"How about my thumbprint ID?"

"They used that as well."

"But how on Earth could they have got that?"

"Difficult," Lymington said. "But not impossible."

"Okay, so here's an important question—nothing to do with coffee, by the way, but if you want a coffee, just help yourself." He pointed to the circle on the low table. Lymington didn't move. "Difficult question, but important: What makes you think that it wasn't actually me who did it?"

"Ah." Lymington looked relieved. "Whoever did it hacked into your personal data first but left a few digital footprints behind."

"Enough evidence for you to identify him?"

"Yes, but I'm not quite there yet."

"Could it be just about anyone in the building?"

"No, not anyone, but we do have a lot of experts here and quite a few of them have the skills to do it."

"And any idea *why* he did it? I mean, apart from maybe trying to get me into trouble, what was the aim? Did he make any changes to the inject?"

"No, none at all. Just did searches and looked at some of the new sections."

"Which new sections?"

"He did a search on epi-languages and found one that he examined in more detail."

"Which one?"

"One that's new to me, actually. Unusual, not in the regular format. But I'm pretty sure I can get it translated and then examine the content."

Duro said, "No." Then he stood up quite abruptly. Lymington, taken by surprise, got to his feet, too. "This may seem a bit odd," Duro went on, "but I want your investigation to stop now."

"You don't want me to check the epi-language?"

"No. Terminate the whole investigation."

"But I haven't identified the hacker yet."

"Not necessary. You see, there's some issues which I can't reveal to you but which mean you need to stop everything, the whole thing."

"Well…"

"And I want to thank you very much indeed for what you've done this morning. An excellent piece of work, which is much appreciated. And I'll make sure you get a substantial bonus for it."

"Oh, that's hardly necessary."

"Well, I disagree. You've saved the company from a major problem. I've got a feeling, you see, that I know who's responsible, and I'd like to make a few inquiries myself. Now, it is possible that I'll come back to you, but for the moment it's over. Okay?"

"Well, obviously, if that's what you want—"

"It is. And one more thing. I know you've put in an intense period of work this morning, so please take the rest of the day off."

"Oh, I really don't need to…"

"Brian, I insist. Don't even go back to your team now. I'll get Melissa to go and tell them that you'll see them tomorrow."

"But surely—"

"No buts, Brian. Off you go. Take a break. You deserve it."

•••

After Lymington left, Alex Duro realized he had to work out his next course of action very carefully. The most likely person to have used his security data to hack into the Politics update was Peter Roundhill. He would have wanted to find out why the inject wasn't going to be checked. Duro now understood that saying the new update was very similar to the last one was a mistake. Big mistake. Roundhill would have suspected something.

The location screen revealed that Roundhill wasn't in the building. Within a couple of minutes, Duro was on floor thirty-one, talking to Mark Ridgeway.

"Peter's not in, is he?" Duro asked.

"Well, he wouldn't elaborate, but he sounded okay. He just said it was the recurrence of some medical issue and needed to get it checked, and he'd probably be back this afternoon."

"Oh, good. Well, I hope it's nothing serious." Duro looked around Mark's office. "Comfortable here?"

"Yes, it's great. I really like it."

"Well, I'm glad about that. But look, there's just one other thing. You must be keen to get started on the injects again—getting the injects yourself, I mean. And doing an assessment. After all, that's what we hired you for..."

"Well, yes."

"But the thing is, I've had a chat with the head of our medical team and told him what you've done already—the review of the Religion inject—and he's quite concerned."

"Concerned?"

"About your health. You see, Dr. Broadhurst's aware that an inject every few days isn't a problem. But when someone's required to do a review of all the data in the inject, just as you were—and we're aware that it's a completely new approach—then the brain activity is very intense. You might not be fully aware of it, but it is, and doing a check on another inject within a few days of the first one is not on. *Definitely* not on. In fact, you shouldn't even be here. You should be at home, resting."

"But... well, I've already had some time off and I feel fine."

"Well, that's good news and I'm sure everything'll be okay. However, I'm sure you understand that I've got to abide by what Dr. Broadhurst says. We look after our staff in this company and you're clearly going to be a major asset so we want to take good care of you. So I want you to go home now and not come back till the day after tomorrow. Then we'll reassess the situation."

"But I... I really do feel perfectly well—"

"Yes, as I said, that's good, but your brain could be under acute stress even though you feel fine. I don't want to take any risks here. So…" He smiled. "Off you go. And don't worry about anything. I'll sort it out with Peter when I see him this afternoon."

Duro waited until Mark had tidied his desk, picked up his bag, and was in the elevator heading to floor level. Duro then used his senior ID pass to get into Peter Roundhill's office. He closed and locked the door and sat at Roundhill's desk. There were several screens in front of him. He touched what he reckoned was the main one, and a password was requested. He took a phone from his pocket, flicked through his app list until he found passwords. Employees of Eden Rich didn't know that every piece of technology in the building—all computing devices, communications systems, inter-company raysings, even the heating system, *all of them*, had two passwords, not one. The second password was known by two people only: Alex Duro and Victor Pelling.

Trust? What did trust mean? Duro *did* occasionally think about this issue, but quickly put it to one side because the answer was easy: *trust no one*. No doubt there were people you could trust. Brian Lymington was probably one example. He was so totally dedicated to the company that the best way to make him really happy was to ask him to work twenty-four hours a day. But as a general rule, no, don't trust anyone. And here was proof he was right. When the screen opened for him, he ran a search on activity for the past twenty-four hours, and yes, it was clear Roundhill had been in the office working until three o'clock that morning. Duro deleted all traces of his own use of the screen, closed it down, then wiped it clean of any fingerprints he might have added to the pure glass surface.

Back in his own office, he searched Peter Roundhill, opening the security coverage within Roundhill's office. He skipped through all the previous evening until, as he expected, everything went blank at 8 pm, after Roundhill left. And it remained blank for the rest of the evening and into the early morning.

Roundhill was clever. He knew the monitoring system shut down at 8pm so, if he came back into the office later, there'd be no vizi-recording. *Except he's not that clever.* Duro switched to another camera—one not known to Roundhill—and saw he'd returned to the office at 9 pm and continued working. Duro managed to see the screen that Roundhill was working on, and there were intermittent flashes of data as Roundhill shifted in his seat. Duro flipped forward until he reached a point at about 2 am when he could see two windows on the screen, one with 17 as its heading, the other with 18. Roundhill was comparing the Politics updates. Yes, Roundhill had discovered Victor's secret. *What a bastard.*

3.3.

Victor Pelling opened the secret drawer in his office desk and took out the photograph he kept there in contravention of the company rules he'd created himself, which did not allow employees to bring personal items inside the building. He'd already switched off all surveillance systems within the office. He sat down on one of the armchairs in his leisure area and looked hard at the photograph of a little boy with a pale complexion, spectacles with round lenses framed in black, and thick black hair with a fringe at the front. It was a photo of his son, Jim.

He couldn't remember if Jim's hair in this photo was his real hair or the wig he wore during the last few months of his life. Probably the wig. His hair had never grown back.

Pelling found that he was retrieving the photo from the secret drawer more and more often these days. Also, as was happening now, he would start to have a conversation—one-sided, of course—with his son, who had died twenty years before. "I want you to know that the success of this company, my success, it's all down to you, Jim."

He paused for a few moments. "I'm sorry, of course—desperately sorry—about what happened to you. I know it was really awful but… well… I know I've told you this before, but I'm going to tell you again. And again. And again. It helped us learn how to do it properly… how to help other children all over the world. Without you, I'd never have been able to do it. And now I'm going to be president of this country. Difficult to believe, I know, but I am, I'm absolutely sure of that. And I'm going to have more power to help people, offer more education, get everyone heading in the same direction so we can be more and more successful and much happier." He paused again.

"All down to you, Jim, all down to you. There'll be statues of you erected all over the country, all over the world, in fact. I guarantee that. The least I can do, I know. The least I can do."

●●●

Alex Duro also had a secret drawer in his office desk, and, similar to Pelling, he had only one item in it. However, it was a very different item from Pelling's. It wasn't a photograph, it was a phone. A special type of smartphone—its use could not be detected by any of the surveillance systems inside the Eden Rich Tower.

He could only use this phone to contact one person. The person he contacted was someone he had actually met many years before, a man who had set up a very strange system which, at first, Duro reckoned would never be used. It turned out he'd been very wrong. And now he needed it again.

He took the phone from the secret drawer and made a call. There were voice recognition systems in place for the caller and receiver. Their identities were shown on the phone screen, not photographs, just the special names they had both created and were only known by each other. No passwords or codes or any further identification required. "Got a job for you," Duro said.

"One job?"

"Well, three, actually."

"Three? And when do you want the work done?"

"Within twenty-four hours. Within the next six would be even better."

"Here in this city?"

"Yes, all three. And not here in our building now. They're either at home or on their way home."

"Should be possible then. Send me the details in the usual way."

"Will do," Duro said. The phone call ended.

Within the next couple of minutes, Duro sent the details which were the names of three people: Lymington, Roundhill, Ridgeway and their addresses. Most people would think that Duro's request was appalling and Duro himself was slightly upset about what he felt he had to request. But he convinced himself that what he had asked to be done was absolutely essential. It was important to be aware that the future would be in a much better state when this job was done.

●●●

Malcolm, Guard 17, got a phone call. He was surprised and, up to a point, unhappy about the request that had been made. Of course, it wasn't really a request. It was an order. He left the ERC building and walked quickly to one of the nearest streets, where he got into a car with a driver and two other men in the back seat.

●●●

Mark was at home in his flat. He had lived there alone for six months. He had been looking forward to joining the ERC, was happy—yes, very happy—that they had taken him on but a little confused about what they were now requiring him to do which, technically, was nothing at all.

Of course, maybe Duro was right about the impact of that inject survey that had lasted sixteen hours. But Mark felt okay. Better than that, actually: he felt fine. *Curious*. Anyway, he was sure he would enjoy his next few days. He had the opportunity to meet some of his friends. In fact, today he was going to meet—

His phone rang. He didn't recognise the number and there was no indication of who the caller was.

"Hello, is that Mark?"

"Possibly. Let me know who you are."

"This is Malcolm."

"Malcolm? Oh, Malcolm, Guard 17, am I right?"

"That's right, yes."

"Well, great to hear from you."

"Thank you. And you're at home right now, are you?"

"Yes."

"Great. You see, I've been sent to pick you up. Something urgent at ERC that they need your help with."

"Really?"

"Yes."

"But they haven't contacted me."

"No? Well, you're likely to get a call when you're on the way to ERC. But anyway, please come down as soon as you can. We're waiting for you on the road by your flat."

"No problem. Down immediately."

Mark made his way downstairs and, as he left the main door of the block of flats—his flat was on the third floor—he saw Malcolm waving to him.

"Hi, Malcolm. Great to see you."

They shook hands.

"Ah," Mark saw that on his left wrist, Malcolm was wearing the watch he'd given him a couple of days before.

Malcolm tapped the watch gently. "It's great," he said, smiling. Then he added, "Sorry we had to come and pick you up, but they're desperate to have you back at work today."

"Quite a surprise," Mark said.

Malcolm shrugged. "Not a surprise to me." He opened the back door of the car. Mark got in next to two men in the back seat.

"I'm not coming with you," Malcolm said and shut the door.

The car moved away quickly. Malcolm just watched it go. He shook his head gently. "Well, that's it," he said to himself quietly.

He began to walk down the street toward the nearest station. When he reached a corner, he saw a litter bin. He took the watch off his wrist and tossed it into the bin.

• • •

Soon, Duro got a phone call. "Job complete," he was told.

"Excellent. All three?"

"Yes, all three."

"Good. Well done. Pay on its way."

Duro put his phone back into his secret drawer. Then he sat down. Yes, he was fully convinced that what he had arranged was pretty awful but absolutely essential.

Lymington, Roundhill, and Ridgeway: all three were now dead.

One thing that Duro *didn't* know was that Malcolm, Guard 17, worked for the private company that he had contacted on that special phone in his secret drawer.

3.4.

Duro contacted Pelling. "Victor, I thought I'd better let you know that we've had a couple of resignations."

"Important ones?"

"Not particularly, but people you've met recently. I thought you should know about it. Brian Lymington and Peter Roundhill."

"Really? That's a bit of a surprise. Both good guys, if I remember rightly."

"Yes, they are. Anyway, both were feeling they needed a break, maybe quite a long break…"

"Overworked?"

"Not at all. Well, both did long hours but purely voluntarily. Anyway, I agreed that they should go, but I told them we'd take them back if they ever wanted to return. Gave each of them a decent bonus, too."

"Good. That was the right thing to do."

"Oh, and I had another chat with Dr. Broadhurst about Mark Ridgeway. You know, our new man with all the injects—"

"Yes, is he okay?"

"Well, thankfully he is but Broadhurst's not convinced that that kind of job's possible. Long term there might be some critical implications so I've had a word with Mark and I've extended his sick leave to two months. That was Dr. Broadhurst's suggestion. Then, if we still need him, we can reassess his situation. So, again, I've given him an excellent bonus. He'll be okay."

"Good," Pelling said. "Of course, we might not need him again. Not after the election, I mean."

"Agreed."

"Okay. So, well done. Thanks for sorting all that."

4.1.

The election of President Victor Pelling was a shock to political analysts all over the world. Two days before the election, opinion polls had given him a rating of 3%. The next day, it had shot up to 39%, and quite a few people thought there had been some technical hitch in the data collection process. Pelling was pleased that only one political commentator suggested that there might be some link to the Politics update, which had been issued free the night before. The commentator confessed that he had no idea what this link might be. Pelling found this reassuring, but he noted the commentator's name.

On the day of the election, exit polls suggested that Pelling would win by getting 58% of the vote. He received 63%. This figure astonished everyone. Pelling himself was disappointed. *Only 63%?* Alex Duro had to remind him that he'd won.

When it became clear he'd won, he arranged a press conference. He invited journalists, cameramen, political commentators, TV and social media presenters, and anyone with a link to news promotion to attend the conference on the ground floor of the ERC Tower. Close to two hundred people attended.

The press conference was called for 11 am. At that time, not everyone was ready—some camera equipment wasn't set up—but Pelling began anyway on the dot of eleven o'clock. Standing alone on the stage with only a single microphone, he began without a greeting. He said, "I wish to thank everyone who voted for me. I will work hard, not just for them but for everyone. And, in order to work hard I'll be based here, in the ERC Tower, because this building has the best communication systems in the country. I will not be occupying the presidential palace. I'm going to arrange for it to be opened to the public."

This statement prompted a lot of comments among the audience. Pelling ignored this and carried on: "I've arranged for my first meeting with some of those I've chosen to head up the governmental departments. This meeting will take place here, in this building, at ten past eleven, so this will be a short press conference."

The response to this statement was disbelief, unrest, and some anger. "Ten minutes?" someone shouted. "Just ten minutes?"

Pelling looked toward the journalist who had shouted. Then he glanced at the digital clock on the far wall. "Eight minutes and twenty-three seconds," he said.

The noise from the audience rose. There were more shouts. "This is crazy!" "What the hell's going on?" "Ridiculous! Ridiculous!"

Pelling waved for silence. "Do you want me to leave now, or would you like to listen?"

Everyone quietened down. Almost. Enough of them, anyway, for Pelling to continue. "There will be a government statement tonight at eight o'clock. Then, there'll be one statement every Friday that will list the issues that have arisen during the week and how they've been dealt with. There'll also be an indication of progress on manifesto promises, reaction to worldwide incidents, and so on…"

"Just one press conference a week?" one of the journalists in the front row called out.

"No, not a press conference, *a statement*. This is my first press conference and my last."

"What?" This from several of those present.

"There won't be anymore from now on, just a weekly statement."

Laughter and a lot of anger followed this.

When the noise had quietened down again, Pelling said, "Let me tell you why."

"Bloody good idea!" someone shouted out.

"Leaders in the past," Pelling went on, "spent more time talking about what they were doing than actually doing it. Not good in my opinion. I want to spend my time getting on with the work that's required to deliver what I've promised in my manifesto. So, from now on, there"ll be a weekly statement but no more press conferences." He paused, said, "Thank you," and stepped back from the microphone stand.

More noise followed: voices of complaint, shouts of anger. Pelling turned away and prepared to step down from the stage. "Wait, Mr. President! Wait!" one of the journalists yelled, his voice audible above the general turmoil. "We have questions! We have questions! There's things we need to ask!"

Pelling shook his head but then returned to the microphone. The audience got quiet again. "One thing I can see," Pelling said, "is that we're into the eleventh minute, so you're already interfering with my schedule of government business. But I'm happy to answer *one* question. Just one."

The journalist in the front row who'd shouted out looked confused and angry. "You're saying we can only ask you one question?"

"Correct," Pelling said. "And you've just done that." He gave a smile that suggested disinterest with a hint of cynicism. "Good morning," he added as he stepped down from the dias and headed off stage.

•••

Within minutes, all elements of social media were full of this news—the fact that there would be no news! Well, no press conferences, just weekly statements.

It was pointed out that there was no indication of how long these statements would be and only the most meager of suggestions about the kind of issues they would cover. What upset everyone in the media most was the fact that there would be no opportunity whatsoever to question the president himself about what was going on.

It took only half an hour for a petition to be set up which demanded the president should be available regularly—at least two mornings or two afternoons a week—to respond to questions raised not just by the media but by members of the public as well. By eight o'clock that evening, thirteen million people had signed the petition.

Then everything changed.

At eight o'clock, as promised, came the first statement. It was quite short. In fact, it covered only one subject: education.

Pelling announced that, as president, it was essential for him to concentrate all his energy on governing the country. This meant that he would have to distance himself from his commercial activities. Consequently, he would step down from his position as CEO of Eden Rich Corporation. He would hand over the running of the company to one of his deputies. However, his final act as CEO was to declare that for one year (at the very least) and starting soon (date to be announced shortly) all ERC injects and updates would be free. This action would be the first country in the world in which all education—at all levels—would be free. To everyone. A further promise was made to those who had already paid for future injects and updates: they would get their money back.

The reaction on social media was far greater than the earlier response to Pelling's statement about press conferences. There were immediate expressions of shock, wonder, joy, praise. The petition about the president's methods of communication, or lack of them, was forgotten.

4.2.

Pelling learned from Alex Duro that about ten percent of parents still refused to allow their children to have injects. They funded schools and employed teachers to instruct their pupils using traditional methods. Duro discovered this figure had risen from eight percent over the past six months. A little worrying. It was reasonable to predict it would rise further. Duro ensured that this information, obtained by one of ERC's research units, was not made public. He and Pelling had a long discussion about it.

"It's a question of control," Duro said.

"Well, of course it is," Pelling said. "But the best way to get control is to be positive, make offers, lure people in. That's why I've gone for free injects. A lot of people will be persuaded to do it that way rather than pay for schools and teachers. You know, carrot rather than stick."

"Most of the schools are community-based," Duro said. "Run by collectives. They give their lessons in their homes and, generally, the tutors don't get paid. Or they're paid in kind."

"Or they're the parents of some of the kids," Pelling said.

"That's right, yes."

"I did a bit of research, too, you know." Pelling smiled. "I'd like to see the figures for next month. How many of these schools have closed down? How many inject virgins are there? You know the sort of thing."

"No problem," Duro said. Then he added, "But there is one issue, possibly quite a big one. I'm thinking of inject deaths. After all, a lot of the parents who arrange traditional schools are doing it because they had a kid who died at the first inject. Or they've got friends or relatives who lost a child."

"Yes, I'm aware of that."

"So, if they decide to go for free injects and there's a few more inject deaths—even just a few—then there could be more trouble. Most of these people are well-informed, have high-level media links—"

"How many?"

"How many what?"

"Well, let's start with inject deaths. How many last year?"

"Hold on." Duro picked up his phone, worked his way through several windows and said, "A hundred and twenty-three."

Pelling expressed something that was a mix between an exhalation and a sigh.

Duro said, "Down on the year before, though. The figure then was a hundred and fifty-four."

Pelling thought for a few moments. "Not good, is it," he said. "How many people know about this?"

"Difficult to know the exact figure," Duro said. "We've kept it as quiet as we can. There'll be hospital doctors and nurses who've got an idea of local numbers, but not the range over the whole country. We've kept an eye on social media and deleted texts, photos, videos, etc. that've started to publicise this kind of data."

"Not sure that's such a good idea," Pelling said.

"No? Well, I can tell you it's worked so far."

"Well, I want you to stop doing that."

"You do?"

"Yes. Stop immediately." For the first time in this conversation, Pelling's tone was decisive, firm. "In the future, if you've got any plans for stuff like that, ask me about it first."

Duro thought about this for a few seconds and then said, "Okay."

"Look," Pelling went on. "I know these figures—I mean, the inject deaths—these figures are high, but we need to massage them a bit and then allow them to be available. Not broadcast them, but if there are enquiries, then people are free to find out."

Duro, animated, voice rising, said, "Come on, Vic, don't be ridiculous. You put me in charge of these figures ten years ago, and all this time I've kept them secret because of the potential problems. If people find out about this, then it could be the end of ERC for a start and the end of your presidency as well. Christ almighty, you want that?"

Pelling remained quite calm although arguments with Duro, like this one, were rare. He said, "New world, Alex, and we've got to move gently into it. Look, take car accidents, for example. How many people die in car accidents each year?"

Duro shrugged. "Don't know the exact figure."

"Well, I do. Last year it was just under fifty-six thousand."

"It's come down, then."

"Yes, it has. Driverless cars are proving to be much safer. But then, when the figure was about one hundred thousand a year—and everybody knew that, by the way—it was reported in all the media."

"Lots of complaints," Duro said. "Protests—"

"Yes, but did people stop driving? Did they? Did they want cars to be banned?"

After a few moments, with the hint of a wry smile, Duro said, "No, they didn't."

"Exactly. Ban driving? Ban all vehicles? Not a chance. We accept it, you see. Thousands die each year in car accidents but that's okay because society couldn't exist without cars. So what I'm saying is that hundreds of millions of people get educated by ERC injects each year—we're heading for billions worldwide, in fact. The fact of the matter is a hundred people died because of this, well… it's the price we've got to pay, isn't it? And every year the number's being reduced. People will accept that. Cancel all education because a tiny fraction of one percent die from injects? No. No way. No one's going to agree. So what I'm saying is that we need to be open about this. Can't you see that?"

The conversation ended there. Pelling left for his first meeting with the people he'd chosen to take responsibility for each of the manifesto projects he'd decided upon.

Duro, feeling considerable discomfort following the revelation of Pelling's change of view about aspects of ERC's work they had previously fully agreed on, made his way to what Pelling had set up as the Vice President's suite in the tower at level one-hundred-nineteen. This was a luxury he enjoyed much more than he'd expected. Pelling had been very generous. Such large, beautifully decorated rooms with furniture that was perfect in what it offered. Armchairs, for example, that adapted immediately to your body shape when you sat down. Very relaxing.

Duro sat down but didn't relax. It was clear to him that his relationship with Victor Pelling was under stress. A couple of weeks ago he, Duro, had been one of the top men in a big company run by Pelling. Now he was Vice President of the country and Pelling was President! How the hell had that happened?

Well, he knew, of course, how it had happened. He knew about the subliminal messages placed in the Politics update. He understood the logic of the events that led to his current position, but it would take time to get used to this new role as Vice President, although he had already started to feel good about it.

Duro could see a few problems ahead. The subliminal messages, for example. Difficult to keep that secret. There were lots of people out there who were trying to discover how Pelling had come from nowhere to win the election. No doubt someone would figure it out fairly soon. Then what would happen? Would Pelling's popularity be so high that people would be happy to accept how he came to power? Very unlikely. No, there had to be tight control of information and this was something that, to Duro's concern, Pelling was shifting away from. Tell everyone the truth? No, no, no. That would bring disaster. Just keep people happy and tell them very little. Tell them nothing. Or tell them just what they wanted to hear.

Duro stood up. The armchair was the most comfortable he'd ever sat on, but he had to avoid relaxation. There was another big problem—one he'd set up himself. He'd lied to Pelling. This was something he'd done before but always relating to minor issues that didn't have a major impact on Eden Rich.

But this lie was a big one. He'd seen no way of avoiding it.

When Pelling had asked him for last year's number of inject deaths, he'd amended the figure by… well, quite a margin. The number of people—mostly under fifteens—who'd died from injects worldwide wasn't a hundred and twenty-three, it was closer to twenty-three thousand.

4.3.

Some of you may be surprised… well, no, perhaps *all of you* are surprised that you are here for the first full meeting, the *only* meeting—I'll explain that later—of all heads of government departments. You can see from the list I've issued what I've got in mind for each of you. And yes, some of you are people I admired from the last government, but most of you are completely new to the positions I'm offering you. I've done my research, you see, and I know what your superior qualities are. It's those qualities, those specific skills, that have enabled me to link each one of you to the position I believe is best for you.

"By the way, I also know that some of you—well, all of you, all of *us*, me included—have some negative attributes and have done some dubious things in the past. Now, I'll make a promise: if any such issues arise, I'll ignore them. You see, I want to get on with things, get things done. Bit of a cliché, but the future's more important than the past. I hope you agree.

"Now, I need to make a few things clear. First, the position I'm offering each one of you is the *only* position for you. If you think you'd be better taking on a different role in the government, the answer's no. For example, if two of you had a chat and felt it would be better all around if you swapped roles, the answer is no. You either take the job I'm offering or forget it. Now, I will say that I'll be happy to discuss the scope of each position. I look forward to having one-to-one discussions with each of you about the range of your duties. No problem. But, if it's already clear to any of you that you don't want the position I'm offering, then please leave now."

Pelling stepped back from the microphone and looked round the faces of the thirty-eight people who made up the audience. They were in the same room in which the very short press conference had been held. Many of those present were CEOs of successful businesses, some were scientists, some were celebrities well-known for specific skills. A few—very few—were politicians from previous administrations. Almost all of them were men.

Someone raised a hand and stood. "Mr. President, may I ask a question?"

Pelling stepped forward to the microphone again and, after a moment's silence, said, "No." The man sat down. During the next half minute no one left the room.

Pelling continued. "Good. Now, it may already be apparent to you—I hope so anyway—that my view of governmental leadership differs greatly from the traditional one. I'll be spending very little time talking to the media about what we're doing. I just want to spend time doing it. I'd like your approach to be the same. Also, I hate meetings. This meeting we're having now—if you can call it a meeting—is the first and most likely the last we'll have during my period as president. You can all meet together if you wish, or groups of you can meet up—that's fine. But I won't be present at any such meetings. I'll meet each of you one-to-one. That's the way I prefer. You see, for me, it's all a matter of trust. For example, I've known Vice President Duro for many years and I trust him completely. He's not here right now because he doesn't need to be. He's getting on with his job.

"Finally, are you all honored to be asked to join the government?" He raised a hand quickly and said, "Rhetorical question. I don't want to hear an answer. I want the answer to be inside your heads and I want the answer to be no. I think that kind of thing is highly emotional stuff and it's bullshit. We're not here to congratulate each other or praise each other or anything like that. We're here to get started on a job and do it well."

Pelling stepped back from the microphone. He looked around the group before him for about ten seconds. He didn't smile. He left the room.

●●●

"They probably think I'm turning into a dictator," Pelling said to Alex Duro when they met up later that day. "What do you reckon?"

"I think you're already there," Duro said, smiling.

"Really?"

"Well, I hope so. I'm thinking *benevolent dictator*, of course. It's the only way to get things done, after all."

"Agreed. When you think of some previous governments spending most of their time just pissing around and achieving nothing. Just get on with the job."

"Got to be the right job, of course," Duro said.

"Well, I know that. So, what do you reckon? Our group of thirty-eight. Have we asked them to do the right things?"

"I agree with most of it."

"But?"

"Comes down to what we discussed earlier. Control."

"You want more of it," Pelling said.

"Yes."

"Well, having a level of control is helpful, I agree."

Duro shook his head. "Not helpful. Essential."

"So, what type of control is essential?"

"Control of population," Duro answered. "Who does this, who does that, who goes where... Fix the size of the population, who comes in, who goes out. Control of crime..."

"Double the police force?"

"We talked about this before, didn't we? No, triple it."

Pelling smiled and then stood up. They were in Pelling's office suite on floor one-hundred. He walked across the room to the nearest window and looked out over the city. He turned and said, "Can I get you anything? Tea? Coffee?"

"No thanks," Duro said.

Pelling looked out over the city again. It was a bright, cloudless day, and the air over the city and into the distant landscape was clear. Tall buildings, silver, white, even taller buildings, then suburbia beyond with lots of green—street trees, parks, roof gardens. "Never seen it as clear as this," Pelling said.

"Looking good, eh?"

"This view, yes." Pelling returned and sat down opposite Duro. "You lied to me," he said.

Duro's immediate reply was, "Yes, I did."

"Why did you do that?"

"Control of information," Duro said. "That's the most important of the lot, and you seem to be letting it slip away."

"About twenty-three thousand inject deaths last year."

"That's correct, yes."

"How the hell can we keep that quiet?"

"Well, what have we done for the last... more than a decade?"

"We?"

"Okay, it's me, I've done it. You told me all those years ago you wanted me to keep the figures and ensure there were medical advances to sort out any problems. You didn't want to follow this issue, did you?"

"No, I didn't. I know that."

"Why did you want to find out the figure now?"

"Change of job. Need to know."

"And how did you find out?

"Not easy," Pelling said. "But, remember, I invented most of the systems we use. Managed to locate the right file."

"Okay, so you're technically miles ahead of everyone. No one else is going to find out."

"I don't agree. I think they will. Now that I'm President—oh, and you're Vice President, just in case you've forgotten—all ERC data will be under even more intense scrutiny than before. Can't you see that?"

"Yes, I can. Precisely why we need to keep hold of all that data. Keep it to ourselves."

Pelling shook his head. "What about leaks? Whistleblowers? It's not just you and me who know the systems."

"No, but only you and I know the whole thing. Anyway, there's never been any leaked information."

"Quite remarkable when you think about it," Pelling said. "But look, we're moving into a different era, Alex. You've got to understand that. We've got to be more open. Oh, don't get me wrong, we've got to do it slowly—"

"How the hell can we do that slowly? Tell them that three years ago two people died from injects and the year after that five people died and then last year twenty-three thousand people died? Good stuff, Vic. Good stuff."

Pelling's expression was one of anger under control, but he started breathing heavily. "We just need to get the figure down, Alex."

"No problem," Duro said. "I'll give you this year's figure now if you like. Let's see... five thousand? Ten thousand?"

Pelling was silent for a while and then, quietly, said, "We need the real figure, Alex. the actual figure. The true figure."

"Okay, look, I'll tell you what I'll do. I'll give you regular updates of this year's figures. Monthly."

"Weekly."

"Fine. I could do it daily if you want. Hourly?"

"Stop taking the piss, Alex. Just let me know the figures weekly. The correct figures. Remember, I can always check them."

"So you don't trust me anymore, then?"

"Well, you *did* lie to me, didn't you?"

"Yes, yes, I did," Duro said, his voice rising. "But to *protect you*. Can't you see that? Difficult to believe, Vic—difficult right now, anyway—but I'm actually on your side."

Pelling looked away. He closed his eyes for a moment. After another short silence, it was Duro who spoke again, his voice firm but measured, not angry. "There's a major problem here, Vic. We've talked about it already, but you seem to be deliberately ignoring it. You've just announced that, starting soon, all injects will be free. Now, don't get me wrong, I think that's a great idea, but think of the implications. Lots more people will go for the injects. Free education? Terrific. And when I say lots more, I mean hundreds of millions, maybe even a couple of billion worldwide. And even if we can find out the problem that's killing some of them, it'll be too late for this year's figures. There'll be lots more dead, *lots* more. Twenty-three thousand last year. This year? Thirty thousand? I'd say that's the lowest figure possible. Fifty thousand? Let's face it, Vic, whatever it is, we can't possibly make that figure public. If we did, then ERC, the presidency, everything we've built up over the years, all of it, completely fucked. Is that what you want?"

• • •

Later, Pelling stood up and walked over to the window he'd been at earlier during his discussion with Alex Duro. He placed his feet as close to the base of the window as he could and looked out across the city and then down to the street below. For the first time in several months, he felt a little surge of vertigo. He looked up at the sky. It didn't help. He turned away from the window, disturbed that a hint of vertigo had returned, if only for a moment or two.

More resolution, more determination, more of that was needed and not just to do with this little blister of physical nervousness that had invaded his body. Perhaps that was linked to the enormous change in his general situation. When he'd said to Alex Duro that the two of them were entering a new era, he'd merely wanted to suggest a shift in their working relationship, but now he was beginning to realize that there were big, big changes ahead.

Before the election, he'd convinced himself that running a country was no different from running a business, particularly given the size of ERC. After all, the annual turnover of ERC was greater than the GDP of several countries. CEO of Eden Rich? Big job. President of the country? No, not a bigger job, just a very different one. Maybe... Christ almighty, maybe it wasn't such a good idea after all.

He walked over to one of the desks, opened his thumbprint-protected drawer, and took out the photo of Jimmy. He sat down and gazed at the photo for several minutes. He got upset every time he looked at it, but so far, he'd never cried. Not a single tear. This time? No, still no tears. For years he'd felt that weeping might help, but help with what? Some kind of acceptance of what he'd done to his son? Forgiveness from Jimmy? Dependent, of course, on some kind of spiritual link to the dead boy, something transcendental, supernatural and... well, he didn't believe in any of that shit.

But he wanted to cry, and he couldn't.

He put the photo back in the drawer and sat at one of his screens. He checked his schedule. In half an hour, he'd meet Alan Lerret, his Finance Adviser, then Brian Southwell, Home Affairs, and then... oh, two or three others before John Verne...

So he had a few minutes alone, time enough to write a speech in preparation for the video Mike Easton would record for him. How to begin? Easy. How to finish? Not so easy. And the content? Important that it should be positive, direct, and honest—well, as honest as he could manage. And most important of all? Keep it short.

He went back to the desk to take out the photo of Jimmy. He sat down again and propped the photo at the base of the screen. "You're going to have to help me with this, Jimmy," he said, then began to dictate his speech.

4.4.

At eight o'clock that evening, after he'd seen seven of the thirty-eight of his governmental advisers—he refused to call them ministers; he was in charge, they were advisers—and his broadcast video had been recorded, he asked Alex Duro to come up and watch the video.

"Video?" Duro said.

"I've recorded something I want to broadcast later tonight, but I think you should see it first."

"So you've already changed your mind? I mean, it was going to be Friday statements only, wasn't it?"

"Very slight change of plan."

"Not a good idea," Duro said. Then he added, "What's it about?"

"Come up and watch it," Pelling said. "It's only a few minutes long."

Duro arrived five minutes later and sat down to watch the video. The recording had been made there, in Pelling's ERC Tower suite. He was seated with his back to the window that faced east over the City. A fine net curtain had been placed across the window. His background, therefore, was one of tall, muted buildings, glinting softly in the sunlight with the occasional helicopter floating past quietly. In the video, Pelling seemed relaxed for only the first three minutes. After that, he gave the impression of being a little strained, with a level of unrequited exploration of his own emotions. It soon became easy to guess why this change had occurred.

Good evening. Once again I'd like to thank all of you who voted for me and gave me the opportunity to become your president. My winning of the election was a shock to many but not to me. I was convinced that what I offer this country would be recognized as the best way forward, and so it is.

I'd like to make it clear that I'll be a very different leader from those in the past. My time as the CEO of Eden Rich Corporation and my dedication to the spectacularly successful reform of the education system has led me to understand one essential aspect of leadership: the most important thing is to do the work, not spend hours and hours talking about it. Consequently, I won't often appear on television or other social media outlets. There will, of course, be regular detailed updates of what I and my government advisers have been doing, but I want us all to concentrate fully on the work of government rather than spend time recounting details of each and every task.

So this is my main message: I will work hard to fix problems and improve all aspects of life. As I said before I became president, I've already created a superb education system that has helped everyone—not just children, but *everyone*—to acquire an amount of knowledge that is many times more than what could be learned in the old traditional system.

The main reason I wish to speak to you this evening is because following my announcement of ERC injects soon being free to everyone, I learned there have been some rumors. While hundreds of millions of people worldwide—mostly children—have received first-class education through the systems offered by Eden Rich, a tiny, tiny fraction of one percent have become ill after receiving their injects. Now, I regret to tell you that these rumors, up to a point, are true. The actual figures for those who became ill as a result of injects are difficult to determine, but it's become clear that some injectees—a very small number—have been adversely affected.

There are two things I wish to say about this.

First, with the increased authority I have as President, I have set up a medical team to investigate what has been happening. I've set them a target of three months to come up with a solution.

Second, I wish to tell you about a little boy named Jim. This is a photograph of Jim at the age of eight. Jim was struggling at school, unable to retain very much of what he was taught. He became a sad little boy, depressed and miserable because he was so far behind his classmates. His problems increased to the point that Jim's entire future was in doubt. It was then that his father chose, as a last resort, to have him receive an inject.

The result was amazing. Jim's knowledge of all subjects increased to the point he became a walking encyclopedia—which, of course, is what happens to all children these days. Jim's complete demeanour changed. He became happy, vibrant, outgoing, a really wonderful child. But later, he became ill.

At the time, there was no indication—none whatsoever—that his illness was linked to the injects. But it's very sad to report that Jim did not recover. He's no longer with us.

It's only in the last few days that there's been the suggestion of possible links between injects and certain illnesses. My medical team will examine this carefully and arrive very shortly at a definitive answer. My commitment to this process is total, and my monitoring of the medical team's progress will be rigorous.

There's a specific reason for this, which you may have guessed already: Jim was my son.

After a silence of fifteen seconds or so, Pelling said, "There you are: four minutes."

"And four seconds," Duro said. "I timed it."

There were three people in the room: Pelling, Duro, and Mike Easton, who had recorded the video. It was Mike Easton who spoke next.

"Are you sure you don't want some kind of... well, semi-formal ending to it, Mr. President? A valedictory message of some sort?"

"Valedictory message?"

Duro said, "Goodbye, good luck, goodnight..."

Pelling smiled. "Actually, I do know what a valedictory message is." He turned to Mike Easton. "No, none of that. It's done."

Duro said, "Could I ask you to leave us for a couple minutes, Mr. Easton? The President and I need to discuss this."

"Sure, no problem."

"But don't go away. There's a lounge down the corridor to the left. If you could just wait there for a few minutes—"

"Fine."

"—and please remember that everything to do with this broadcast is entirely confidential."

"Of course."

"Good."

When Easton had left and Duro was sure he was in the other lounge and well out of hearing range, he said to Pelling, "Absolutely not."

"What?"

"That broadcast would be a complete disaster."

"Well, I don't agree, but come on, tell me what you think is wrong."

Duro shrugged. "Too many lies in your honesty."

"What the hell do you mean by that?"

"Well, let's take a very obvious point. You're a scientist, right? You invented injects, and your son became ill after he'd had an inject, but you couldn't imagine there was a link between the two? No, no, no. Nobody's going to believe that. Also, it becomes clear from what you've said that you used your son as a guinea pig. And he died. So you killed your son."

Pelling's anger was immediate. "How dare you say that!"

"Oh, for Christ's sake, Vic, I'm not saying it. You're saying it. That's what everyone will understand from what you've said."

"Oh, don't be ridiculous."

"No, that's the conclusion they'll come to. No question about that. And look, another thing. You've only found out in the last couple of days that some injectees die? Oh, come on. Are you assuming that everyone out there is stupid enough to believe that? How long have we been doing this? ERC was established over a decade ago, and it's only now that we've discovered problems? No." He shook his head. "No, no, no, *no*. But it's your basic approach that's completely wrong. You've managed to convince yourself that if you bare your soul to the nation about what happened to Jimmy, everyone will be overcome by compassion at such a desperate tragedy. Well, you're wrong. They'll see you as a murderer, and they'll fucking stamp you to death. Maybe even literally."

There was a long silence now, interrupted by Pelling, who took a tissue from his pocket and blew his nose. After returning it to his pocket, he said calmly, "Well, I can't agree, Alex. I think it'll work, and I want it to be broadcasted tonight."

After a short pause, Duro said, "Look, we mustn't fall out over this, Vic. I mean, it's your broadcast, it's your decision, I accept that. But I'd like to make one request. Don't broadcast it tonight. Take a little while to think it through. Give it twenty-four hours. Then, if you still think it's the right thing to do, okay, go ahead and do it. But please, *please*, leave it until tomorrow evening and broadcast it then."

Pelling thought about this for several seconds and said, "Okay."

"Good." Duro stood up. "I'll go and let Mike Easton know, and I'll remind him to keep his mouth shut." Then he left the room.

● ● ●

Duro went down to his office, took his special phone from his private drawer, and contacted the only person he could contact on that phone. There was an immediate response to his call.

"Update," Duro said. "Got another job, Top priority."

"Higher than the last three?"

"Yes, you'll need all your resources for this one. You need to complete it within the next twelve hours."

"Okay. Send us the details."

"Will do. There are two. One will be very easy, but the other will be very difficult. Surrounded by security all the time."

"Don't worry. Whatever security group it is, one or two will be from us."

"Of course they will. Good. Anyway, with this job, there's got to be no mistake, not even the tiniest error. The future of the country depends on it."

5.

Duro turned to one of his screens and flicked through to his favorite 24-hour news channel. It appeared there was only one subject being covered.

A commentator stood in a bright city street with a background showing stationary police cars with their emergency lights flashing, areas cordoned off by black and yellow tape, crowds of people in the distance with flashing phones. The commentator was a young man with a short, dark beard.

"—wasn't the standard armored vehicle. Police are still investigating why this was the case. Normally such a "medium-sized bomb blast"—I'm quoting Sergeant Max Horton, the head of the bomb investigation team—such a blast would hardly damage an armored vehicle and would certainly protect all those inside. It's clear President Pelling was ushered into the wrong vehicle, though why this happened is still unclear. The result is that all three inside the car—the driver, President Pelling and his personal assistant, James Portland, all died instantly as well as four pedestrians who happened to be close to the car and two members of the motorcycle security squad. Sixteen other civilians were injured, two of them critically. We have a statement now from Vice President—Now President—Alex Duro…"

Duro appeared on screen with an expression of deep sadness.

> What's happened today is completely shocking, appalling. There's no words to describe how dreadful I feel right now. My thoughts and prayers are with President Victor Pelling, who was a close friend of mine for many, many years, and my sincere condolences go to all his relatives and friends.

I wish to say no more at this time apart from the fact that I'm fully aware of what President Pelling's plans were for his administration of the country, and although it is a dreadful shock to have this position thrust upon me, I promise to carry through President Pelling's plans to the best of my ability.

Back to the commentator who said, "No terrorist group has claimed responsibility for this attack, and so far the police have no indication of who might have been responsible. Nevertheless—"

Duro turned off the screen. He was smiling. He stood and walked over to open his security drawer. He took out his special phone and made a call. "Well done," he said.

The Decline of the Death Artist.

> "After the first death there is no other."
> —*Dylan Thomas*

> "After I got to number twenty-two, a world record, I realized that what I'd done had no value whatsoever."
> —*James Pilgrew*

For several years, Drennan preferred to die by the sea. He felt that the sea was the setting for his finest moments. In Greckle Bay, for example, the scene of his Great Trilogy, he would wade, barelegged, out to the platform and enjoy the early morning light and the coolness of the salt water.

During this slow walk of sixty meters or so, he insisted that all his medicants were hidden below the platform and that the crowds on the huge semicircular stand behind him were completely silent. He wanted to see no one and hear only the gentle shifting of the waves and the calling of the seabirds. He craved solitude at that time and, even though he knew this was an illusion, held onto it for the two minutes it took him to reach the platform.

Arriving at the ladder, he placed one foot on the first rung and slowly rose from the sea. The climb was twenty meters, and when he reached the top and stepped onto the bare open-sided space, he turned to face the land. This was the signal for wild cheering to erupt from the crowd in the giant amphitheater and those on the grassy banks and rocky promontories to either side.

Four hundred thousand of his fans in fifty tiers a quarter of a mile wide shouted and screamed and applauded. The chant of *"Dren-nan! Dren-nan!"* began, reaching a crescendo as he turned away and stepped onto the central dais. Flags of all nations flew from the top of the stand. In the sea beyond the platform, two huge screens rose and flashed into life. There was Drennan himself, tiny on top of the platform, a giant in each screen as he turned to face the crowd again.

He raised his hands, and the cheering stopped. From beneath the platform, the medicants arrived to set up the apparatus and complete the arrangements. Then they stepped to one side. Drennan removed his shirt so that all he was wearing was a white loincloth. For about a minute he stood, eyes closed, composing himself. Then he said quietly, "Yes," and there began the gentle orchestration of his death.

In the only interview he ever gave, he was asked if it hurt.

"Hurt? Of course. It always hurts."

The interviewer was the journalist Muriel Lindberg from the webfold *Data! Now!* which specialized in close analysis of contemporary cultural events. Lindberg was twenty-five at most, and Drennan—then ninety-two—tried hard not to appear condescending.

"Of course it hurts," he went on. "You're conscious all the way through—well, I am—and it takes even these tretta drugs a few minutes to kick in and kill the pain. During that time, I'm in agony, screaming agony..."

"But you never actually scream, do you?"

"I did once, but now I try hard to stay silent and keep my eyes open. Eyes open, mouth shut. That's what's expected of me. I mean, anyone can die screaming or yelling or whatever, but it's my job to show that you can master the situation. That is, I die, but I die with as much dignity as I can. I control death, do you see? But yes, there's lots of pain, and that's how it should be."

"How it should be? What do you mean by that?"

"People have to be aware that I actually might not make it back, that the pain might be too great. There has to be the possibility of insuperable damage, permanent fatality."

"You mean some people want to see you die? Die permanently, I mean."

"Of course. That's an essential part of the event. Remember what happened to motor racing."

"Motor racing?" Lindberg repeated.

"Disappeared about a century ago."

"I've heard of it," Lindberg said. "I'm just trying to see the connection."

"Cars driven very fast round a track. Why did people want to watch that?"

"Well, to see who was the best driver, I suppose."

"You think so? I'm not so sure. I mean, there was competition, certainly, but that's not why most people were interested."

"No?"

"No. They wanted to see crashes. Bits of metal flying all over the place. Wheels bouncing up in the air. Flames. All that kind of thing. And the bit that was really thrilling was seeing people getting killed. Then all these safety procedures came in and the technology sorted everything out. All the drivers were completely safe from then on. So people began to think, *what was the point anymore?* Risk-free motor racing? Boring as hell. That was the end of it."

"And then along came the death artists?"

"Yes. A logical development, don't you think? Forget all the other stuff and get right to the nub of the matter."

"Death."

"That's right. We need to acknowledge that people like to see people die."

"But you don't die; you come back to life."

"That's part of the spectacle, yes. But there has to be the chance that I won't make it. Otherwise… well, they might as well pay to watch me drink a cup of coffee."

"So what do you get out of it? What does it all mean to you?"

"It's an art form, and I aim to be the best artist there is."

"Really? You know, I've never actually been that comfortable with the word *art* in this context."

"No? So what would you call it?"

Lindberg shrugged. "A kind of fairground show, I suppose."

•••

That interview with Muriel Lindberg was on Drennan's mind some thirty-two years later when everything was finished, all done, and his days as a death artist long gone. He was on his way to visit a man called James Pilgrew, who lived on the outskirts of Gracetown.

Drennan's trip was the result of a request—more of a summons, really—from Pilgrew, with whom he'd had no contact for quite a number of years. Pilgrew had also been in the death business, and the last time they'd met they'd fallen out over their differing attitudes to their life's work or, as Pilgrew put it in a tired old joke that Drennan grew to resent, their death's work.

"You don't really like people much, do you?" Pilgrew had said to him.

"Depends what you mean by *like*."

Pilgrew laughed. "I think you've just made my point. You don't really respect them, do you? I mean they're just… I don't know, *numbers*, ciphers. They turn up, pay money, and you do something that, apparently, they enjoy watching."

"Isn't that what you do?"

"Well, yes, but I like to get closer to people."

"How can you possibly get closer to half a million people?"

"They expect more from me than just turning up, performing, and being dragged off to hospital. I make a point of meeting them—well, some of them—and trying to understand what they truly want from me. You don't seem to be interested in that."

"Not in the slightest," Drennan said. "Anyway, I know what they want. It's drama with a bit of mystery. I'm not their friend; I'm this distant guy who performs a sacred act for them."

"A sacred act?"

"Sacred… yes… something they can't quite understand but realize is of tremendous significance. And distance is critical. I don't tell them anything about me, and I refuse interviews, and the crowds at my deaths get bigger and bigger."

"I can remember at least one interview," Pilgrew said.

"I only gave one," Drennan said. "And that was a mistake. Muriel Lindberg. Not very bright. Made no real attempt to understand what I do."

"Well, I struggle with that myself," Pilgrew said. "I mean, what is it that motivates you? You live alone, you've got no contact with anyone other than your medicant team, you don't interact with any media…"

"That's right."

"But *why?* What do you get out of this isolation?"

"I like to concentrate on my art," Drennan said.

"Art?"

"We're death artists, aren't we?"

"Oh yes, we are," Pilgrew said. "Well, that's what they call us. But I've never really thought of myself as an artist."

"No? So what are you then?"

"I'm a performer, an entertainer."

This reply rankled, not least because Pilgrew had been—and still was at that time—Drennan's inspiration. Pilgrew was the best. Drennan had always said this because of Pilgrew's dedication, the care, and the attention to detail he brought to every death. The Egyptian Death was still the best there had ever been. Even when someone told Drennan that his Great Trilogy was the pinnacle, he'd say, "No, no, look at Pilgrew's Egyptian Death. Supreme quality in every department. Unsurpassable." And here was Pilgrew saying, as Muriel Lindberg had suggested, that what he did was little more than a fairground attraction.

●●●

Pilgrew lived a few miles from Gracetown, which, in turn, was a hundred and fifty miles from Brake City, where Drennan had his home. Drennan took the fast shuttle and then a helicab to Gracetown North Base.

"You know this is as far as I can take you, sir," the pilot said.

"I'm aware of that, yes. I know all about it," Drennan assured him.

"And I'm required by law to check you've got the correct protection."

"No problem." Drennan took from his backpack a large plastic tub of Quatrophilidide and held it up for the pilot to see.

Noticing the size of the container, the pilot said, "Planning to stay for a while, sir?"

"I'm not sure," Drennan replied. "Better to be safe than sorry, don't you think?"

"I'll need you to take two tabs before leaving you."

"Sure." As the helicab settled gently onto the landing stage, Drennan released two pills from the tub and swallowed them dry. "And I'll set the medi-alarm too," he said as he pressed a button on the tub's lid. There was a single beep, and the lid flashed. "Everything's in order."

"That's excellent, sir."

As he watched the helicab rise and bank toward its base in Central Gracetown, Drennan wondered if he'd ever used that expression before: "Better to be safe than sorry." Even if he'd never actually used the words themselves his whole approach to his life's work—care, precision, accuracy—embodied their meaning.

The high perimeter fence around the toxizone had several signs fixed to it warning visitors about the dangers of entry and listing the precautions to be taken. Drennan had done everything required of him, the Quatrophilidide being the final item. He placed his hand against the ID plate, and the entry gate spoke to him: "ID confirmed, but immunity not yet complete. Try again in two minutes and fifteen seconds." Evidently the Quatrophilidide needed more time to kick in. Drennan waited, tried again and the gate swung open.

One of the questions he wanted to ask Pilgrew was why the hell he'd chosen to live in such a god-forsaken place. Living permanently in the toxizone was possible but hardly recommended. Pilgrew must need stacks of these plastic tubs of pills to keep him alive.

But, before he could ask any questions, he had to get there—*there* being a cabin on the shore five miles away, and the only transport available was that provided by his own body. He had to walk. Leaving the perimeter fence behind,

Drennan set off along a path that led through a small wood and then up onto the top of a bare hill.

Soon, the little vegetation there was thinned out even more. For twenty minutes he passed through fields that had once produced high yields of corn, wheat, and other cereal crops but were now abandoned: bare earth and stone with little islands formed of grass tufts and stunted trees. Then, half an hour into his walk, he reached a steep incline from the top of which he looked down onto a bay in the shape of a near-perfect semi-circle.

For a moment, the sight confused him. Then he sat down on a rock as the shock hit.

But I know this place, he thought. His heart was beating fast and he put his backpack on the ground at his feet while he tried to calm himself. *This place... it's found me again.*

There was the huge grandstand, curving round the bay—a great construction now in ruins—seats destroyed or removed, those remaining bleached by the sun and salt spray. The flag staffs around the top edge remained, but only the faded tatters of two or three flags were in evidence. The merchandising booths, the reception modules, the private viewing stages—all collapsed. The once-bright colors had become washed-out shades of pastel. The beach beneath the stand was clogged with detritus, unrecognisable shards of metal, wood and plastic. Out in the bay itself, the platform was long gone, pushed away by the tide, but one of the gigantic screens was still there, lying flat in the shallow water, visible a couple of feet below the surface. This was Greckle Bay, the scene of Drennan's Great Trilogy.

Almost as disturbing as the sight of the ruins in front of him was the surrounding silence. He had insisted on silence before each event but now he found it intimidating. There were no birds here, no birdsong, and the gentle wind didn't manufacture any whispers as it moved through the trees because there were no trees to interrupt its flow, just a few scrappy thorn bushes, leafless and dying.

The Trilogy had been his greatest triumph but had ended his career. It was generally accepted by those in the business that you only had so many deaths in you—ten, maybe fifteen if you were lucky. Pilgrew reached a remarkable twenty-two; Drennan's final Trilogy death had taken his total to seventeen. Apart from the fact he had no idea about how to follow the Trilogy, that last death had not proceeded as planned, and his medicants, among others, had advised him to quit.

The three deaths had all involved sloping laser guillotines. In each case his body was sliced into two pieces. The first death involved a single swift diagonal cut from right shoulder to left hip bone. This resulted in breaks to the collar bone, ribcage, and spine as well as the hip bone itself. Several internal organs, including the heart and lungs, were also bisected.

Because of the extent of the damage caused in this death, Drennan's recovery, though assured, was complicated and took longer than usual. He was hospitalized for seventy-two hours, and it was six days before he was restored to full health.

The second Trilogy death, a month later, was the mirror image of the first—a cut from left shoulder to right hip. The recovery process was similar. It was during the third death that things went wrong.

It was to be by far the simplest act but the most spectacular. The laser guillotine was set to strike Drennan horizontally through the upper chest. He would be holding onto a bar above his head, and after the laser passed through, there would be a moment when his lower body fell away, and his upper body stayed in place for as long as his hands remained grasping the metal bar. This was to be the spectacle, a body halved as never before, residual strength assuring a few seconds of stillness before death encroached. But it didn't happen like that.

At the instant the laser beam hit the left side of his chest, Drennan let go of the bar with his right hand, and his arm fell away. But only his elbow dropped below the plane of the laser; his right hand was still up by his shoulder. Consequently, the laser cut through his upper chest at the wrong angle and continued to slice his right arm in two places—just above and just below the elbow. As his lower body slipped away, Drennan swung to the left, dangled by his left arm for three seconds, and then dropped to the platform, landing on top of his lower body and his right hand. His elbow, completely severed, tumbled over the edge of the platform and into the sea.

Although Drennan's medicants were trained to cope with a wide range of eventualities, this came as a shock and it took them nearly three minutes to stabilize Drennan's condition. More blood had been lost than expected, more bones, more muscle, and sinews damaged. There was also the question of recovery of the elbow and the consequent risk of unforeseen infections.

Drennan left the hospital after an unprecedented two months of treatment. He was told later that on two occasions during the first week, his life had been in serious danger, incredible though that might seem. Many of his followers really thought he was going to enter perma-death. And later, when he recovered fully, it was suggested that he might consider retiring from the death business. Even his medicants, who were due to lose income if Drennan quit, pointed out that he was undoubtedly the greatest death artist who had ever lived, and he had absolutely nothing left to prove. And he didn't need the money anymore; he was already very rich.

Drennan considered the issues for a couple months and decided to take the advice he'd been given. At the age of ninety-eight, he retired from the death business.

Now, thirty-two years after his last death, he was on his way to visit James Pilgrew—his sometime rival—who he still regarded as a friend, even though he hadn't seen him for years.

Pilgrew was one of those who had advised him to quit.

• • •

After a mile of walking along the coast from Greckle Bay, Drennan began to tire. He reminded himself that, at one hundred and thirty, he was still a young man. But then, young and old were words that held little meaning anymore. Nevertheless, it annoyed him that he felt tired. He was fit and healthy, and yes, he was young. Then he remembered the Quatrophilidide. Maybe tiredness was a side effect of the drug. Yes, almost certainly, that was it.

He could see a building in the distance, the first thing other than ruins that he'd seen on his walk. He assumed it must be where Pilgrew lived. As he got closer, he saw that it was quite small and uneven in shape, constructed of slabs of material of different sizes with little regard for what Drennan thought of as *stable architectural techniques*. It was like something from a shanty town or an enlarged version of a child's den.

A man with dark grey hair was sitting outside in a chair which was an old-fashioned metalframed, wicker construct. Across his knees lay a walking stick.

The man turned, rose stiffly and smiled as Drennan approached. "You're here," he said. "You actually made it. Well, Dren, you're very welcome."

They shook hands.

"You know, I'm struggling to recognise you," Drennan said.

"It's the hair, I suppose. I'm getting old." Pilgrew smiled.

"There's no such thing as old any more," Drennan said.

"No? Well, we can argue about that later. Come inside."

The impression that Drennan had gained from the outside of the building—of something unconventional, unplanned, thrown together using a variety of materials—was confirmed when he went in. It was like a beachcomber's hut, a single room with a very old core-stove in one corner, a bed to one side and a table with two wooden chairs in the middle. There was also a cupboard and what looked like a wardrobe, both made out of zyolon. The floor was made from pine planks, the walls lined with layers of heavy canvas. There was only one window; made from plastic sheeting, it was translucent, not transparent. However, with the door wedged open, there was plenty of light inside.

"Did you actually build this yourself?" Drennan asked when they were seated at the table.

"That's right, yes. I just picked up material from the abandoned buildings along the coast, the ruins of the Greckle Bay Arena. You must have seen all that on your way over."

"I did," Drennan said. "I'd forgotten it was here."

"Well, the scene of your greatest triumph."

Drennan shook his head. "Not so sure about that."

"Do you remember the platform?"

"You mean my platform out in the bay?"

"Yes."

"Oh, I remember it well," Drennan said. "But I try to forget."

"You're sitting inside it," Pilgrew said.

"What?"

"I took a lot of the boards from it when it crashed onto the beach. Used the pieces for the walls and roof."

Drennan looked up and said, "Christ."

"Sitting inside yourself," Pilgrew said, smiling.

Drennan stood up. "I think this was a mistake, I'll be off." He stepped toward the door.

"No, no, come on, Dren..." Pilgrew struggled to his feet. "I'm sorry. Really. No, I apologize. I didn't mean to be flippant."

"You always were, you know," Drennan said as he stood in the doorway. "You always made light of everything, even your own achievements. You always played down what you did."

"I was objective. I never tried to build it up into something it wasn't."

"And I did?"

Pilgrew steadied himself against the table. Quietly he said, "Yes, to a certain extent, you did."

"Well, thanks for that," Drennan said, but he didn't move. He stayed in the doorway.

"I'm sorry, Dren, I really am. I didn't mean to make fun of you. And I really want you to be here. So please stay."

After a few seconds of hesitation, Drennan returned to the table and sat down. "Tell me," he said, "why on earth do you live here?"

"It's quiet."

"Well, I'll bet it is. Not a lot of people want to live in the middle of a toxizone."

"I'm the only one I know of in this one," Pilgrew said.

"Exactly. But look, if you want a quiet life, why don't you… I don't know… buy ten square miles of land somewhere or an island maybe, and build yourself a proper house. I mean, you're a rich man, after all."

Pilgrew started to laugh. "A rich man? Me? Where'd you get that idea?"

"Well, you made a lot of money, didn't you?"

"Oh, I certainly did. I made a lot but then I lost a lot. Now I'm completely broke."

"Broke? But how the hell did that happen? Millions used to watch you. Millions *paid* to watch you."

Pilgrew shrugged. "At one time, maybe."

"The Egyptian," Drennan said.

"You remember that?"

"Of course I do. You were my hero—"

"Hero? Christ." Pilgrew's gaze dropped to the table top.

"That's what you were to me," Drennan insisted. "Along with—what was it—a couple of billion other people."

"Well, I did make a lot of money out of that one," Pilgrew said. "But there was a bit of a problem afterward."

"A problem?"

"Yes. The Egyptians kept it quiet because they didn't want it to affect their tourist trade, but there was quite a bit of damage to the Great Pyramid. You know, setting up the platform and everything and then taking it down. And the blood—" He shook his head but at the same time he was smiling.

"Blood?"

"Well, quite a bit of it, you know, spilling over the stones at the top of the pyramid—"

"Oh, come on, a liter or two…"

"Yes, I know, a tiny amount, relatively speaking, but the crazy thing was that the stuff we used to clean it off did more damage to the stone than five thousand years of weather. The Egyptians weren't happy. I got sued for… well, just about everything I had. That was my *first* bankruptcy. It took me three years to get the cash together to stage the next death and do you know how many people turned up for it?"

Drennan shrugged.

"Three thousand. Well, three thousand one hundred and four to be exact."

"I remember, yes. It was around about that time it all fell apart."

"Certainly did. Remember those kits you could get? All those idiots dying in their backyards as a kind of party piece? *DIY Death* and all that shit. I was glad some of them didn't make it. Of course, you were well out of it by then."

"That's right. But you… I mean, you started before me and continued after I quit. And you were one of those who advised me to retire—"

"Oh, partly self-interest, I admit," Pilgrew said. "With you out of the way, I reckoned more people would come and see me."

"But they didn't."

"No. As you say, it was pretty much finished by then. No risk, no spectacle. Actually, I blame the government." He laughed. "If only they hadn't made that stupid announcement. *Death is abolished.* Christ, that was the end of it."

"Pure politics I thought at the time," Drennan said.

"Oh, I agree, but that didn't matter. It was official. Death abolished! Ironic, don't you think, that the abolition of death did us both out of a job?"

"Well, as you said, I was out of it by then."

"Yes," Pilgrew said. "But I couldn't stop. I began to realize that I needed it. And now, after all these years, I still miss it, you know."

"I do, too," Drennan said, adding, a moment later, "sometimes."

"With me, it's all the time." Pilgrew smiled, and his smile was amused but wry. "Now that I can't do death, there isn't much point in living." He stood up. "Let's go outside, shall we?" He took hold of his walking stick, and they left the cabin.

"This is the kitchen garden," Pilgrew said ten minutes later, after having walked slowly a few hundred meters inland from Pilgrew's make-shift house, and approached a walled enclosure.

"You created this?" Drennan asked.

"I built the wall, yes."

"Quite something."

The garden was about ten square meters, and the wall was not quite two meters high. It was built using assorted bits of rubble that Pilgrew had collected from nearby ruins.

They stepped into the garden through a wooden gate.

"Tomatoes," Pilgrew said. "Sweet corn, potatoes, broad beans…"

"But isn't the soil toxic?"

"I brought in some topsoil."

"How did you do that?"

"Had bags of it delivered to the edge of the zone and then loaded it onto a boat."

"A boat?"

"A rowing boat. I'll show you later."

Drennan looked over the expanse of the garden. "You must have needed a lot of soil."

"About a tonne," Pilgrew said. "Took me about twenty-five trips in the boat to get it all here."

"Amazing."

Pilgrew approached the row of tomatoes, picked half a dozen, and put them into a canvas bag. "Dinner," he said as they left the garden. "Well, part of dinner."

"What do you do for protein?" Drennan asked.

"I catch fish."

"Isn't the sea toxic as well?"

"Oh, it's improving. Anyway, I row quite a way out from shore. I get mackerel, cod, sea bass—"

"But you've got to get other stuff in, haven't you? I mean, you can't be completely independent, can you?"

"Unfortunately not. So yes, I have to make a trip to Gracetown every month or so to stock up on things. Hate going there."

As they approached the cabin once more, Drennan said, "So, are you going to live here for the rest of your life?"

"The rest of my life?" Pilgrew laughed. "Well, maybe a couple of hundred years, then I'll think again."

"Not forever, then?"

"Forever? You don't seriously believe that's a possibility, do you?"

"No, of course not," Drennan said. "I mean, bits of our body will wear out sooner or later, and that'll be it no matter what the government tells us."

"Well, yes. As you were saying, the abolition of death isn't a medical triumph, it's a political statement. But there's one thing they haven't told us."

"Oh? What's that?"

"Well, if you abolish death, you've also got to abolish birth."

•••

Dinner consisted of fish—sea bass that Pilgrew had caught while fishing not far from the promontory at Greckle Bay—and the tomatoes picked in the garden. Drennan didn't enjoy the meal. He admitted to himself, but not to Pilgrew, that he was conditioned to the taste of the instant meals that were his usual fare at home. As they finished, Drennan's medi-alarm beeped. He took two more Quatrophilidide pills.

"So what do you do here?" Drennan asked. "I mean, when you're not fishing or gardening."

"I spend a lot of time watching the sea."

"In case it runs away?"

"Well, it does run away twice a day, but it always comes back, or at least it has done so far."

"Reliable, then."

"Nature generally is reliable, even when we mess it up."

Drennan said, "I still don't understand why you live here."

"Maybe you will by the time you leave. And, who knows, maybe you'll want to stay." Pilgrew laughed.

"Unlikely."

"Plenty of material here," Pilgrew went on. "I'd even give you a hand to build your own cabin. Not too close to mine, of course…"

"Well, no."

Later, they went out for a walk along a narrow track that meandered among the sand dunes.

Progress was slow. Drennan could see that even with the walking stick, Pilgrew was limping. There was something wrong with his right leg.

Along their route, there were clumps of marram grass, and occasionally they encountered the spiky silver-blue heads of sea holly, though Drennan couldn't have named either plant. Finally, the track reached the top of another beach of white sand streaked with lines of grey pebbles and empty bleached seashells. Along the high tide line tangles of green-brown kelp were drying out in the late evening sun.

In the distance to the north they could see the towers and domes of Blaetsev with a concentration of air traffic like a swarm of flies above the city.

"I hate the sight of that place," Pilgrew said. "But I take a walk this way sometimes, as a kind of penance, I suppose."

"How far away is it?" Drennan asked.

"About twenty miles. Sometimes it's blanked out by fog or heat haze, which is the way I like it."

"You never go there?"

"Never. As I said, I go to Gracetown occasionally. I can just about handle that."

● ● ●

That night, Drennan slept in Pilgrew's bed while Pilgrew slept outside in a sleeping bag laid out on a pile of grass collected from the area near the sand dunes. "There aren't any predators around here," he explained. "And hardly any insects. All quite safe. Anyway, I often sleep out in the open, so no arguments, please."

Drennan woke early the next day feeling rested and refreshed. Pilgrew brewed some coffee.

"Sleep well?" he asked.

"Yes," Drennan said. "Very well."

"You see, you're getting to like the place. You'll want to stay. I guarantee it."

"It's got its attractions, I suppose," Drennan said. "But no, I'm not tempted."

"Pity."

They sat down at the table and began to drink their coffee. Drennan's medi-alarm beeped. He swallowed another two pills. "What about you?" he asked Pilgrew, holding up his stock of Quatrophilidide. "I imagine you've got tubs and tubs of this stuff."

"Well, I have, yes."

Pilgrew volunteered no further information. After a few moments, Drennan said, "I have a theory."

"Go on."

"While I've been here, you haven't taken any pills at all, have you?"

"No, I haven't."

"So... so I think you've stopped taking them. Am I right?"

Pilgrew raised his right hand as if to take an oath. "Guilty as charged."

"When did you stop taking them?"

"A couple weeks ago."

"In anticipation of my visit?"

"Your visit has something to do with it, yes."

"So tell me," Drennan said.

Pilgrew sipped his coffee. "Wanted to talk it through. Examine things with someone who would understand."

"What exactly are the *things* you want to examine?"

"The implications of the way we're heading. I mean, this abolition of death and the inevitable reduction in the birth rate... Well, how do we get new ideas? Fresh thoughts? Don't they understand that we'll just end up in a rut? If people don't die and people aren't born... we just get nowhere."

"People need to die is what you're saying."

"That's right, and sooner or later, they'll figure it out. So I reckon they'll start by setting an age limit. You know, we'll be allowed to live to a certain age, then they kill us."

"Kill us?"

"Choose any phrase you like. Comes to the same thing."

"Well... so, if you're right, how long will they give us, do you think?"

"Who knows? Five hundred years? Four hundred? Two hundred?"

"Two hundred's a bit close," Drennan said.

"Maybe, but then, you've got money, remember."

"What's that got to do with it?"

"Oh, come on, Dren, you'll be able to buy time."

"Buy time? You really think it'll come to that?"

"Of course it will," Pilgrew said. He placed his empty coffee mug on the table. "Everything's negotiable. Always has been. When you get a bit too close to terminal age, you just find someone who's a lot younger and a lot poorer, and you do a trade. You buy ten years off him. You go up to two ten, and he goes down to one ninety. One ninety will seem a long way off when you're only thirty or forty—and anyway, maybe later he'll get rich and be able to buy some years back from some other poor unfortunate sod. I can see time-trading becoming a major industry."

"Even if you're right, what's it to do with you stopping taking your pills?"

"Well, I just don't want to live in the kind of world we're heading into," Pilgrew said.

"But... we're a long way from anything like that right now, surely?"

"It's already started."

"You think so?"

"I do get news here, you know. There are government announcements daily about the restructuring of the future. *Refuturing*, they call it." He laughed. "God, some of the words they manage to come up with. No, no, I want to go now before it becomes unbearable. And anyway, I'll be making room for someone else."

"I can't believe this," Drennan said. "You actually want to die?"

"Yes."

"Permanently?"

"Oh yes," Pilgrew said, smiling. "This time it's for keeps. Ironic, isn't it," he went on. "This'll be my final death, my slowest and quietest and, you could say, my most significant—and there won't be anyone to witness it. Of course, you could come back in a couple months and watch me die, if you like. That's how long it'll take, I reckon. My right leg's kind of dead already."

"I noticed you struggling with it."

"Yes, well... anyway, you've never seen me die, have you?"

"I told you," Drennan said. "The Egyptian."

"Well, you saw a recording—"

"No, no, I was there. I was actually there."

"Really?"

"I told you, you were my hero. And on that occasion, you were magnificent."

Pilgrew looked at him in surprise. "You actually mean that?"

"I do, yes. It was an astonishing performance. After I saw you, I changed my whole approach. I did nothing for two months but think about what I'd seen. I watched the film of it again and again. I examined every detail of what you did and calculated its effect on the full performance. It was—well, it was a revelation."

"My god," Pilgrew said. "I don't know what to say…"

"And I began to realize that it wasn't just the attention to detail," Drennan continued. "I mean, the meticulous way everything was carried out. No, it was more than that. You see, you made the event itself seem almost incidental. It was less important than your presence, your attitude of calm, your reverence for the act itself. You knew what it meant. You knew it wasn't just a fairground attraction, whatever you say about it now. No, it was a lot… a lot *more*."

"Christ, well…" Pilgrew picked up his coffee mug, remembered it was empty, and moved it to another position on the table. "Well, this time it'll be a paltry, dismal affair, I can assure you."

"You don't have to do it, you know," Drennan said. "You can still change your mind."

"Actually, I can't."

"What do you mean?"

"It's too late to go back on the pills. Too much damage done already. That's why I gave them up two weeks ago—just in case you tried to persuade me against it."

"But they can do anything now. You know that as well as I do. They can fix you. Christ, that's what they did for us all those years."

"We had *money*," Pilgrew said.

"And I've still got plenty of money even if you haven't. I can get you the best treatment—"

"No."

"But why not?" Drennan's voice rose. "Dying like that'll achieve nothing, not a damn thing."

"It'll mean something to *me*, even if I'm not around to enjoy it."

"Now look—"

"No, you look. I've made up my mind, and that's that. I asked you to come here because I thought you'd understand, given what we've both been through."

"That's it," Drennan said. "I don't understand."

"No? Well, you will," Pilgrew said, though his tone was less than convincing. "Yes, I'm sure that you will."

•••

Drennan left the next morning. He agreed he would return in the days before Pilgrew died; he agreed to be present for his friend's death.

He returned to Brake City. For some days, his mood was sombre. He didn't leave his home.

Then he took a helicab to Blaetsev. He tried to persuade the pilot to fly over the toxizone so that he might see Pilgrew's cabin, perhaps catch a glimpse of Pilgrew himself, but he knew this wouldn't be allowed. The flight path got no closer than five miles from the zone. The pilot assured Drennan that he took no risks.

Drennan hadn't been to Blaetsev for two years. He was astonished at how much it had changed and was still changing. Every street had partially built buildings or sites cleared for redevelopment. Near the city center, he saw a building being demolished which, only a few years before, he had witnessed in the process of being constructed. Screens around the site displayed footage of the new building, which had not yet been built. It would be bigger than the old one; it was a key element in the city's regeneration.

When Drennan got home, there was a spilmail message waiting for him. A tired voice said, "I haven't changed my mind, but I need a bit of help with something. I've only got maybe a couple of days left, so I'd like you to come over as soon as you can. If you would. Please."

•••

When Drennan reached the cabin a few hours later, he found Pilgrew lying on his bed. He was very thin, his face narrow, his skin pale. He was weak and looked old. But he could still speak, albeit slowly.

"I realized," he said, "that there should be nothing left of me, no corpse or pile of bones to be taken care of. I mean, it's best for me just to disappear altogether. So, a burial at sea, that's what I want. But I still want to experience it, Dren, don't you see? I want to feel it, not just drift off into a coma and then die here and have you dump my body in the bay. I want to understand what it's like to *really* die, not to die as we used to do it, knowing we'd be saved. I don't want that. I need to experience the door closing without any possibility of opening again. Do you understand?"

"Yes," Drennan said. "I think I do now."

"Good." Pilgrew breathed quietly a few times. "Help me to the boat."

The distance from the cabin to Pilgrew's boat—beached just above the high tide line—was only a couple of hundred meters away. Supported by Drennan, Pilgrew managed to walk halfway before he slipped down to his knees. But he was so emaciated now, so light, that Drennan could carry him the rest of the way. The tide was in, so Drennan didn't have to push the boat far before reaching the water. He went back to Pilgrew, who was sitting on the white sand, lifted him, waded out to the boat, and helped Pilgrew settle into the stern.

"Row round to Greckle Bay," Pilgrew said. "You remember Greckle Bay, don't you?"

"Of course I do, yes."

It took Drennan about half an hour to row the mile to the promontory at the north end of the bay. During this time, Pilgrew said very little. Then, when they reached the bay, he said, "Maybe you could row out into deeper water."

Drennan did as he was asked.

"Now, pass me that belt." Pilgrew pointed to a long leather strap that was lying in the bottom of the boat. As Drennan lifted the belt he saw that several pouches had been attached to it—all of them stuffed with pebbles. The belt was quite heavy.

"Better help me with it," Pilgrew said. "We wouldn't want any accidents now, would we?" He managed to smile.

Drennan fixed the belt around Pilgrew's waist.

"Everything in the cabin is yours, by the way," Pilgrew said. "Be assured, however, that its total value is zero." Without saying anything more, he allowed himself to tumble backward into the sea.

Sitting in the middle of the boat, Drennan made no attempt to look over the side. He waited several minutes as the boat drifted slowly around in the ebbing tide and then began to row. He headed toward the ruins of the Greckle Bay Arena and then turned to follow the coast back to the cabin.

He beached the rowboat and went into the cabin. He found no message, no final words, no documents of any kind. The table was bare. There was the stove, several chairs, a cupboard containing some clothes, and there was the bed against one wall.

Drennan sat down on the bed and looked around the cabin at everything that was left of Pilgrew's life. Then he leaned over, undid his shoelaces, and slipped his shoes off. He swung his feet up onto the bed and lay down.

Then he fell asleep.

Acknowledgements.

With thanks to Angela, Janet, Jennifer and Martin for their help and support.

About the Author.

David Shaw Mackenzie is from Easter Ross in the Highlands of Scotland. His several careers have included social work, teaching, systems analysis, painting and decorating and fish packing. These activities have led him to various parts of the Middle East, Latin America, mainland Europe and the Island of Mull on the west coast of Scotland. He now lives in London with his wife, Rachel.

His short fiction has appeared in several major literary magazines and anthologies including several editions of the annual *Best Short Stories*. His first novel, *The Truth of Stone*, was short-listed for the Saltire Society First Book Award. Two more novels have been published: *The Interpretations* and *The Last Wolf*.

Printed in Dunstable, United Kingdom